CAMINO
BEACH

AMANDA CALLENDRIER

CAMINO BEACH

LAKE UNION
PUBLISHING

Text copyright © 2017 Amanda Callendrier

Published by Lake Union Publishing, Seattle

www.apub.com

Amazon, the Amazon logo, and Lake Union Publishing are trademarks of Amazon.com, Inc., or its affiliates.

ISBN-13: 9781477848524
ISBN-10: 1477848525

Cover design by David Drummond

Printed in the United States of America

For girlfriends everywhere—especially mine

Roxanne was the kind of friend who borrowed that sweater you would never see again. She was the kind of friend who would tell you to dye a pink streak in your hair, that it would wash out, except it didn't because it was actually paint. She wore too much makeup and skirts that were too short, and she bit her nails to the quick and picked the split ends off her long red hair while the rest of us were trying to pay attention in English class. She listened to eighties rocker chicks like Debbie Harry and the Go-Go's and would dance around her room until she ran into a wall. She kissed anyone who wanted to kiss her at parties and polished off whatever was in the cup you handed her. She dragged me into more trouble than I have been in before or since, and I loved her.

Sometimes, in the middle of the night, I can almost smell her watermelon shampoo and feel the hard angle of her elbow when she was pushing me toward the edge of the law. I hear a Stevie Nicks song and feel my eyes close into the rhythm of the guitar. I hear the roar of her El Camino in my driveway, and I am pulled out into the night and the uncertainty of a Roxanne adventure. And I want to hold on to her tight, tight, and say, *Please don't go.* And sometimes, I wake up, and my throat is sore, as if I've been yelling, *I'm sorry, I'm sorry, I'm sorry*, and she doesn't hear me. And the truth is that she doesn't know how sorry I am, because she vanished like a ghost into the night. Sometimes I wonder if she was ever really there at all.

It's a warm fall Friday, apples and football in the air. I am cutting class with Kristen, but it's not really cutting because we're decorating for the football game. I have no business doing this, since she's the cheerleader, not me, but it keeps me out of gym class, which I hate.

I'm bubble lettering our team's name. Kristen says, "What the hell are you doing?"

"I just wrote 'TIGERS.'"

"Your bubbles suck. They're not even attached."

"What are you, the Poster Police? What makes you so sure yours look better?"

Kristen rips the poster away from me. "Give me that."

A smooth voice interrupts us. "This looks like more fun than push-ups."

"You'd better believe it," says Kristen with a paint pen stuck in her mouth. I've already looked up to see that this is actually a teacher, even if she looks like no teacher I've ever seen.

"I am just so sorry to put an end to it, then." Big smile. This woman is so good-looking it hurts. Cascade of red hair, bright-green eyes, and she doesn't even need makeup. She's wearing our gym uniform, too, and it looks as good on her as it does even on tiny Kristen, head cheerleader. We both take a moment to gawk.

"I'm responsible for decorating for tonight," says Kristen with a confident grin. She adds, unconvincingly, "Sarah is helping."

"Not now, ladies. Come on back to class." She turns around, and the two of us cannot help but ogle her as she leaves.

"Who *was that*?" says Kristen, and we follow, more out of curiosity than duty. Coach Miller's replacement, is what it looks like to me. Miller was the best. He was eighty and didn't know how to take attendance. Also, all you ever had to do was say, "I have my period," and it would get you out of anything you didn't want to do.

We go into the gym and line up. We had dressed for it even if we had no intention of participating.

This new teacher says, voice all honey, "We'll start with fifty push-ups and fifty sit-ups." Everyone groans and drops. She turns to the two of us, at the end of the line. "And for you two, let's say two hundred."

"What?" says Kristen. "We'll never finish before our next class!"

"You'll remember that next time you confuse gym and art." She doesn't smile this time.

"Bitch," mutters Kristen.

"Oh, you have no idea," says this random girl I've never seen before, sitting behind me. She's also a pretty redhead. Is there no shortage of those today? "Wait till you get to know her. It gets worse."

"How do you know?" I ask.

"She's my mother," says Roxanne.

Chapter One

I knew something was up when Kristen came over to my place. She always said my place was too far away, too close to downtown, and that there was nowhere to park. In fact, there were plenty of street spaces, but Kristen didn't know how to parallel park, and a Range Rover didn't improve her skills. She hated coming over; I got it.

When she buzzed downstairs, I asked her over the intercom who it was.

"It's me, dumbass. Can I come up? What number are you again?" Kristen had a husky, instantly recognizable voice, like she was a pack-a-day smoker. She wasn't, but she did yell a lot.

"I don't know anyone named Dumbass. If you knew me, you would know which apartment I live in." I smiled into the receiver and waited just a few moments before pushing the button. A huffy little sigh came through the speaker. I had detected a note of hysteria in Kristen's voice, and the fact that she hadn't even called was worrisome. I hoped she hadn't decided that she and Chris were "on a break" again and that she wanted to sleep on my couch. She'd done this once a decade ago after they were first married and hung up half her wardrobe in my living room for a week. But I had a house then, and a husband of my own. Since my divorce, I'd moved into a small apartment, and Kristen's wardrobe had tripled in size. I loved having her around, but some warning would be nice.

I opened the door to my best friend in all her Kristen splendor, white sundress and massive stilettos. She was still shorter than me. Kristen wore her hair halfway down her back and blown straight, just like she did when we were young, and was a perfect platinum blonde like then, too. She said she didn't color her hair, but I was fairly certain she had been highlighting it that shade as long as I'd known her. We'd been friends since middle school homeroom. I was lucky to have her by my side for the transition into high school because she was so golden that my popularity was assured.

Kristen had her I'm-on-a-mission look, but her eyes were red. I decided to stop teasing her on the off chance there was really something wrong. "Pour me a drink, wouldya?" she said. She looked around my place, which was roughly ten times smaller than hers. "Shabby chic. Nice painting, though." She hadn't been here since she'd helped me move in two years ago. She said that she would never again help someone move who owns more books than clothes—books are heavier. It was even worse now. I owned my own bookstore, and the warehouse was so far away that boxes of books often ended up sitting around my living room. Kristen was having some trouble navigating around them.

Though the décor left much to be desired, I had a gorgeous abstract over my fireplace—black and red and silver, some squares, some splatters. Not even Kristen could criticize that one, since it was a Kristen Calhoun original, vintage from 1998, the last time Kristen had done any sort of painting at all. She'd traded in a career as an artist for a career as a professional wife, and now she spent a lot of time volunteering at her kids' school.

My refrigerator had a bachelorette emptiness: too clean, with nothing in the crisper, and some of those ready-made meals stacked up on the bottom. I was doing okay in the condiment department, and I was hoarding an old bottle of Shiraz from the last time my neighbor Jack and I had felt like cracking something open. Diet Coke occupied a whole shelf, but that wasn't the kind of drink Kristen was talking about.

Kristen peered in, horrified. "You have to be kidding me. What do you eat?"

I gestured toward my lonesome-me ready-made meals. I'd had it all once, and not that long ago. Matt, in his own estimation at least, was perfect, but when someone considers himself to be perfect, he wants everyone around him to be perfect, and that's a lot to live up to. I was glad I didn't have to put up with him anymore, other than our back-and-forth dog custody arrangement. What I had to put up with instead was everyone feeling sorry for me and trying to set me up with any available man without a prison record. My mother might even be willing to compromise on that one, now that my biological clock was reaching the end of its ticking.

"We could go out?" Living in the Gulch, a neighborhood that had sprouted up suddenly in yuppie splendor about a decade ago, I had something that Kristen did not—a staggering choice of chic bars and restaurants. Kristen, out in the burbs, had to take her car if she wanted to go to TGI Fridays or Applebee's. She didn't see anything wrong with that.

"Let's go," said Kristen. "Please change your shirt and brush your hair first." My blue oxford was halfway untucked, but I couldn't see the problem with it otherwise. I had to agree with her about the hair.

While upscale was more to Kristen's taste, we settled for casual sushi down the street. Kristen had probably come down here to complain about her husband, Chris. Chris loved his family in an abstract, photo-on-his-desk kind of way but was allergic to any real contact at home. This sent Kristen into an I'm-going-to-divorce-his-ass tailspin every couple of years. He wasn't a terrible guy, but he was one of those good old boys who couldn't talk about anything besides football and the size of his boat. He was the kind of good old boy who drank three Old Milwaukees when he came home from work every night and then passed out with his feet on the couch. They were college sweethearts, and he did love her. We just make peace with a different idea of love as we get older. Some of us, that is. Others buy single-girl apartments in the middle of town.

"What has Chris done this time?" The restaurant was busy for a Wednesday, but we found two available seats at the bar.

"Nothing. Well, other than threatening to buy a new jet ski. Why? Is that why you think I'm here?"

"Well, that's usually when you need me." I was kidding her. We saw each other all the time. We were just usually more civilized about it and made plans first.

"Sarah, that is not fair. It has been years since that time I came and lived with you."

She pulled out an invitation, written in perfect bubble handwriting that was instantly recognizable as that of the head cheerleader, even twenty years later. It was reunion time. "Oh, God," I said. "We don't actually have to go to that, do we? We see these people all over Nashville anyway." I didn't see the point of dressing up to do it in our old gym.

"I want to talk about Roxanne," said Kristen.

Of course.

Roxanne had disappeared right before graduation. She'd left town so fast that we never got the chance to say good-bye. And now it was reunion time. This was bound to happen.

Suddenly I needed a drink, too. Just the sound of her name, all these years later, made me feel queasy, like when you've been pulled over and you're waiting for the cop to come to your window and give you a ticket. You know you haven't done anything really wrong, just driven ten or so miles over the speed limit, and that you'll have to pay a fine. Still, there is a moment where you feel like you've done something really, really wrong and that maybe they're going to haul you in for it.

"Can we get beers first?" I said uneasily. I fumbled in my bag for my wallet, past a Moleskine journal, past a dog-eared copy of *The Road*.

This was an empty gesture, since Kristen has paid every tab since the millennium. I wondered sometimes how often Kristen thought about Roxanne. Was it as often as I did? In the early years after we graduated, I thought about Roxanne all the time, but the urgency had faded over time, like my guilt. Kristen, at least, was blameless. I wished I could say as much for myself.

We ordered Sapporos, and Kristen put the invitation on the table. We stared at it for a moment. Kristen was right that it was impossible to think about attending that reunion and not think about Roxanne. We knew everything about everyone from our graduating class. Nashville was not as big as it seemed, and most of these people had not gone far. Some of our old classmates were now teachers at our high school, and my friend and neighbor Jack was even the principal. My banker went to high school with us. One of the former cheerleaders owned the salon where I got my hair cut. They were everywhere, except the one person we wanted to see.

"I want to find her," said Kristen, sipping her beer. "I just need to know what happened to her."

"She's probably living it up in Hollywood," I said nervously. Roxanne had always talked about getting out of Nashville, making it big. She was beautiful, too beautiful, and drama was second nature to her. I'd scanned soap operas for years, hoping to see her as an extra, at least, in the background somewhere. I hoped that she hadn't landed in some juvenile detention facility instead.

"What if she isn't?"

"Then, I guess she's just doing something normal," I said.

"What if she's dead?" asked Kristen.

"Jesus, Kristen." But I, too, had thought it. At first, I had thought I would feel it if she were dead, would at least know that the world had dimmed a little bit without her frenetic energy in it. I had broken the connection between us, though, and maybe I wouldn't feel it ever again, so completely was it severed.

"Why would she have left without saying anything?"

I knew why. And if Roxanne had known what I'd done, I was the last person that she would have called.

One day she was in biology class with us, and the next day she was gone. She had been caught cheating, and soon after her mother told us she had decided to send Roxanne to boarding school, that the structure would be good for her. We never really believed that, and we didn't understand why she wouldn't tell us where the school was. We had gotten out the Yellow Pages and called around, but, well, Google hadn't existed back then. After we called information for Clarkson, the only boarding school we had heard of, we quickly ran out of ideas. At the end of the school year, Roxanne's mother left, too, and there was no one around to ask anymore. Not even Roxanne's boyfriend, Mark, had a clue. He walked around like a zombie until he graduated and went on to play football at the University of Tennessee.

"The thing is," said Kristen, "do you really get thrown out of school for cheating? And we were a month away from graduating. Who changes schools then? It makes no sense."

Now, this was easy to see. I hadn't believed it, not then and not now. I just thought she would get detention for a couple of weeks, or maybe that she might flunk the class. Neither of these were game changers in Roxanne's world. I had thought that there would be consequences, but not that consequence.

A couple of boys wearing Vanderbilt caps sat down next to us. There was a lot of random high-fiving. This was clearly not the first stop on their party bus. "Ma'am, is this seat taken?" one of them asked Kristen.

Kristen looked over at me and rolled her eyes. "Don't you hate it when people call you 'ma'am'?"

It was nice when well-behaved southern boys said "ma'am" and "sir," but I was with Kristen in wishing that they wouldn't say it to me.

"It's not taken, on the condition you don't call me 'ma'am' anymore."

The boy looked stricken. "I'm sorry! I didn't mean to. I was just . . ."

Kristen laid a manicured hand on his arm. "It's all right, honey. My friend and I would rather not think that we're old enough to be your mothers."

"Y'all are way hotter than our mothers!" yelled the other one. "Will you do a sake bomb with us?"

"What's a sake bomb?" I asked.

They looked incredulous that, at our advanced age, we did not know what a sake bomb was. "It's a shot of sake, in a beer."

I could not imagine anything more disgusting.

"Sure!" said Kristen.

"No, thanks," I said. "We're kind of in the middle of something here."

Four beers appeared. Chopsticks were placed on each of them. Tiny cups of sake were placed on top of those. "You're not really going to drink that, are you?" I asked Kristen. "Why don't you leave Kappa Alpha over there alone so that we can finish this conversation?"

Kristen ignored me and turned her attention to the two college boys. "Now, how does this work?"

The bartender rang a bell and shouted, "Sake bomb!" Everyone in the restaurant turned to look at us. I hoped they didn't think we were the mothers of these young men. I also hoped their actual mothers were nowhere nearby. The bartender turned toward us. "Okay, then. I say 'sake,' and you say 'bomb.' Then you bang the bar with your fists, and your shot falls in. Then you chug your drink."

"Oh, dear," I said. I didn't know what it was about hanging out with Kristen. It shot me straight back to high school and all the accompanying bad behavior.

"Sake!" yelled the bartender. I jumped in my seat.

"Bomb!" we yelled back.

We all banged the bar with our fists, and a tidal wave of beer rushed over our forearms and pant legs. The boys were already done, and Kristen halfway through, before I had the wherewithal to pick up my glass. When I had finished, Kristen and I looked at each other. Kristen raised an eyebrow at me.

"Delicious?" said Kristen.

"I was going to go with 'surprisingly refreshing.'"

The bartender set up another round, and we sake-bomb-shouted our way through the whole ritual again. This was a lot easier than talking about what we needed to talk about.

One of our new companions, whom I had temporarily forgotten, turned to us. "Hey, we're going dancing at Acme. Do y'all want to come?"

"We are in the middle of a very important discussion. We couldn't possibly come out dancing," said Kristen, as if she had not just chugged two beers next to these very same young men.

"Also, we're very old," I said, and Kristen glared at me. They wished us well and then headed on their way. I noticed that they had not paid their tab.

"Where were we?"

"So why didn't we go looking for her, then?" Kristen said.

"Kris, what were we supposed to do? We were seventeen. What resources did we have then, anyway? Once we had called around in different cities a few times, where were we going to look?" I didn't mention that, at the time, I'd been terrified to see her again.

"We should have gotten in our car, and gone!"

"Where would we have gone? It's not like we could have just looked her up on Facebook or LinkedIn." She probably wouldn't have agreed to speak to me if we had.

"We could have gone to Myrtle Beach."

"Why on earth would we have gone back there? We tried that old beach house, but the number had been changed and no one was listed. She was gone! Besides, we had to graduate, and head off to school."

"You were too busy getting ready to go to Sewanee to look very hard."

"Excuse me? You also were otherwise occupied. There were Vanderbilt cheerleader tryouts, sorority pledging events. Don't act like you weren't elsewhere, too."

"I know!" moaned Kristen. "It's my fault. Why didn't I do something?" She looked like she might start crying. *Oh, Kristen. It wasn't your fault. If only you knew . . .*

Kristen sat still for a minute. "Hey, can we have another one of those sake things?"

"Don't you think we've had enough?"

Kristen ordered them anyway. We just knocked our sake cups in this time, without bothering to shout about it, and drank in silence. "It's just that I don't want to go to this reunion thing without her. What's the point of seeing all those tired old faces, but not her?"

"God, remember her awful El Camino?" I said.

Kristen started to laugh. "Camino Beach!" That old nickname. "It was the coolest car in the universe, so ugly it was awesome."

"How long did she have that thing? A month?" I started to giggle, too. The sake had finally kicked in.

"Oh, at least two or three, don't you think? It made it to spring break."

"We should get one. Don't middle-aged men buy sports cars when they turn forty? This could be our midlife crisis car. If we find Roxanne, we should get an El Camino." We had loved that old car, fantasized about our cruising options. Nothing said "white trash" like an El Camino, with its low-riding two-seater body and truck bed. It came in colors that resembled bodily fluids—shit brown and mucous green—and there hadn't been a new model since 1987.

"We should get an El Camino and go find Roxanne." The sake was speaking, not me. I did not want to go find Roxanne, not really. I definitely did not want an El Camino. But I had forgotten who I was sitting next to, apparently. When your best friend had lots of money and no impulse control, you really needed to watch what you said.

"Sarah, yes! Let's do it! I'm going to look up El Caminos!"

Kristen's phone was out, already scouring the Internet for El Caminos. Kristen had not changed much since high school, really. She might as well have been organizing a liquor run for a party with someone's parents out of town, except we didn't have smartphones back then, which made things more complicated. And more satisfying.

"So, when are we going to start this quest?"

What bullshit excuse could I cough up? I had an author I adored—local favorite Amy Pritchard—coming into the shop on Saturday, and my parents' anniversary dinner was on Sunday. The next weekend was the much-anticipated high school reunion. In principle, I could get away some during the week, but I had major inventory work to do and some shipments arriving. I tried to explain all this to Kristen.

Kristen looked up from her phone. "Are you going to help me or not? The reunion is next weekend."

"Yes, sure. I'll help you." I was banking on the strong likelihood that Kristen would not fully remember this conversation in the morning.

"It doesn't sound like you're going to help me with all that *na-na-na* anniversary this and *blah-blah* store that. Are you in or out? Do I need to find another friend?"

"Who else are you going to find?" I said. "No one cares about Roxanne. Not even Mark. He can probably barely find pants to put on in the morning." Roxanne's ex-boyfriend had disappeared from our lives as quickly as Roxanne had. Except we hadn't missed him, that lunkhead who didn't even have the decency to ask us about her.

Kristen sniffed. "Maybe I will, then. I mean, how important is this stuff you have to do? We have been putting this off for twenty years, Sarah! It's now or never."

It wasn't now or never. If you had put something off for twenty years, odds were it could wait another week or two. "You don't have a job," I said. "You don't understand." I understood the pull of Kristen's plan, even though I was afraid of what we might find. I was dying to know what had happened to Roxanne, what she had become—if she was okay. Turning an abstract desire into a real mission would need more thought than a conversation over a few too many drinks on a Wednesday night, though. I wasn't sure I was ready to do that kind of thinking.

"No, all I have is three kids. Maybe I should ask them to drive themselves to school and soccer practice. I'll ask Jackson if he'll make dinner." Jackson was three years old. Point taken.

"Okay, okay. If we dig something up, I'll take a day or two off." I hoped I could stall her this way, but we hadn't talked about Roxanne like this for years. All of a sudden, there it was again between the two of us, a Roxanne-size hole.

Kristen whipped out a manila folder from her giant Louis Vuitton tote. It had a label—"WILDER, Roxanne." She opened it up to a home deed. I'd been had. "What's all this, Matlock?" I asked, feeling sick.

"Oh, this is just what our PI turned up," she said casually.

"You hired a private investigator?"

"Do you have a better idea?"

I had several—Google being the first one, but Kristen explained that she had tried all of that.

I peered at the document. The house was in Myrtle Beach, not the street where we used to stay but at an address that I didn't recognize. It was a city we had checked before, but nothing had turned up. "Man, what if she was there all this time and just had an unlisted number?"

"The investigator couldn't find a phone record, and really, nothing else in Myrtle Beach, but he came up with this pretty fast. It's a start. He's still looking, but I figured we could go down there."

"When?"

"This weekend."

"Already! God, you don't waste any time. Why not tomorrow morning while you're at it?"

"Because we're going to go buy an El Camino tomorrow."

"What? That's insane. No, we're not. Let's go back to my place, and you can sleep on the couch, sober up. This will all seem clearer in the morning."

Kristen looked at me levelly. "It has never seemed clearer to me than right now."

Could I afford to let Kristen go on this mission without me? What if she found her, and Roxanne told her what I did, all those years ago? Because Roxanne knew, had to know. Would I lose another best friend, too? When you're unmarried, your friends are everything. If I went with Kristen, I could explain everything. I could tell Roxanne that I didn't know what I was doing back then, that I didn't know what would happen, that I didn't know she would leave. I was young, and I didn't know. I could tell her all this in person if we found her, if she was willing to speak to me. *If.* But would it be enough?

November 1996
Parking Lot, Briley High School

My lab partner in biology tells me his girlfriend told him about Roxanne's new car. There is no way Roxanne has a new car since she can't keep a job for longer than a month and her mother sure as hell won't give her any money. Kristen and I think this guy is just making shit up, but we're still going to run outside and look in the parking lot after class. If Roxanne has wheels, no one should know before us.

We see it as we run down the steps—this beat-up 1980 El Camino, and nobody but Roxanne would dare show up with a car that badass ugly. Roxanne can do whatever she wants, and it always looks cool. The juniors will start buying El Caminos if this is for real.

She sees us coming and honks the horn. "No way!" I say. "This is not your car!"

"Do you think I'm getting in that nasty piece of shit?" Kristen has a new BMW convertible and can afford to be picky. Her blue eyes are wide, and she's making no moves to get in this car.

"Suit yourself." Roxanne snaps her gum and jerks her head at me, and I'm not going to miss the chance to see the inside of a real El Camino. All the guys who hadn't yet made it to football practice pour down the steps in droves to see this redneck marvel. A few climb in the truck bed. There's Kristen standing all by herself, and it doesn't take long for her to change her mind and cram into the front seat with the two of us. We have to shake off all the boys to get out of there, but then again, we always do.

"How did you afford a car?" says Kristen.

Roxanne rolls her eyes. "Kristen, this *el crappo* only cost five hundred dollars."

"This still begs the question. How did you afford a car?" I ask her.

Roxanne shrugs, like, of course she has five hundred bucks lying around. I guess we don't really want to know how she got the money.

"Why an El Camino?" Kristen cannot imagine why anyone would buy such a thing on purpose. Her eyes are wide with privileged horror.

"Honey, this isn't picking out the color of your new BMW. How many cars you think are out there for sale for five hundred dollars?"

The car reminds me of my parents' Oldsmobile from the eighties. And a truck bed! Think what we could do with a truck bed! You could haul stuff, or get on back there yourself. Kristen has her neck craned all the way around like an owl, inspecting. "You could have a party in it, it's so huge."

"I'm gonna put me a lawn chair in the back of that thing." Roxanne laughs.

"Plonk down a six-pack next to you." Kristen's eyes gleam.

"Why don't you put some sand in the back of it and call it Camino Beach while you're at it?" I ask. We roar with laughter, and all of a sudden we have a new spring break goal. Camino Beach.

Chapter Two

Hangovers, at age thirty-eight, are not pretty. I woke up with the intense desire to vomit and the equally intense desire to not do so, as it would serve as proof that we had behaved badly. I hauled my carcass from bed and padded into the kitchen, where Kristen was already in full workout gear.

"I'm going to shower, and we're going," she said, pouring herself a liter-size glass of water. She didn't look sweaty to me.

"Did you put on mascara to go running?"

"Just a little eyeliner. What? I might run into someone." Her eyelashes looked like Miss Piggy's to me, doll-like. Just a little eyeliner, my ass.

"Where are we going? I need to go to work. As soon as I'm sure I'm not going to die."

"Duh. We're looking at El Caminos!"

"Ha-ha." She hadn't forgotten, after all.

"Okay, I'll be out in a jiffy. Go put something on that makes you look poor. Not hard! I've got the address of a dealer." I gave her the finger, or rather gave it to her butt, since she was already on her way.

The evening's discussion came back to me in the form of a stomachache. Were we going to do this? She had an address, she had a file:

Roxanne was still around. What would it look like if we showed up, unannounced, after twenty years, in an El Camino?

"Sarah, go put on your fucking clothes," called Kristen from the bathroom. Had Kristen already mulled this over, rationalized it? But Kristen didn't rationalize anything. She acted, then apologized. I made some toast, thought hard about how I could get out of this. I really did have a lot to do at the store this weekend. My mind went easily to the tasks waiting for me at work. I had to pay bills, unpack boxes. Get the store ready for a reading. I wasn't halfway through my toast before a fully realized Kristen emerged, long hair as smooth as if she had just left the salon, wearing a different sundress and shoes. How did she do that?

"Sarah!"

I bit into a piece of crust, chewed slowly. It was time for a little intervention. "Kristen, I just cannot do this, okay? It's great that you found her, but you know, I have a life."

"No one in the whole world has a life besides Sarah. Everything revolves around Sarah! What about the reunion?" Kristen could be a real pain in the ass.

"What about it? I don't have to go to that stupid thing. You can go if you want to. Roxanne has been gone for longer than we knew her." My voice sounded hollow.

"And that makes it okay?"

"Well, no, but I just don't know what I'm supposed to do about it now." I hoped I sounded casual.

"Figures," said Kristen.

"Figures, what?"

"Figures you would give up."

I breathed in and out a couple of times. "What's that supposed to mean?"

"It means," said Kristen evenly, "that you quit on this all those years ago, and you're quitting now. It means that you're a giver upper."

I laughed edgily. "Fine. I'm a quitter. What about you? How come it took you twenty years to get this started? Don't get all come-to-Jesus on me."

"I made a mistake. And I'm going to fix it—before next weekend. I'm not showing up without her." I had to watch out whenever Kristen put both hands on her hips.

"Good for you. I'm going to work."

"What do you think people are going to ask us at the reunion?"

I wondered if all that mascara helped Kristen keep her eyes open extra wide. Scary, really. It was hard to look away. "Is this a rhetorical question?"

"No! What do you think they'll ask?"

"Oh, I don't know. Am I married? *No.* Do I have kids? *No.* Do I have an exciting career? *No.* And so on and so on. Sounds like a great time." I needed to throw that invitation in the garbage is what I needed to do.

"Wrong! They're going to ask you one thing—have you heard from Roxanne? What are you going to say?"

"No?" What could I say, that Roxanne probably hadn't wanted to speak to me in twenty years? That I hadn't taken the initiative to find a private investigator to do this search and reassure myself that she was okay? That maybe we hadn't been such great friends in the first place? What could I say, except that it was my fault?

I was not going to the reunion.

Now I had to face the possibility, though, that Kristen might find Roxanne without me. What if Roxanne told her everything? Was this a chance to make it right? Before I knew it, I heard myself say, "Okay, I'll look at a car with you. But no promises."

NashVegas Oldies wasn't far, a five-minute drive up Eighth Avenue, somewhere in between the old comedy club Zanies and downtown, in a questionable neighborhood that had been revamped into what Nashville imports called Sylvan Park. The saleswoman standing outside looked oddly familiar. "Is that Montana?" I asked. If my hunch was correct, we'd have to deal with the clingiest person we knew back in high school. We could hope that she had improved, perhaps more than we had. Montana had sat on the outskirts of our lunch table for a couple of years, occasionally running for class office, and we hadn't done much to acknowledge her existence. She hadn't changed much, still with a riot of curly hair, hips wider than they used to be, glasses more fashionable.

She recognized us immediately and screeched, "Sarah Martin! Kristen Calhoun! I can't believe it!" She hugged Kristen, who was a little stiff, giving Montana the butterfly finger-patting hug that meant *Please go away*. Why was she so glad to see us? She didn't need our votes anymore. Still, there was something about seeing someone who knew you all those years ago; as if just by osmosis, you could be young again and things would be as they were.

"Um, do you have an El Camino for sale?" I asked, after we had gotten all of the what-have-you-been-up-tos out of the way.

"El Camino!" said Montana. "Yes! Of course! I forgot all about y'all in that crazy old car. You wanted to turn it into a beach! Ha-ha! Well, let's go take a look at this baby, see if she's sand-worthy." Kristen and I followed her. "Whoa! If you're looking for an El Camino, I bet y'all are planning to roll up at the reunion in this thing." Montana smacked a wad of gum as she talked.

"You bet," I said unconvincingly.

"Oh, y'all are such badasses. I love it. How's Roxanne? I can't wait to see her. Can't wait!"

I wanted to say that we hadn't found her, that this was the point of looking at El Caminos, but Kristen said, "Oh. You just wait and see." I stared at her, wide-eyed. She winked at me. This was vintage Kristen— say it, and then make it true.

Our El Camino was out back, so we had to walk past a red-hot '65 Mustang and a super retro-looking roadster. I said, "Hey, I think that's the car that Daisy mowed down Myrtle in."

Kristen said, "Huh?"

"Um, American literature called. You missed class."

"Sarah, we're looking at El Caminos. Stay focused."

"Never mind." This El Camino was sitting out back for good reason. The beige paint job had seen better days, and there were spots of rust around the joints. Still. There it was, all low-down, with that extra-long truck bed. I started to snicker.

"Montana, does this thing actually run?" I asked. It would take a lot of sand to fill one of these things up if you wanted to make a rolling beach. We had never made it that far before.

"Oh, yeah! I got the keys right here. You want to fire her up?"

I looked the thing over skeptically. I wasn't at all sure that it would make it around the block, much less on a wild-goose chase. But Kristen had already taken the keys and jumped in the car. I shook my head at her as she put the keys in the ignition. The engine roared spectacularly to life. Kristen put the thing in reverse, and I took a step back. She slammed on the brakes hard to avoid hitting the wall on the back of the lot, and the bumper fell off.

I put both my hands over my mouth, either out of shock or to keep myself from collapsing with laughter. Kristen jumped out of the car and shut the door hard.

"Kristen!" said Montana.

"Kristen what? Were you going to let me drive this piece of shit down the road and kill myself?"

"You made the bumper fall off!"

"I didn't make jack shit fall off! I hit the brakes! What was I supposed to do, run into the wall? Bet it would have wadded up like a Kleenex. Forget it. Here." Kristen threw the keys at her.

"Hey, why don'tcha try out the Mustang out front?" Montana was getting desperate.

"Nope, gotta be an El Camino or nothing," I said, intercepting Kristen's exasperated glare.

"Well, sorry, y'all! See you next weekend?"

I was about to say that I didn't know if we'd see her, but Kristen had already said, "See you then," with an airy wave.

We climbed back in the car. "That's that," I said.

"So, we're going to head out to Donelson now," said Kristen, looking at her phone. Donelson was about thirty minutes from downtown Nashville, near Opryland, an amusement park that had ceased to exist about twenty years ago. Rides like the Screamin' Delta Demon and the Wabash Cannonball were razed to make way for an outlet mall. This didn't stop people from continuing to call the area Opryland. There isn't much else out there, other than Andrew Jackson's old homestead and a bunch of hicks.

I opened my mouth to say that we should just quit now, but Kristen wouldn't hear it. Besides, this one was probably not going to run either. How much could you expect from a thirty-year-old car? And then I would be off the hook.

The next El Camino belonged to someone named Jimmy, who answered the phone by making a loud spitting noise and then saying just, "Yep, Jimmy." I asked him if we could come and visit, and he said that we could: "Sure thang, sweetie."

We hopped on the interstate and were in Donelson faster than I would have thought possible. Jimmy flapped a fat hand at us as we rolled up the driveway.

Kristen turned to me, panicked. "Should we leave? What if he offers us some beef jerky to eat?"

"We'll say we'll only eat it if it's homemade. No Slim Jim shit for us, thank you. Only the best."

Sitting in the middle of that dump, this El Camino did not qualify as an old junker. It was painted shiny purple and had giant new-looking tires, defying all expectations—if we even had any expectations. This could be it. An El Camino that looked like this one might even run. I shifted around nervously in the car.

Then what? Are we really doing this? Thinking an El Camino would be a funny gimmick and buying one were two different things, and you crossed a line when you opened that checkbook. If Kristen bought the car, I would have to go with her. I was committing myself to finding Roxanne. And to finding out what had happened to her.

"Sarah! The car is a symbol."

"A symbol of what? Dixieland?" I knew exactly what she meant. An El Camino meant high school. It meant Roxanne. It meant reliving my life in reverse, going back to where I was twenty years ago, cruising with my high school best friend.

Jimmy ambled over to the passenger car window and rapped sharply on it, beaming at us with an almost complete set of tobacco-stained teeth. I winced.

"Hi, there, Jimmy, is it? My name is Kristen, and that's Sarah behind the wheel."

"Hoo boy!" Jimmy whistled. "It sure is my lucky day, two pretty ladies comin' to visit."

"Ready to show us your other pretty lady?" Kristen sounded like she had been talking cars her whole life. There was a lot of sass in that tiny body, and she had the confidence to pull off bigger loads of bullshit than this one. She flicked that long blonde hair and then stepped out of the car. Jimmy was a goner; he'd probably end up giving her the car.

I hopped out, too, and Kristen was already in Jimmy's clutches; he was steering her toward his El Camino more gallantly than I would have thought possible. I trailed behind both of them, impressed into silence. The car looked almost new: eggplant with a metallic sheen, mirrors gleaming.

I must not have been paying attention because Kristen froze me with eyes like the pool in her gated community. "Sarah. Please say hello to Jimmy. He's telling me all about his baby. He calls her 'Elvira.'"

"She runs like a dream. She was an original showroom car, ain't got hardly no miles on her. You wanna take her around the block? Y'all, listen!" crowed Jimmy, and the Oak Ridge Boys blasted out of the car. "This one has its original cassette player!"

My heart's on fire, for Elvira . . .

"Yeah, boy!" shouted Jimmy. Had listening to music at this volume damaged his hearing? "Ready to go for a spin?"

Kristen and I looked at each other. We had wanted to climb back in an El Camino for twenty years, although this didn't seem like the right moment to start talking about that sand fantasy. Kristen bolted faster than I did, made it to the passenger side door, and shouted, "Shotgun!" just like we were seventeen again.

"Dammit! I am not riding in the back. I am *not* riding in the back!" She always made me ride in the back!

"Hey, don't y'all worry. I'll get on back there. You'd better be in the driver's seat." I exchanged a look of horror with Kristen as Jimmy opened the door for me to climb behind the wheel. Kristen was already inside and turned to look out the window, shoulders shaking with laughter.

"Giddyup, then," I said.

Jimmy climbed in the back, the car sinking under his not insignificant weight. He leaned over to my open window, breathed Cheetos into my ear, and hollered, "Now, this baby still runs like a dream. You ready?"

I had forgotten what cars were like in the seventies and eighties, wide stretches of bench-like seats that felt like couches. No one used car seats for children. People didn't even use seat belts, and you could slide back and forth on the leather whenever you made a hard turn. I gave my seat an experimental bounce. The dashboard was so high I had trouble seeing over it, and at five eleven, I could see pretty high. Kristen must have felt like she was in a hole. I put the key in the ignition—a big, heavy one, no remote-control door locks on this one—turned it, and the engine roared to life. The gears, which were on the steering wheel, took me a minute to locate, and I put Elvira in reverse, hoping that I wasn't also turning on the windshield wipers.

It was thrilling to ride in one of these; this one was a lot nicer than Roxanne's, impeccably preserved. I glanced over at Kristen in delight. I punched the accelerator, and we peeled out of the driveway, gravel flying. It ran great for such an old car, better than my much newer sedan. I had to take the corners wide, since the Camino had a lot of length. It had power steering, surprisingly, and maneuvering the big wheel felt a lot like docking a boat.

"Why did you name her Elvira?" Kristen had to stick her head out her own window and yell.

Jimmy gave the question some thought. "Well. I wanted to give 'er the name of a great country lady. I thought about Loretta, tried it out, but it just didn't stick, ya know? She didn't seem like a Tammy either. And Dolly. You cain't name a car after Dolly, not even a car as great as this'un. And one day, I dunno. I was listenin' to the radio, and that song came on, and I went, yeah!"

"How fast does she go?"

I floored it, and we took off down a straightaway. No problem for fifty on a back road. I was having so much fun; it felt more like an amusement park ride than a car. Kristen started snorting with laughter again as we pulled back into Jimmy's compound. We all climbed out, and Kristen turned all business. Now that we had been in the car, it seemed impossible that we wouldn't have it. It was a jewel of an El Camino. The most beautiful El Camino I'd ever seen.

Kristen and Jimmy were mumbling about the deal, and all of a sudden, I heard Jimmy say, "Ten thousand." I gasped.

"Ten thousand!" yelled Kristen. "You've got to be kidding me! You said five in your ad."

Jimmy shrugged, smug. "Changed ma mind."

"That is false advertising," I said prissily.

"What I *sa-yud*, was that offers could start at five thousand. When folks see Elvira, they can tell that five just ain't enough."

"Let's go," I said.

"Wait a minute." Kristen thought for a moment. I hoped she wasn't going to call her husband Chris and ask him to donate to our retro spring break fund. "I have a deal—you sell for seven, and we get you Dolly's autograph."

Jimmy had a terrible poker face, and he lit up. "Really?"

"You bet," said Kristen. "We know people." *What people?*

He hesitated a moment. It was three thousand bucks, after all. Of course, ten thousand was probably all bluff. No one was going to pay that. "Y'all promise me you can get that autograph?" He frowned.

"Easy as pie," said Kristen. "We have a big-time songwriter friend." "Big-time" was an exaggeration. We had an old high school friend who played at local clubs occasionally. I doubted she had ever met Dolly. I held my breath, hoping he would go for it and afraid of what would happen if he said yes. If he said yes, we were off on a cockeyed road trip, with an expiration date of next week's high school reunion.

"Wellllll . . . All righty! You got yourself a deal! Y'all are gonna take good care of Elvira, I know it. I got this good feeling."

"Hi-ho silver, away?" said Kristen.

I swallowed hard. It was a long way back to Kristen's house in Brentwood, but not nearly as long as the walk from the driveway to the front door, when Kristen would have to confess her purchase to her husband.

I was in this now. Maybe Roxanne wouldn't be there. Maybe we wouldn't find her. Or maybe we would find her and everything would be just the way it was before. Maybe there was a logical explanation for why she left school without even saying good-bye, one that didn't involve me. Maybe she didn't even know that I had betrayed her.

February 1997
Math Class, Briley High School

I hate it when Roxanne cheats off me. I don't even like to sit next to her when we're in class together because I know she might take a peek anytime we have a test. We don't have many classes together because I'm Advanced Placement everything, and Roxanne is Advanced Placement nothing.

If Kristen is with us, there's a good chance Roxanne will try to look at her paper, too, and this gives me a fifty-fifty chance of not having to be the one who gives Roxanne the answer. My papers are better than Kristen's; I hate to say it, but it's true. It's almost better if Roxanne doesn't get answers from me because all the teachers know there is no way she is going to get everything right.

"Psst." The whisper is hard on my right.

I stare daggers at her, clench my jaw, and shake my head. She is going to get me in trouble and fuck everything up. I need a scholarship if I want to go to Sewanee, and I'm pretty sure they don't hand those out to cheaters.

Roxanne winks at me, makes a sad face, pushes her bottom lip out in a pout. I try hard not to crack a smile.

"Ladies," Mrs. Griffin calls out. "Silence." *How does she know?*

Roxanne shoves her paper to the leftmost corner of her desk with insistence. Written on it is "5 or .5?" I do not know how someone can make it this far in school without knowing how to do simple conversions. Roxanne knows how to mix margaritas and bake chocolate chip cookies. I mean, she gets the concept of ratios. But anytime there is a question with a number on a piece of paper marked "test," everything she knows just flies out of her brain.

I look over at Kristen and hope that she is going to do this so that I don't have to, but Kristen has done the smart thing and has her left arm covering her whole paper and a sheet of blonde hair covering that. It is the Kremlin, and Roxanne is not getting through. Kristen does not look over, not once. I know Kristen wants to get into Vanderbilt, but her grandfather has his name on a building there, so I'm pretty sure she has nothing to worry about, even if she gets a B instead of an A in statistics.

I mouth, *Fuck you,* at Roxanne, but I write, really lightly, ".5" on the right corner of my page. Mrs. Griffin is on the move, walking around desks, and Roxanne better get her head down. I look straight at my paper and nowhere else.

I finish all the problems in the time we have left, and the bell rings. Mrs. Griffin tells us we have to stop working right now, bring our papers to the front of the room. She says, "Miss Wilder, I'll thank you to stay after class." I glance over at Roxanne.

She didn't see, no way. But still, I erase my mark fast, blow off the eraser shavings. I am sure you can't see it, and if you can't see it, it didn't happen.

Kristen is waiting for me outside, rolls her eyes. "Goddammit. If she gets in trouble again, she is going to ruin spring break! If she has to spend the weekend in detention, we'll have to leave two days late."

We're not sure how or why our parents agreed to let us drive out to Myrtle Beach next month. I guess they know we're leaving soon one way or another. We totally want to take Roxanne's El Camino, just because it's so funny, but my parents think that pile of junk would never make it down there in one piece. They say we have to take their Ford Taurus, or Kristen's BMW. Guess which one we pick.

Roxanne bursts through the door, a fireball of red curls and explosion of papers. "Please tell me you did not get busted," I say. I hope she's not going to rat me out.

"Easy breezy. I just *swore* there was nothing going on."

"Did she buy it?"

"Oh, sure," she says, and for her, it's finished, just like that.

"I have to buy clothes. Who wants to come with?" says Kristen. Roxanne and I exchange a look. We do not have Kristen's clothing budget, and new clothes are not a necessity or a possibility.

"I have yearbook," I say.

"I have play rehearsal," says Roxanne.

Kristen continues, "Dad's got my car today, says he wants to make sure the oil is changed and all that. You know, our big trip is coming up soon." Roxanne and I exchange another look. I work two nights a week at Dairy Queen so that I can get gas money. Roxanne babysits. Not very well, I think.

Roxanne leans in and grabs Kristen's arm. "Oh, honey. He didn't need to take your car in. We are totally driving the El Camino."

Chapter Three

When life was not going as it should, I turned to two things: work and Jack. Jack was the closer of the two when I got back from our El Camino adventure, since he lived across the hall from me. I banged on his door before unlocking mine, and I heard a dead bolt sliding back and two latches clicking open. Jack smelled of oranges and Dr Pepper, and his curly hair was cut back to a manageable length. He was tall enough that I had to look up when we made eye contact.

"Sarah, are monsters chasing you?" Jack raised an eyebrow suspiciously, and I barreled past the door and into his arms. I shouldn't have done this, because Jack was always on the hunt for romantic interest. But he understood, and even though I said Kristen was my best friend, Jack deserved the title more. I'd known him just as long, since we all went to high school together. He was here for me through everything.

"Yes," I mumbled into his barrel chest.

"Sounds like someone has been reading science fiction again." Jack pushed me gently away.

"Not true," I said. "Literary fiction this week. Jonathan Franzen again."

"That's a lot of book. Maybe you'd be better off reading science fiction. Hey, would you like ice cream? Ice cream is the balm to all hurts." I nodded. "Then you'll tell me what's the matter?" I nodded again.

Jack owned ice-cream bowls. I couldn't think of any other man who owned ice-cream bowls; they looked like little round waffle cones, and they were just the right size for two scoops. Jack always said that ice cream tasted better out of an appropriate bowl, and he was right—as he is about most things. He gave me one scoop of cookie dough and one scoop of chocolate, my favorites. I said, "We bought an El Camino."

"Excuse me? It sounded like you just said *you bought an El Camino*."

"Yep."

Jack's eyes widened. "What? Why? Do you think you might have a brain tumor? I hear people sometimes behave illogically when they have tumors."

I delivered the next punch. "Kristen bought it. She wants to go find Roxanne."

"Aha. Is this about our high school reunion?" Jack was now the principal of our old school and was overseeing the event. My own sparkly marker invitation had been lying around for weeks, and every time Jack saw me he asked if I was coming. I never had an answer.

"Yes. No. I don't know," I said. "We may or may not also have had three sake bombs last night."

"I don't even want to know what a sake bomb is, but it sounds like an excuse for a wildly inappropriate purchase. I don't know why you and Kristen have to behave like a couple of sorority girls every time the two of you are left alone."

I soaked in the dad lecture, feeling a scowl etch itself on my brow. "Anyway," I snapped, "that is just background information. Just setting the scene here. If you're going to get all judgy, we can stop talking about it."

"No, no. Go on. It was a healthful and merry libation, your sake bomb choice, no doubt. Please continue." I ignored the sarcasm because of the smile he was trying to hide.

Jack was the only person who knew why I might be dreading this confrontation. I'd spilled it one New Year's Eve, along with an entire bottle of red wine. The evening was blurry for me, but not for Jack. "Well, this is a good thing. You should go, resolve your issues, see your old friend," he said.

"Yeah." I didn't sound convinced.

"Sarah, it was not your fault. Wherever she ended up, it wasn't your fault. Roxanne made her own choices that had nothing to do with you. And that crazy mother of hers." He put a comforting heavy paw on my shoulder. "Gorgeous, both of them, but scary! Something was bound to happen there."

"I guess so." I didn't believe it, and I wasn't sure if Jack did either, or if he was just trying to make me feel better. "If it wasn't my fault, why didn't she ever call?"

Jack shrugged. "Who knows? People start over, and maybe they don't want to bring the past with them. You don't know that it had anything to do with you. This is a great idea, the more I think about it. If you weren't also in an El Camino, that is. Where did you even find one?"

I told Jack about Jimmy and about running into Montana. See, Jack would remember Roxanne's El Camino, but he just didn't ever ride in it because he wasn't part of our group and was, well, kind of a tool back then. Jack was on the debate team, not the basketball team, so he didn't have a shot in the world. Literally. Air-ball city. We became friends near the end of senior year while working on the school newspaper together. By then, being cool meant less to me. After Roxanne left, I stopped hanging out with a lot of the popular group because I got tired of everyone asking me if I had heard from her. I enjoyed Jack's company more than the football jocks I'd spent my time with before anyway.

Jack said, "When are you going? And where?"

"Um, tomorrow? Myrtle Beach. So, do you think you could . . ." If Jack couldn't watch my dog, I'd have to get on the phone to my parents.

I heard some pounding. "Is someone at the door?"

Jack scratched his head. "Well, I don't know why they wouldn't use the doorbell." But he got up and ambled over to see who it was. When he cracked the door open, a blur of beige and black, about midshin height, shot through and hurled itself at me. Rhett Pugler.

I picked up my dog, who covered me in a bonkers slobber bath. My ex and I may not have had children, but we did have a pug. The joint custody arrangement that followed the divorce was as complicated as if we had been parents. Rhett Pugler liked the park near Matt's house, but he could come to work with me. Matt took him to obedience classes, and I let Rhett Pugler sleep on the bed. A lawyer would have agreed that splitting custody was the way to go. It was my two weeks.

Jack had still not fully opened the door, and I shook my head and waved my arms. *Don't open it,* I mouthed. Jack opened the door all the way.

"Hello there, Matt," Jack said. "Don't know if you see it there, but that thing on the right next to Sarah's door is a doorbell. Works better than knocking." I coughed.

"Hello, Jack. It works when the person is inside the house, like that person is supposed to be because that person has an appointment with another person."

Matt had drawn himself up to his full six four, which meant that he could look down on us in more ways than one. He was a great-looking guy, I had to admit it, longish blond hair and a goatee. When I first met him I thought he looked like Wesley from *The Princess Bride.* I could never get him to say *As you wish* to me, though.

"What are you even talking about?" I said. Matt couldn't stand Jack. I think he believed that we were secretly living together, and the two apartments were just a front. Matt had even hated Jack when we were married, all those inside high school jokes that he wasn't a part of. He could deal with it from Kristen, but couldn't bear the thought that I was such close friends with another man.

Matt. I had given up a medium-paying job as an editor to start my store, and I'd thought Matt was going to lose his shit. I had to take out a loan, and he was not on board for that. He had just paid off his own student loans five years earlier and remained traumatized by the idea of debt. He said that it was a risk, and ridiculous. But when the space had opened up in an area I loved, I just couldn't imagine anything else being there but books. What if someone else took it and put running shoes there, or a Chinese restaurant? I had always wanted to surround myself with books all day long, and none of my English-major career options had yet allowed me to do that. It turned out that editing a trade newsletter involved no books. I felt no pull toward teaching, which involved students. I wanted my own space, and I ended up insisting. The chasm between me and my husband just got bigger and bigger until those books all piled up to create a big wall between us.

"So, I'll see you in a couple of weeks, then? I'll bring RP back to you." I hated it when he said "RP," which made me think RIP. My dog liked to be referred to by his proper name. Matt still lived in our old house out in Crieve Hall. When I wasn't busy being annoyed with him, I felt sorry for him. I was the one who'd ended our marriage, not him. Not that he didn't have his part in it—all the criticizing and complaining would wear on anyone. No one is perfect enough for Matt, especially not me.

"What are you going to do about this weekend?" said Jack, and I looked at him like I might stab him in the throat. If Matt caught wind of our crazy El Camino trip, he would run along back home with Rhett Pugler in his arms. I missed my doggie; if Jack were busy, my parents would be happy to watch him for the two days I'd be gone.

Jack realized what he had done as soon as it was out, but it was too late. "What's going on this weekend?" asked Matt.

"I mean, Matt," I swallowed and petted the top of Rhett Pugler's head, "that, um, I have to leave him at home when I go to Mom and Dad's anniversary event. And also when my author Amy Pritchard comes." It wasn't a lie, what I'd told Kristen. My parents were celebrating an anniversary, and I did have a big event at the store. I was just going to have to bail out on both of those if I were heading to Myrtle Beach instead.

"So, why don't you leave him with me?" I noticed that Matt's collar was ironed neatly down. He used to do that with mine when we were married. I didn't wear so many button-down shirts anymore now that I had to do my own ironing.

"And you can't bring Rhett to your parents' dinner?" They were going to the restaurant in Belle Meade where we'd celebrated every family event as long as I could remember.

To a nice restaurant? Jesus. "No, Matt. I think they have a 'No Pugs Allowed' sign outside."

"Oh."

"I'm kidding." Did he really think there was a sign?

"Oh. Well, where is he going to stay?"

"He can stay at the house for two hours alone, I'm pretty sure."

"I don't know," said Matt, like a dad leaving a baby with a new sitter.

"Look, it's my turn. He'll be fine. Like always."

Matt nodded brusquely and turned to go. "Are you well?" he asked suddenly. *Well.* It sounded so grandfatherly.

No. I wasn't well. I was having a midlife crisis. I was going on a misguided road trip with my unhinged friend to find out if a bad choice I'd made in high school had ruined someone's life. Matt had heard Roxanne stories. I had shown him the yearbooks, the old scrapbooks. He just hadn't heard all of the Roxanne stories that mattered.

"Yeah, sure."

"Business going okay at the store?" I get a lot of satisfaction out of the fact that business was going okay. Better than okay. I'd turned a profit the past two years. Unfortunately for Matt, the two of us no longer had any financial ties.

"Yeah, yeah. Good."

In the early days, Matt would come by the store every now and then and roam around without buying anything. I think my offerings were not stuffy and old enough for him, all of those new titles and shiny covers. He liked for his books to smell musty.

"Well, okay, good-bye, then." He shuffled off down the hall, and I thought of him going back to our old house. I wondered if he still slept on the left side of the bed, or if he slept in the middle now. Or on my side even. Had he taken over my side of the closet with his quirky ties?

"Are you doing okay?" I called to his back, and he whirled around. The guilt was talking.

"Yes, great! I got a promotion even."

"Really?" I said without interest, and Matt started to explain the difference between "associate" and "full" professor. I knew the difference, and I knew it was a big deal. I inched out the door and leaned against the wall of the hallway while he finished.

"Congratulations!" I said brightly, hoping that would bring us to the end, and he hugged me, a hug that lingered. I backed out of it as graciously as I could. "Okay, bye now!"

"Take care, Sarah."

I watched him go (the view was not bad). It was not so long ago, that life, but it seemed ages ago.

Jack poked his head out the door. "Are you done here?"

I nodded.

"Please tell me that you are not getting mopey over that one again."

I shook my head.

"Do you need a hug again?" Jack held out his arms with more insistence.

I shoved him. "Don't get fresh. You need to trim your beard, by the way."

"No second thoughts. It was the right decision, getting rid of that guy." He held out his iPad, which displayed a map.

"What's that?" I said, as Rhett Pugler sniffed around my feet.

"It's a road map to Myrtle Beach. I've decided I'm going with you."

"What? Why?"

"It will be great amusement! Like in high school! Also, you need someone to make sure you come back in one piece." Jack had never been on a road trip with me in high school, much less with Prom Queen Kristen Calhoun. Maybe he was hoping to live out some high school fantasy. And Roxanne was every guy's high school fantasy.

"I really do not think that is necessary." On the one hand, it was shaping up to be a girls' trip, and he might ruin it. On the other, we might indeed need someone to make sure we made it back in one piece. And if Kristen decided to stop speaking to me, I could use an ally.

"I'll take Friday off. I can be your bodyguard."

"And can I call you Al?"

"Huh? Oh, ha. Yeah. I'll be your long-lost pal." I loved him for getting a Paul Simon joke. "My roommate from college lives in Myrtle Beach. I can stop over and say hello while we're there," said Jack.

I raised an eyebrow suspiciously. "What's his name?" I said. Sounded like Jack was trying to get in on the action. I worried sometimes that staying in that high school all the time stunted his opportunities for a social life.

Jack was peering at the iPad, pondering road options. "Sorry?"

"What's his name?"

"Oh. Bert. Robert."

"Bert? Really?" I didn't know anyone named Bert other than the *Sesame Street* character. Sounded made up.

"Yes, really. I'll give him a call."

"How many seats do you think there are in an El Camino? I don't even know where we're going to put our stuff. I mean, I'm fine putting a tote bag under the dashboard, but I doubt that is going to cut it for Kristen, who will need different shoes for each day."

"I can drive. I'll take your stuff."

"Now, that is just stupid. Why?" I had to admit, though, that there was great appeal to the idea of keeping our bags in a warm trunk, plus Jack could change a tire in no time and always kept jumper cables in his car. I have called upon both of these services.

"It would take a lot more than my trunk to carry all of *your* baggage, Sarah." Jack deadpanned. Score one for him.

Kristen wouldn't mind; she was always glad to have an extra man around to flirt with, and she thought Jack was cute, like a hall monitor. Besides, I knew better than anyone that the odds of an El Camino making it all the way to Myrtle Beach were not good.

"All right, you're in," I said and enjoyed watching his face light up. "But just so you know—this is a *girls'* trip. You are here to aid and abet on that venture. No testosterone-y moves."

"Yes, that is me. One of the girls."

"Do you want to borrow a dress?"

"Get out of my house," said Jack. "Pink polo is the best I'll do. Bright and early tomorrow."

I felt a little flutter of excitement walking out the door. So much could change in twenty years. None of us were the same as we were. Who would she turn out to be?

March 1997
Roxanne's, Green Hills

It's eleven, and we're already supposed to be at the pool. Roxanne's subdivision of condos backs up into a more posh subdivision with megahouses and a giant pool. We have to climb two fences to get there, but we're fine—we've done it before. I can clear the fence, no problem, and Kristen's short, but she's a gymnast. Roxanne is practically liquid. Maybe she slips through the bars for all I know.

Roxanne told Mark to meet us there, and he'll probably bring Kevin and Joey. At least I hope he will because if Roxanne is the only one with a guy, Kristen and I will be pissed. I'm not used to staying at Roxanne's house, and she swears her mother doesn't care if we go out. Mrs. Wilder isn't even here—she's on a date. She said before she left, "He's a doctor—a heart surgeon," with a gleam in her eye. I tried to look impressed because it was obvious she wanted us to be.

But we're stuck because these two can't finish their homework.

Kristen's pre-calc problems are almost done. She's decent at math, but a little in over her head here. Roxanne has some English paper to write, and I do not know how we're going to get her to cough that up.

For once, she's serious, red hair piled into a knot on the top of her head. She's nearsighted, and she has her glasses on today, not that she'd be caught dead in them at school. "Just write something!"

I plead. "It doesn't have to be good. Just finish, and get it done on time."

Roxanne's English class is reading *King Lear*, and she has to write a short story on the themes of family and betrayal. She can create her own characters, do anything she wants. This assignment is so easy, I don't know why she doesn't have a million ideas. In my honors English class, we have to read *Waiting for Godot*, which despite having half the words, is twice as hard.

Roxanne scratches her head with a pencil. "Which daughter is the good daughter? Gonorrhea?"

"Goneril!" shouts Kristen.

I explain slowly, "No, Cordelia is the good one. Goneril, not so much. Remember it that way. We don't like Gonorrhea."

"What makes Cordelia the good one?"

"Because she's loyal," I explain. "The king can trust her."

"So?" Roxanne shrugs. "Maybe that just makes her dumb. I thought her dad wasn't so great."

"The king, you mean. That's not the point."

"What is the point?"

"Shhhhh!" says Kristen, who is one problem away from being finished.

"We are not getting anywhere. Can't you just think of some characters to put in a story?" Of all the days, Roxanne picks now to start questioning Shakespeare. "Just think of a way someone, like our age, could be loyal to her dad." Roxanne doesn't have a dad. I mean, I guess she does, but she doesn't know where he is. "Her family, I mean." Her mom is not so great either. Shit. "Or her sisters, or friends, or whatever—anybody! Just pick someone!"

"Sisters!" Roxanne brightens. "I like that. Can I name one Sarah and one Kristen?"

"Yes, fine," I say, looking at my watch and checking to make sure I put a towel in my bag.

"I'd better not be Gonorrhea!" yells Kristen from behind her math book, and we all start laughing.

I let her work for a while, flip through the channels. There's a rerun of *21 Jump Street* on—Johnny Depp, ooh. I wonder how long the guys have been there, if they'll wait. Of course they'll wait.

Roxanne has her nose in her notebook. "My girls are going to conquer the kingdom and take it away from the king!"

"Um, I think you're a little off topic there," I say. "I mean, it's fun, but it doesn't really sound like *King Lear*."

Roxanne's forehead wrinkles up, and she goes back to doodling. Thirty minutes later, she has three characters, but only three sentences written. "Oh my God," I say. "Just give me your notebook. We're never going to get out the door at this rate."

She hands it over mutely. I knock this puppy out in twenty minutes.

We leave through the front door. We've just got the one bag with three towels, swimsuits on under our clothes. It's still chilly in the night air of early spring, but we don't care. We don't think we'll get caught, not this time, but Mark hasn't been here before, and he and his friends are going to have to be quiet. There are houses all around, beautiful three-story brick—all of them—and if anyone in those houses hears us out this late, the police will get called.

The first gate is easy; someone left it unlocked, and we go right through. The second one is harder, a stone wall that we have to hike ourselves over. I tell Kristen I'll give her a boost, but she takes it at a run, vaults over it like it was a pommel horse. "See ya, suckas!" she calls. I go next, and clamber to the top. I give Roxanne my hand and pull; she weighs nothing, and she's up and over before I can climb down. We see Mark and Joey standing by the gate of the pool, and they don't even hear us coming, we're so stealth.

We're not alone at the pool; there are splashes and waves and giggles there already, so our outing is dead. We'll end up in a parking lot somewhere, hanging out with Mark and Joey until Kristen and I get bored and go home. Kristen is glued to the bars of the pool fence with Joey and Mark, and I run over to see what she's looking at.

There's a couple there. They have left their clothes in a trail that begins by the gate and goes right up to the water's edge— a pair of pants, a sock, a tie, a bra. When she emerges from the water, I'm speechless at the perfection of her body. I wonder if and when I've seen a naked woman up close, and I think that maybe I haven't because I'm so disturbed by this vision. It is disturbing mostly because I know who it is.

It takes me a moment to recognize her, too long to turn around and warn Roxanne that the pool is occupied before she sees that this is where her mother has ended up with her date. Nothing surprises Roxanne, or us, about her mother anymore, but I don't even want to know how long Mark has been standing here, which is gross. All this goes through my head at the exact moment that Roxanne arrives at my side.

I don't know what to do, so I say, "Let's go," and then I pinch Mark really, really hard. I can't read what is happening on Roxanne's face. Her green eyes turn to steel, and she doesn't even notice her boyfriend and his dopey friend gawking at her mother; it's like they're not even there. She unlocks the pool gate latch and goes in. I hiss, "What are you doing?" but then I see.

She gathers up every piece of clothing within arm's length, what-ever she can get without being seen—the pants, a dress in the grass, a stiletto-heeled pump—and slithers back through the gate. I wonder how she's going to get back over the wall with all that, but there's a dumpster nearby, and she just pitches everything in. I see her slim fin-gers scrabble for purchase on the wall, but she finds a foothold on the stone, and she's up and over before we even realize that she's gone.

Kristen looks over at Mark and Joey, both so riveted by the scene that they haven't said one word the whole time. "You're morons, both of you."

Chapter Four

If you had told me even a few years ago that I would turn into one of those crazy dog people, I wouldn't have believed you. I got Rhett Pugler shortly before the divorce, not a planned thing. An author came into the shop, a romance writer, with this drooling ugly beast, and the thing had just had puppies. She had sold all but two of them, and she was waiting to meet someone, hoping he would sign on for the job of dog owner that very evening. She asked me to come look at the puppies waiting out in her car: "the cutest little things!" She was one of our most popular local authors, and I needed to humor her to make sure she would continue to give readings. Given the appearance of the mother, I did not have high hopes for the babies.

Instead, I found a smooth, wriggling ball of smooshy face adorableness, with eyes as big as golf balls that saw right through me. I picked it up and was a goner. I told the author to cancel her meeting with the prospective buyer, went back inside, and emptied my cash register, forking over most of the morning's contents to the owner of the ugliest dog I had seen in some time. My student employee Aidan said, "You know that the thing you are holding is going to grow up to look like that other thing, don't you?"

"Frankly, my dear, I don't give a damn," I declared. "He is a wonderful little gentleman of a dog, and he will grow up to look only like himself."

Rhett Pugler looks exactly like his mother now.

Matt claimed to be angry about my impulse purchase. This ill will lasted less than twenty-four hours, the time it took to fall in love with my dog. We competed for Rhett Pugler's attention, and I'm not sure, even today, that I won.

If he wasn't what she would have asked for in a grandchild, Rhett Pugler was nevertheless my mother's only grandchild, and she treated him as such. When I had to go out of town, she watched him for me and let him eat whatever he wanted. He could double in size if I left him for as long as a week.

She agreed to watch Rhett Pugler this weekend, after a long silence when I told her I couldn't make their dinner. I hadn't exactly told her where I was going. My mother always disapproved of Roxanne, so I didn't especially want to enlighten her about our destination. I wouldn't even consider mentioning the Camino, which was likely to be considered (correctly) unsafe and silly. She hadn't forgotten what happened in 1997.

My parents have lived in the same place for decades, in between two of Nashville's universities—Belmont and Lipscomb, neither of which tempted me. Belmont seemed to get all the musician types, and Lipscomb got all the good girls. I didn't fit in there. My parents' neighborhood was somewhere in between genteel and bad. When I was young, it was closer to bad, but real estate next to the city had done well lately and hipsters were fixing up those old houses. My parents lived in between two of them. They always had some sort of microbrew or homegrown tomatoes in the fridge from one of their younger neighbors.

My dad was sitting at the kitchen table, bent over a sudoku puzzle, when Rhett Pugler and I came in the side door. Dad was a postman and was still delivering the mail, even though his vision was not what it used to be. He peered at his puzzle through thick lenses. "Hi, baby," he said.

"Aren't you going to say hello to me, too?" I teased.

"I didn't even see this gentleman!" he said. "How long do we get to keep our granddog?"

"Just a weekend." I could confess my secret to Dad, who was likely to not care either way. "Kristen and I are going on a road trip to see if we can catch up with Roxanne. Jack's coming, too."

"Roxanne." He whistled. "Been a while since I heard that name. Well. That's nice. You drive safe. And you're not going to come to dinner with us old farts?" This was my parents' forty-fifth anniversary weekend. Forty-five! To think that people could be married for longer than I'd been alive. I felt bad for missing it, but it would have been just me and four other older couples. They'd be just as happy with Rhett Pugler instead, not having to explain my unmarried, childless status.

"I'm sorry?" I offered, and Dad smiled at me. He knew I wasn't that sorry.

"Your mom's out back in the garden," said Dad.

I took Rhett Pugler off his leash, and he jogged behind me to the garden, snorting gleefully as soon as he got a glimpse of my mother.

"Rhettie Dog!" she shouted, turning away from her roses. She swept him up in her arms as if they were old lovers and planted a kiss in the middle of his flat face. "Who's my dog? Who's my dog? You're my dog! That's right! You are!" Rhett Pugler soaked it all up, panting ecstatically.

"Hi, Mom." I wasn't sure she saw me at all.

"Hello, dear." My mother had already tucked Rhett Pugler underneath her arm, and the camps had been reassigned, the two of them together. "Where are you off to this weekend?" She wiped a smear of dirt from her cheek. My mother is not just an enthusiastic gardener but excessive. The backyard is beautiful, overflowing with roses, rhododendrons, and hydrangeas. She works at a garden shop and spends most of her paycheck there, hauling sacks of dirt home.

I could have lied about my destination, but I felt too old to lie to my parents. Mom was going to give me a hard time about this. "Kristen and I are driving out to Myrtle Beach. We think we know where Roxanne lives." She did not have to hear about the El Camino, about which she would have lots of opinions—none of them good.

"Roxanne! You've got to be kidding." She grimaced. "Poor Roxanne. Bless her heart. That poor, lost girl. What is she doing with herself?" Back then, she hadn't worried about Roxanne being poor or lost; she just hadn't wanted her to interfere with my future.

"Mom." I wished that I could tell her that she had been wrong, that Roxanne was now a successful doctor or lawyer. I didn't know, though, and maybe she had been right all along. "I don't know. Kristen looked her up, and we're going to see if we can get her to come to our reunion. It's coming up, you know."

"Reunion, Lordy, that's right. I can't believe it's been twenty years. I wonder what everyone will look like. I hope you have a date to bring, other than your lost ex-friend."

"If I don't find anyone, I can always go with Jack." My mother likes Jack almost as much as she likes Rhett Pugler. This should get her off my case.

"Sarah, this is a terrible idea."

"Jack will be a perfectly acceptable date."

"Roxanne, I mean. It's a long way out there to Myrtle Beach. Why do you have to do that? It's better to just leave the past alone. You know, I always thought it was a good thing that she took off when she did. You were getting ready to head off to Sewanee and needed to focus on school."

I felt a twinge in my stomach and decided to play down the anticipation of the reunion. "I just need a weekend away from the store, some good weather. It will do me good to put my toes in the ocean. We don't even know if we'll find her. I just thought a weekend in Myrtle Beach would be fun."

"Well, in that case. You're probably right. You do need some sun; do you know how pasty you are?" My mother is always tan. She's outside in the yard every day while I'm inside with a book. "Do you think there are any available men in Myrtle Beach? That's not so far away."

"We may meet up with Jack's old roommate," I offered, even though I wasn't sure I believed in his existence.

"Keep your eyes open," she lectured, pointing at me. "You'll be forty soon." As if I didn't know. "Do you know how many good eggs a forty-year-old woman has left?"

"Two?" I snapped. Here we went with the eggs again. She loved bringing this up.

"That's about right. And pregnancy is much riskier when you are over thirty-five. You are at a higher risk for birth defects, placenta previa, and diabetes." It was early in the day to be talking about birth defects.

I sighed. "All right, Mom. I'm on the lookout. You'll take good care of your only grandchild, right?"

She lifted up his paw, made him wave good-bye to me. He didn't even look in my direction. The two of them had digging to do.

The next morning, I packed a quick bag. I wouldn't need much for a short weekend away. Hotels always had toiletries, and I could wear the same jeans twice. I looked around my apartment for something that needed care in my absence, and found nothing. I unplugged the coffee machine. I locked my door and turned to knock on Jack's, which opened while I was still knocking. "Jesus, have you been sitting next to your door all night?"

Jack, freshly shaved, heaved his bag out the door. He looked ten years younger without beard stubble, newly baby-faced. Jack was going on a road trip with Kristen, and he might even wind up seeing Roxanne, both of whom were worth a nice shave and a shower. I sniffed Vetiver. We took the elevator downstairs to our building's parking garage, Jack humming a little. "What is that supposed to be?" I asked grumpily.

"You know," said Jack. "I don't even know." He hummed a few more bars.

"I think it's 'Morning Train.' Stop."

"'Morning Train'?"

"You know—*My baby takes the morning train, he works from nine till five, and then . . .*" I am not actually a bad singer, when forced. I catch Jack staring at me with a half smile. "Oh."

Jack chimes right in, *"He takes a-noh-ther home again to find me waiting for him."*

"Open the trunk, would you, Sheena?" Jack puts the two bags in side by side. Jack drives a Hyundai, new and bright red, all shiny as if it wanted to be a Mustang. I cannot imagine anyone else other than Jack who would consider buying a Hyundai in a race-car color. I had pointed out that red cars get more speeding tickets, but he told me that he had never gotten one, not once. I saw that he had also packed a cooler. My mother did this, too. If she was going to the mall, or on any errand that would take more than a couple of hours, she had to bring along something, some "cold drinks" as she says. I took a peek in the cooler to see if he had anything interesting in there, or just a bunch of Cokes. Worse: bottled water.

We had to drive to Brentwood to pick up Kristen, in a gated McMansion subdivision with massive fake Tudors and villas and Cape Cods, each of which had a plot of green yard only slightly bigger than a driveway. It looked like every period of history had vomited its progeniture onto neatly lined streets.

"Whoa," said Jack admiringly.

"You like this sort of thing? I thought you had better taste, Mr. Donahue."

"Style, shmyle, seven thousand square feet has to be pretty nice, too."

Kristen's house was one of the most tasteful ones, white colonial with some charm, after all. When we arrived, her suitcase was already sitting on the front porch next to another cooler. What was with these people and their coolers? I was hopeful that Kristen's cooler would turn out to be more interesting than Jack's. We parked the Hyundai next to Elvira. Chris lumbered out of the house after Kristen. He was dressed for work, in the southern-boy uniform of baggy khaki pants and blue sport coat. His tie had not yet been tied. "Hey, you," he drawled at me, engulfing me in a hug. I heard something crack. He looked Jack up and down and stuck out a paw to shake. "So you're the bag boy, heh." Some men might balk at sending their wives on a road trip with some random guy, but Chris had been a defensive back at Vanderbilt and was not easily intimidated. That or he just didn't care. He handed Jack the cooler, which could not have been any more emasculating.

"Chris! The suitcase!" hollered Kristen, and Chris jogged gracelessly, like a bear off to investigate a campground, to go pick it up.

"Where are the kids?" I asked.

Kristen shot me a look. "School? I took them an hour ago." I had forgotten it was Friday.

Chris loaded everything up, and I peeked in the new cooler. "Y'all got y'all some cold drinks." Chris is a southerner who can integrate "y'all" twice into a sentence completely vacant of meaning, which takes some skill, y'all.

"Yep," I drawled back. "Got us some co-colas."

Kristen gave me the finger behind Chris's back. She had packed a shaker, the contents of which were likely to be fruity and strong, three Amstel Lights, and a plastic container filled with strawberries. I closed it back up before Jack could see what was in there. Jack had argued for a predawn departure and could be a real stick-in-the-mud when he was organizing something. He planned for fun, as if it was an entry in his agenda, but every now and then, he would keep that appointment and he was a blast. I hoped we would get to see Fun Jack sooner rather than later on the trip. Putting some distance in between him and his school would help.

"Y'all gonna bring that girl back down to Nashville?" said Chris.

Down? "Yeah, buddy," I said and gave him two thumbs-up.

Kristen rolled her eyes, at me or at Chris. "Chris, hon, we're just going for a visit. You go on ahead to work." *Moron,* she mouths at me. She gave him a quick hug and peck on the lips, and Chris used both hands to squeeze her bottom. "Now don't forget pickup at three. Okay?

And you have to go to the day care after the school. Okay?" Chris nodded slowly in a way that was not at all reassuring. "See you on Monday!" she called to him and tossed me a key ring with a little plastic palm tree dangling from it. "I am going to have to call him every hour on the hour, starting after lunch," she whispered to me.

"Ah, he's got it," I said uneasily, peering at the trinket she had thrown me.

"You don't recognize it, do you?"

I looked closely and saw that the plastic was worn, its paint chipping off, but I could still read "1997, Myrtle Beach" under the palm tree.

"Souvenir. It stayed on my car all through college."

I tried to hand the keys back to her, but she was already sitting shotgun. "Why me?" I complained.

"I've got a date with that cocktail shaker in my first-aid kit. Okay, Jim, drive slow enough for us to keep up."

"Jack," I hissed.

"That's what I said."

I eased myself into the Camino and backed out into suburbia. "Ready to crank up Beach Mix?" I asked Kristen. I turned up the volume, and "Bust a Move" came blasting out.

"Is this the original?" Kristen shrieked in delight.

It wasn't, because we had worn out the first one, playing it over and over in our cars. Thank goodness I had made another copy just before everyone started burning things onto CDs. Whoever knew it would be needed again, in its original format? We also had Modern English, James Taylor, and Tone Lōc to look forward to.

Right away, driving an El Camino seemed like a terrible idea. I had just left the leather interior, integrated GPS, and Bluetooth audio of Jack's car for a flashback into an era where cars were more style than sensibility. This crazy journey that we had embarked upon required a certain amount of momentum and hysteria. If we stepped back from this for even a moment to contemplate it like rational people, we might run back to the safety of our homes immediately.

"Hey, Kristen," I said.

"Huh?" Kristen took a slug out of her shaker.

"Do you remember why we thought the El Camino was so funny?"

"No." Kristen was not really listening. She had spilled a drop of something pink and frothy on her Michael Kors bag.

"Because it is the biggest piece-of-shit car ever."

"Yes." Kristen scrubbed at her bag with her index finger, and then leaned down and licked it.

"Did you just lick your bag? What?"

"I suppose you think I should just let the leather marinate in vodka and fruit juice?" Kristen inspected the bag, properly cleansed.

"No, but an El Camino was the worst car that anyone could imagine driving, especially you. It was never about the truck bed used as a beach. You could get a real truck for that. Don't forget that she bought it because she couldn't afford anything else." I was appalled into silence for a moment before resuming. "I can barely see over the dashboard. People are staring at us."

It was true. People were staring. A baseball cap–wearing, bearded doofus gave us a thumbs-up. "That's amazing! That's exactly why we're riding in an El Camino!" Kristen mused, "How do you think she came up with five hundred dollars to buy a car?"

"Oh my God, I do not even want to know." She probably stole it from purses, bit by bit. I started laughing. "Do you think it will break down before South Carolina?"

"No! This is Elvira! She is fabulous. Billy Bob wouldn't do that to us."

"Jimmy."

"I feel like it was definitely Billy Bob."

"Shame on you. How many miles does it have on it?"

"Let's see—21,837. Not that many! This is showroom stuff, baby! Vintage!"

In front of us, Jack was driving as if he were the one in a thirty-year-old car. We weren't far from the highway, and we were easing onto I-65 going about forty. I tailgated him just to see if he would get the hint, and then blew my horn. Elvira was doing well for now; there was no reason to think we'd need to make the entire trip at this pace. Jack was always so reasonable. I wondered again why he had agreed to come along on this insane journey. What was he going to do once we got to Myrtle Beach and he had to confess that he made up a friend (Bill? Brian?) as an excuse to tag along? Whatever the reason, I was glad we had a real adult with us.

Kristen put her pedicured feet on the dashboard and began to complain about how Chris never took the children anywhere other than sports practice. The kids do play an awful lot of sports, so I was having a hard time at first deciding whether she was complaining about Chris spending too much time with the kids or not enough. Not enough, it became clear, after a story or two. I did not listen as carefully to this because I was still getting acquainted with my new wheels and trying to focus on the road. Jack had picked up the pace, although he still remained staunchly in the right lane.

My phone pinged with a text. "Can you look at that, and tell me what it is?" I asked Kristen. Amy Pritchard was due to arrive at the store, and I hoped everything was going okay. I hoped that my store manager, Evelyn, would take care of her rather than Aidan, who was likely to be a rabid fanboy, peppering her with questions, and that they had remembered to put enough coffee cups out.

"It's your ex-hubby. He says, *Good to see you yesterday.* Anything you want to tell me here?"

"Oh, we just did our doggy drop-off. He looked pretty sad, like he might want to stay for a while. Jack was there, and you know Matt loved that."

"Does he still think you and Jack are a thing?"

I laughed. "Probably. Who cares? I felt bad for him, though. He just looked so . . . lonely."

Was Matt seeing anyone? I hadn't had a real date in about a month and was going into a real drought period. I was sure that dating would get easier now that I was almost forty, but in a lot of ways it was worse. People had had time to acquire routines and habits, routines and habits that were difficult to budge from. When you were in your twenties, you were still moldable, adaptable to the constraints of a relationship and another person's desires and needs. Now, no one wanted to do that. As soon as the going got tough, people retreated to the safety of their own mortgages and furniture. What would it take to uproot all of that? A lot.

"Who cares about that guy? You really need to move on if you still give a shit about that one." Only your very best friends could be this mean to you. I wonder sometimes, though, if other people's best friends were a little bit nicer than Kristen was. "I thought you wanted to get rid of him."

"I do want to get rid of him." I didn't want to spend the early moments of our road trip talking about Matt.

"We've got to find you someone new," said Kristen. "Myrtle Beach, here we come! Want a sip of my drinkie?"

"No!" I did, but it would just have to wait.

I didn't pay too much attention to following Jack, but he must have been watching us carefully, always a few car lengths ahead of us. Kristen regaled me with family life stories, and I relaxed into the hum of her voice. We covered a hundred miles that way, and despite Jack's worst predictions, we made it to Sewanee without stopping once for a bathroom break. I hated to miss a chance to stop in my favorite town, so as we approached, I flashed my lights at Jack. He knew what was on my mind—he always did—and he already had his turn signal on.

Kristen looked over at me, and I hoped she wasn't going to start complaining about my stopover, but she smiled instead, one of those big pearly grins that showcased a deep left-cheek dimple. "Sarah," she said, shaking her head. She knew where I wanted to go.

"Come on, Kris! We need to stop to refuel bodies and Camino. Why not here?"

"Why not? It's your place." I went to college here, at the University of the South. I had dreamed of it all through high school: ivy-covered buildings, liberal arts in the Tennessee mountains. Kristen held out a manicured hand to me, like we were Thelma and Louise. I took it and squeezed. Whatever was in her shaker had clearly taken effect. It was early for sentimentality.

"We'll go to your little place for lunch. I don't mind. After twenty years, a little longer won't hurt."

"Yes! Shenanigan's, here we come."

"Are you scared?"

"Of what? Their chicken sandwich?"

Kristen was staring out her window now. "What she's like. What if she doesn't know who we are? Or what if she's mad that it took us twenty years to track her down? We should have tried harder. We should have tried."

"People lose touch," I mumbled, wondering the very same thing. Would she yell at me, or would she even agree to talk to me at all?

"That bitch just packed her up like an old suitcase, and we let her do it."

"We don't even know what happened."

"No. But I don't believe she ever went to boarding school," said Kristen.

"Where would she have gone?"

We didn't know. I didn't know, and I was afraid. Afraid of showing up on someone's doorstep, someone I had once loved, just to hear her say, *Fuck you, Sarah Martin, where were you when I needed you?*

Where were you?

We're done for the day, and we have thirty minutes before any of us have to be anywhere. Kristen has cheerleading practice, and I have to go work on yearbook. Roxanne is late for rehearsal, but she's lying in the back of her El Camino with her head on her boyfriend Mark's shoulder. She looks like she's not thinking about anything, and I envy her this.

"Y'all better get out of that car. You're gonna break it before we leave next weekend," says Kristen.

"It's already broke," says Roxanne.

"I just hope it doesn't break down on the road." I kind of wish we would just take Kristen's car, even though it is hilarious to do a road trip in an El Camino.

"Calhoun! Do you think we're going to wait for you all day?" Mrs. Wilder yells from the top of the stairs. Kristen is standing right next to Mrs. Wilder's own daughter, who she does not say hello to. It has to be super weird to have your mom at school with you all day. I'd just die if I had to put up with my mom at school and at home. Mrs. Wilder is cool, though. She lets Roxanne do what she wants most of the time, which is why we like to stay over at their house.

Roxanne doesn't move fast for anyone, but Mark does, sits up so fast Roxanne's head hits the back of the truck bed. "Hey!" She sits up and rubs the back of her head.

Kristen rolls her eyes but jogs off to join her coach, leaving us all behind. Mark watches them go, and I can't blame him, really. Both of them are about the best-looking people I know: Mrs. Wilder crazy gorgeous and Kristen like she just forgot and left her princess crown at home for the day. It's a good view, for anyone of the male persuasion. Roxanne smacks Mark in the back of the head with an open palm. I guess she's used to it, though, since Mark practically lives at their house.

"I'd better go, too," I say reluctantly. Our yearbook is going to press next week, and I have to look at final proofs. I wish I could just enjoy the sun on the spring day, not worrying about responsibilities, like Roxanne. It would be nice if she could get us ready to go for next weekend, though. "Hey, why don't you two go check the water, or the engine, or the oil, or whatever you need to check on a car? This is a major piece of shit, and it's got a long way to go."

Mark looks nonplussed at this suggestion. He can spend an afternoon alone at home with Roxanne or waiting at the Jiffy Lube. Not much of a decision.

Chapter Five

When you entered the University of the South, you were supposed to tap the roof of your car to let your angel go, because it had returned home. Alumni even have little angel decals that they put on their cars and figurines to sit on their desks. I dutifully tapped the roof of my car. Kristen rolled her eyes. I bet she was jealous because there were no angels at Vanderbilt.

"You and me and an El Camino in Sewanee? Did you ever think that would happen again?"

Our ill-fated spring break trip. I started to laugh.

"Does Jack know about your plan for a stopover here?"

"Good, you got his name right. He must be growing on you."

Kristen sighed. "I have a hard time with short *J* names—John, Jim, Jeff, Jack. Potato, potahto."

I drove slowly down the main road. In Sewanee, you passed a gas station, a Waffle House, and a Piggly Wiggly—that was "town." There was one decent restaurant, Pearl's, and then you were at the university—all ivy-covered stone on one side, a smattering of fraternity houses on the other. In less than five minutes, you'd crossed the entire campus.

Jack pulled in behind us at Shenanigan's. "Happy?" he called to me from the window.

I nodded, grinning like a Cheshire cat. I was still a Sewanee girl at heart.

"Don't get too settled in. We're on a schedule. Chop-chop." He clapped his hands, a little too close to my face.

"Relax, Jeff," said Kristen. "We've still got plenty of time." Together we climbed the front porch steps to the restaurant.

"Jack," he corrected. "By the way, have I told you yet that the shoes you're wearing right now are spectacular?" Kristen's shoes were pink, open-toed, with a heel higher than anyone needs on a road trip. He opened the door, grasped her elbow, and ever so gently, pushed her inside. He occasionally had some good moves. Kristen beamed at him, and the two of them stared companionably at the menu on the back wall, considering their options.

This place had been here for decades, serving the same kinds of sandwiches. It changed ownership in recent years, and there were a few "Save Shenanigan's" crises and campaigns. Here it was, still, not exactly but more or less the same as always.

I got the same thing every time—a Cool Cucumber sandwich. Put a cold Blue Moon with an orange slice next to it, and I'm in heaven. I'd close my eyes, and imagine that I was just a lunch away from a class I was going to. Kristen and Jack discussed the merits of turkey versus ham, wheat versus sourdough. They decided to get a Shenaniwich and a Serious Grilled Cheese and share. All of a sudden they looked like old chums, and I wondered how Jack was managing to suppress his glee. To share a sandwich with Kristen Calhoun! Maybe their fingers would brush over the crust as they made the exchange. We installed ourselves at an outside table, since the day had not yet turned unbearably humid. Jack plopped a map on the table. I didn't know anyone still used real maps. Jack's car had GPS, so this seemed really superfluous. Put-on, if you asked me.

I chewed my sandwich, tried to tune him out. We would get there when we got there. It felt like a summer family road trip, with Dad as the navigator. With Kristen riding shotgun. Jack filled the "dad" role well for us. It was sad that he wasn't a dad for real. He would have made a good one. Jack was the rare commodity of a never married, real estate–owning, job-holding, almost forty-year-old man. He wasn't divorced, but he'd had a long-term relationship that ended just before they'd made it to the engagement phase. I didn't know if he ever got over it. He now had the luxury of being able to date women far younger, if he wanted. I gave him credit for the fact that he didn't. He spent enough time with teenagers to not want to bother with anyone in her early twenties.

"It's going to take us eight hours." He stabbed the map with his index finger. We'll be in, say, Augusta by late afternoon and outside Myrtle Beach by nightfall."

"Nightfall?" I raised an eyebrow.

He ignored me. "So, here's where you ladies need to fill me in. Surely, you don't want to go banging on someone's door in the evening? They've had their supper, probably getting ready to go to bed."

"They?"

"I don't know. Is there a they?" We turned to look at Kristen. She'd been tight-lipped about our entire venture. Every time I had tried to pump her for information, she'd just said, "Wait and see."

"I don't know either. She's listed under her old name, so maybe not."

"Listed?" said Jack. "You all really didn't try very hard to find her."

"Kristen used a PI," I defended.

Kristen pushed her sunglasses, wide cat-eyed Pradas, on top of her head. "I don't mean in the phone book. That would have been too easy. I mean, the mortgage to her house is in her name. I guess that doesn't mean anything, but if there is a mister of any kind, he's not on the deed."

"Kids?" asked Jack.

"Not that I know of."

"You mean you didn't check the records at the local schools?" he pressed.

Kristen shrugged. "I got what I wanted—an address. I didn't ask for anything more. That's not what I wanted to know anyway. I can hear all the details of the past twenty years—relationships, jobs, dead pets—from the horse's mouth. I just want to see the horse."

"Fair enough," said Jack. "Hey, that would be pretty sensational if we track her down and you all come to the reunion together like old times." That was one way to put it. We were a long way from Roxanne agreeing to tag along with us.

Kristen and I looked at each other, fell silent. It seemed that we were moments from finding her, inches according to Jack's map. I just had to hope that if we found her, she would be willing to see me.

I stuffed the last bite of cucumber in my mouth.

"That was fast," said Kristen. "You're not going to ask for a Blue Moon refill?"

"Two of the three of us have to drive, so no."

"You're not going to ask to go to the bookstore?" Kristen arched an eyebrow.

I loved going to a good university bookstore. I always liked seeing what instructors had put on each semester's syllabi. Sometimes, it gave me ideas. Universities also had author readings and events that were difficult for a neighborhood bookstore to rival. I squirmed in my seat. Yes, I wanted to go. "It's more or less on the way out."

"Can you be in and out in twenty minutes?" asked Jack.

"Jesus, remind me not to invite you on a road trip again. Stop and smell the roses, wouldya?" said Kristen.

"It's Jack."

"What?"

"Jack, not Jesus." Jack smiled coolly back at Kristen. I snorted.

"Okay, thirty minutes." Jack forced a smile, but I knew that our hall pass was limited in duration.

We piled back into our cars for the short drive back through campus, then parked on the main road. The bookstore was not big, but I wanted to see what they had in their windows. Also, I needed a new sweatshirt, which Kristen would probably call too much Sewanee, if she were feeling nice. A pathetic attempt to regain my youth, if not. There was a cluster of books by professors up front, and also the works of authors who had taught at a recent conference. I hadn't heard of all of them and wrote down a title or two that I thought sounded interesting. Naturally, I wasn't going to buy books at somebody else's store. I poked around in the fiction section until Kristen called over, "Hey, there's a student art show at someplace called Guerry Hall. We're going to go check it out."

I had looked around all I needed, and I was pleased to see Kristen showing an interest in art again. I followed them outside. They'd need me to navigate. Kristen had been an art history major in college, in addition to doing some painting herself. I hadn't heard her say boo about art since we were young, though. She used to like the abstract stuff, the Pollocks and the Kandinskys, but now it was flowers, flowers, flowers at her home. She'd talked a lot about going back to work part-time in a gallery, but Chris liked having his "woman" at home. She didn't ever complain about it, but I could sense that old desire in her sometimes.

It was lunchtime, and it looked like the exhibit had just opened, with a decent crowd of students and professors starting to fill up the space. There was everything from watercolors to sculptures to a weird piece of performance art that involved a TV screen and a student dressed entirely in white staring at it. At least, I hoped it was performance art.

I loved being back on campus, but when I'd gotten here the first time, it hadn't felt as good as I'd thought it would. I had been working toward it for so long, I expected an apotheosis of happiness when I arrived. But I was carrying the baggage of Roxanne's departure and missing my trio from home. I did forget eventually, though, in that young-people-amnesia way of thinking only about themselves. I wasn't sure if once I did, that I was left with any kind of satisfaction or sense of belonging in my new place.

Kristen was walking around wide-eyed, worse than I was in the bookstore, and now I was the one trailing behind.

"Ever think about getting back into it?" I asked.

"Yeah," she breathed, staring at a wild abstract, green with spatters of gold. "Chris would hate it, though. He might have to come back home early and fix his own dinner every once in a while."

"Who cares?"

"You're right. Who cares?" Her laugh was too high. "Some of this stuff is so cool. Talented kids." She was looking at a beautiful sculpture of a bird, perched high on a thin wire that was nearly invisible, arching up from a small podium made of glass. It reminded me of Kristen herself, perched high on her heels.

"That one looks like you," I said. "Little thing sitting up high."

She cocked an ankle. "These old things? They are hard to walk in." She held out a foot, so much one of Cinderella's stepsisters, for inspection.

The other stiletto wavered, unused to doing all the work.

Before I could warn her, she did an invisible spiderweb dance, both legs bowing in to catch herself, arms flailing, close, so close, to that little bird. She got her balance back, though, and righted herself.

"Watch what you're doing," I said crossly. Everyone was talking quietly, murmuring, and there was Kristen, arms waving like a circus performer.

"I'm fine," she said. "I was miles from that birdie. Besides, I bet it's sturdier than it looks. I wonder if this was blown here on campus." She stuck out an index finger, ran it along the side of the bird.

"Kristen," I hissed. There were "Do Not Touch" signs everywhere, as if anyone (other than Kristen) needed to be reminded.

"I wouldn't mind owning this thing," she said. I looked at her skeptically. There was no way I was riding the rest of the way to Myrtle

Beach with a glass bird on a stick in my lap. She leaned closer again, her nose almost touching it, and slid her finger down the leg.

"Stop," I said again, and her hand hovered next to the wing before resting on the platform.

But the surface was made of a single pane of glass on one slim pole, and the weight of Kristen's hand tipped that smooth surface, which lurched to forty-five degrees, and down came that cradle, birdie and all.

The crash that ensued was epic, a bomb exploding in the small space.

I closed my eyes tightly, as if not seeing it meant that it hadn't happened. The room was absolutely silent. I opened my eyes one by one.

All that was identifiable of the bird were his feet; the rest was broken into several chunks. I couldn't bear to look at it again, and I couldn't bear to look at Kristen either. The crowd remained frozen, and my eyes found Jack's across the room, horrified, frantic. If we had been in a movie, I would have yelled, "Run!" and we would have hit the door. But my feet were glued to the ground.

A man in a tweed coat, who could have only been the professor in charge of the show, walked slowly toward us. He was wearing rubber-soled shoes, but you could still hear every step.

"I'm so sorry!" I had never seen Kristen look so stricken. Her hands were up around her face, like she was *The Scream*. I realized that mine were, too.

"I suppose it was an accident," he said. His eyes were not unkind, hidden behind rimless glasses. No one moved, still.

"I'll pay for it," cried Kristen. "How much?"

"These pieces are not for sale. They are our students' final projects. I don't think that would help." The crowd slowly dispersed, went back to their conversations. I stepped back a bit. It wasn't like I could pretend we weren't together, but I was in flight mode. Jack was next to the door, and I wouldn't have blamed him if he had made a run for it. He didn't. He wouldn't.

"A donation. Please! Let me make a donation to your program." Kristen's eyes had filled up, wild with embarrassment, and something else, something closer to grief.

The professor shrugged. "If it will make you feel better."

Kristen was already taking out her checkbook, but he held up his hand. "Ma'am, I am faculty here, not the bursar. You'll have to send your check somewhere else."

A girl with a sharp red bob, dressed all in black, had appeared with a dustpan to sweep up the worst of the mess. The glass platform was in a million pieces. The bird had broken more cleanly, and she picked it up piece by piece. I felt physically ill.

Kristen crouched down. "Here, let me help you." But the girl shook her head and went on sweeping. Kristen stood up again. "Are you sure there's nothing I can do? I am so sorry." The professor had returned to his students and his guests. We made our way to the door slowly. What's the old adage about not looking back? Well, we did, looked back to see that the girl had stood up from the ground. I saw the tracks of her tears before Kristen did, and I felt like I had picked up her dream myself and thrown it against a wall.

April 1997
Somewhere near Sewanee, Tennessee

Three people can't ride comfortably in an El Camino. All our stuff is in the back, and I'm scared something's going to fly out. At least I don't have to sit in the middle, like Kristen, but this is such a bad idea. Kristen and Roxanne are singing "I Believe I Can Fly" by R. Kelly as loud as they can, and the wind is blowing our hair around because both of the windows are down. Of course, there is no air-conditioning.

Kristen's BMW is parked in the driveway of Mrs. Wilder's condo. There's no reason in the world why our parents would drive by there and see it, but still. Mrs. Wilder didn't see anything much the matter with us driving Roxanne's El Camino. She was getting ready for a date and just waved at us when we left.

The car is making a terrible sound. *Rumrumrum. Rumrumrum.*

"Sewanee's coming!" I shriek. I so hope I get to go there. I cannot wait.

"Hold your horses," says Roxanne. "You'll be there soon enough, without us, okay?" We don't talk about *after* very much, since *after* means different things for each of us. For Kristen, it's Vanderbilt; for me, it's Sewanee; and, well, we just don't know for Roxanne.

"I have to pee," I say, and Kristen shoots me a squinty-eyed look.

"Sure you do," she says. But I'm in luck because they really do have to go to the bathroom. I don't think they're going to do much more than let me stop at the correct exit, though. We get off at the Golden Gallon gas station in Monteagle. This is better than nothing because there are still Sewanee students here, buying beer, Doritos.

We all go to the ladies' room, and I pick out a Mountain Dew and some Funyuns. My friends are standing outside, next to the Camino, and there's a crowd building around Roxanne. All male.

"Hey, there," says Roxanne to me. "We were just sayin' we wish we could find some sand to put back here, and we'd get in there and call it a beach." She's wearing Kristen's Ray-Bans, and no one can tell if she's serious or not.

Kristen says, behind Kristen's other Ray-Bans, "We'd just love to drive it up and down this street."

There are a couple of Sewanee boys staring at the two of them in admiration, like they'd be prepared to follow them anywhere. But there's this other guy there, too, who looks closer to forty, with gray streaked through his sandy-blond hair. He has an okay face, but a tattoo of a tiger covering his whole arm. The tiger's face ends close to his armpit. He leans his arms on the side door of the car next to Roxanne and says, "Well, why don't y'all just stay for a while?" He smells boozy, even from where I'm standing. I feel little alarm bells go off, and even though I think our El Camino is badass, too, he is not in my vision of Camino Beach.

Roxanne giggles. "Maybe we will! Y'all in?"

"No!" I say, trying to keep a note of hysteria out of my voice. "We have to get back on the road."

"I thought you were the one who wanted to stop off here. How 'bout it, Kristen?"

And that creep's hand is on our door, and I'm like, *nonononononono.*

Kristen glances over her shoulder. I am not wearing sunglasses, and she can see that I am most definitely not in. I can count on Kristen. Roxanne, though . . . we never know what she's going to do.

"Nah," says Kristen. "But we'll see you later."

"That's too bad," he says. I see that he has two gold teeth in front, a canine and that other one next to it, like he's Flavor Flav or something. He does not move from Roxanne's window, and I want to lean over and push him, but I'm too scared.

"Y'all are such buzzkills," says Roxanne.

I lean over and pinch Kristen's arm, and I don't even care if this Camino cowboy sees me do it. "Let's go!" I hiss in her ear.

Kristen gets out the keys, looks over, and says, "You gonna move?"

He smiles that sickening flashy grin. "I'm feeling pretty good right where I am." We all take advantage of the pause to jump in the car.

Kristen doesn't much like people invading her space, and she's the one in the driver's seat now. "Suit yourself. I'm leaving with or without you hanging on." Then she starts to honk. Not just a quick blast, but a long blare that doesn't let up. People in the Golden Gallon start to look at us.

"Aren't you a feisty one?" he says, and he may have even forgotten Roxanne for a second.

"Hey!" shouts Kristen. "I said I was leaving. Get out of my fucking way!" She shifts into reverse and starts rolling. He holds on to the side for only a second before letting go. We get closer to the street, and Kristen peels out of there. I feel my heartbeat return to normal.

"What's the matter with you?" I ask Roxanne. "That guy was a major weirdo. Probably a child molester." "No Diggity" comes blasting out of the radio, along with that engine noise. *Rumrumrumrumrum.*

"Oh, you're always paranoid," she says, and the engine makes a sound like a horse has kicked us.

And the El Camino rolls to a stop.

Chapter Six

The girl left with her sad little dustpan, and I thought about taking refuge in the El Camino rather than watching this train wreck take place. Jack had already beat a path back to our cars, thinking we were behind him. We were off schedule and in danger of derailing completely. I trailed along behind Kristen, slowly.

Kristen caught up with the girl. "Please! Let me do something for you."

"What? What can you do for me?" The girl looked angry now. She had stopped crying.

"I'll buy it from you!" Kristen pleaded. I couldn't bear to watch. She didn't get it. Who knows how much the thing cost? Fifty bucks to make? Even that? It had probably just taken her hours, days, weeks to do. And there it was, with a prize on it, as everyone she knew admired it, until Kristen ruined everything.

"I don't want your money," said the girl. "I don't need it."

"I just . . . I just wanted to tell you that it was beautiful, what you made. I'm so sorry."

"You know what? Fuck you, lady. Why don't you go back home to your Junior League meetings and PTA bake sales?" The girl was sneering now.

I held my breath. The Kristen I knew would never put up with that. But this Kristen just turned around, walked back to me.

I held on to her arm as if we were walking back from a burial (we were), and neither of us said a word. I wanted to tell her that it was okay, that she shouldn't worry about the student, who would be fine. I didn't know that she would be fine. Probably she would always remember the art show that ended in broken glass and the society woman who did it to her. I also wanted to tell Kristen that she wasn't that person, that she was more than PTA and Junior League, though the girl had pegged her—she was both of those. I didn't tell her anything because I wasn't ready to let her off the hook yet. She still thought everything could be fixed by writing a check. We walked back to the car in a silence that was as heavy as the afternoon air.

"You can't buy everything, you know," I said crossly. She wasn't ready to hear it, but I couldn't help myself. Kristen didn't say anything.

Jack was leaning next to the car, waiting for us. He took one look at Kristen and held out his arms. It was so strange to see the two of them there like that, like old friends or new lovers, me on the outside. I should have done that for her, but I couldn't, not yet. She should have kept her greedy paws off the exhibit, and I had told her so. Kristen thought that rules were for everybody else.

I let Kristen stay with Jack for the next part of the drive. Jack had more comfortable seats and better air-conditioning, and I drove Elvira by myself. It was fine; I didn't feel like chatting anyway. I plugged my earbuds into my phone to get some store business done.

Evelyn the manager picked up on the first ring, just like she knew I was going to call.

"How goes it?" I said.

"Sarah. Hello, dear. How are you? How long has it taken you to check in—two hours?" I looked at my watch. With lunch and the art disaster, three and a half. "Do not worry. The store has not collapsed in your extremely short absence."

"Did the new release from Anne Korkeakivi come in? I wanted that on the front table on pub day."

"Done. Has a 'Sarah's Pick' sign on it already."

I thought for a while about some other task that I wasn't on hand to micromanage, and nothing came to mind. The author event wasn't until the next day. "Okay, I guess that's all," I said uncertainly. There was a nice hum behind Evelyn, good traffic for the early afternoon. Doubtful that my absence would affect sales.

"Enjoy yourself, dear. Read a book yourself for a change, and put your toes in the sand." Evelyn was right. Since surrounding myself with books, I read less than ever—no time for it. I did always have a new title on my bedside table, though; it wasn't like anyone was distracting me at night.

We drove the rest of the day until the sun went down, then stopped for dinner at a roadside Cracker Barrel, where we ate in near silence. After dinner, Kristen wandered back to me and the Camino. We didn't talk for a while but turned up the music loud in the hopes that it would drown out that terrible incident. We got tired of Beach Mix. It was only as a teenager that you could listen to songs again and again like that, when they were all ripe with meaning to you and you felt them as intensely as the events they reminded you of. We didn't have any extra tapes, of course, so we ended up listening to the radio. We finally got an NPR station, which suited our sleepy mood. I was starting to worry, like I was going on a job interview or taking the GMAT the next day.

"Look, it was an accident. You didn't do it on purpose." I had to say something. She hadn't done it on purpose, even if her carelessness had caused it.

Kristen nodded.

"You've got to forget about it."

"Oh my God, that poor girl, and her bird. What a horrible person I am! I just ruined her life."

"You didn't ruin her life. She'll make another bird."

"What if she can't?"

"Art is not a well that just dries up. If she made one bird, she can make another, okay?" I wondered if that was true. I had written one great poem in high school. It had won a state poetry contest and then was published in a prestigious literary journal. I was only seventeen years old. It was the last poem I ever wrote.

"I don't know if that's true. Maybe she will never make anything else after college." That had certainly been true for Kristen, but I decided this was better unsaid. "Maybe she'll go on to be a management consultant, and she won't even have her bird as a souvenir from her art days."

"I don't think she'll be a management consultant. She'd have to get a new haircut," I said.

"I just . . . wish I could give her that bird back." Kristen's eyes were welling up again.

I tried changing the subject. "We're not going tonight, right? It's a little late in the day for this kind of surprise. As soon as we find a motel, let's crash."

Kristen wiped under her eyes. We were going to have to move beyond this if we wanted to complete our mission. "Motel? Does it have to be a motel?" she asked.

"A Hilton, a Marriott, whatever."

"So, not a motel. A hotel."

"Hotel, motel, Holiday Inn." We burst into laughter. The tension was finally breaking.

"Do you want to share a room with me or Jack?" I joked. I wondered what they had talked about on the leg they had driven together.

"Jack, for sure." She winked at me. She was starting to sit back up again, after drifting down her seat in misery for most of the ride. She opened up a compact from her purse and checked out her eye makeup. "Nice guy. Great guy, in fact. Cute, too. He looks like Seth Rogen, but a cleaned-up Seth Rogen, like when he's dressed up for the Academy Awards. Why didn't you ever go out with him?"

"Me and Jack? We've known each other too long. Also, not my type." I wondered sometimes if Jack had a lingering high school crush, but we were such good friends now, since we'd known each other forever. I didn't even know how you would start to date someone like that. Plus, he lived across the hall, so it would be like we were living together from day one.

"Maybe you should consider revising your type," said Kristen. "What's he doing, tagging along here, following you?"

"Maybe he's here following you."

"Nah." Kristen shook her head.

"Following Roxanne, maybe."

"Maybe."

We watched the signs for hotels, and I had Kristen text Jack to let him know we were on the lookout for sleeping options. It turned out that on the outskirts of Myrtle Beach, choices tended more toward the motel than the hotel: Sleep Inn, La Quinta. I hadn't seen a Marriott sign since closer to Atlanta.

As soon as we saw the green Holiday Inn sign, we pulled over. We were in Conway, just next to Myrtle Beach. Kristen fanned her face with a paperback. "It is nasty sticky. I hope this dump has a pool. I'm getting in, to wash off the remains of this day."

Jack pulled in behind us, and I walked in to check availability. Sixty bucks a night for a double. The Four Seasons, it was not, but there was a small pool. I went ahead and checked us in for two rooms. When I went back outside, Kristen was doubled over, laughing at something Jack had said. Thank goodness. We needed something to cheer ourselves up. I handed Jack his key. "Where's mine?" said Kristen. I held up our key.

"We have to share a bathroom? Are you serious? What is this, sleepover camp? I'm getting my own room!"

"Fine, princess. Geez, you are a pain."

"Oh, never mind, it's okay. It'll be like old times. So, are we all getting on our swimsuits and jumping in that cesspool out there? Raid our minibars first?"

"I didn't bring a swimsuit," I admitted. It never even occurred to me that I'd be putting on a swimsuit. They both looked at me in disbelief. "I also doubt there is a minibar."

"Sarah, who goes to Myrtle Beach without a swimsuit?" asked Jack.

"Well, clearly me," I said.

"Just get in in your underwear," said Kristen. "It's just us. Who cares?"

I thought it over, looked at Jack skeptically. He rolled his eyes at me. "Sarah, it's not like I've never seen you in a swimsuit. What's the difference if it's underwear?" There was a whole world of difference.

"Come on." Kristen tugged me upstairs to our room and called to Jack. "Meet you downstairs."

We dragged our suitcases upstairs, popped our key card in, and the room was okay, spacious with newish carpeting. The bedspreads were the orange-and-turquoise swirl found only in mid-priced hotel chains, but overall, things were clean and not too faded.

"Hey, hey," said Kristen. "The Holiday Inn ain't bad. It's been a long time since I've seen the inside of one of these." She launched herself onto one of the beds, landing on her back and crossing her trim ankles.

Kristen was so protected, always had been, not simply from danger or starvation but from unhappiness itself, her idea of the world and her own importance in it intact. I wondered how long she would think about the girl in Sewanee. I hoped she would forgive herself for it but maybe not forget about it entirely. Really, the only thing she had never been able to control was keeping one of her best friends with her, all those years ago. And here we were.

Kristen darted in and out of the bathroom in a flash, emerging in a white bikini too small for a woman her age. She looked fantastic. I admired her washboard stomach. Hard to believe she'd had three kids.

"You're not going to walk down the hall like that, are you?" I said, knowing full well she was.

She rummaged through her suitcase and unearthed another swimsuit of a similar size. She looked me up and down with some concern. "You can give it a try, if you want; just know that it's going to be twice as skimpy on you." I frowned at the suit, black at least, but also composed primarily of tiny triangles. "Well, let's see your underwear. How bad is it?" Kristen lifted up my shirt, and I smacked her hand away. "Oh my God." I had this old white cotton bra on. It was a minimizer, so had lots of material. It was probably more gray than white. "What else do you have?"

"That's it."

"Sarah! Who travels with only one bra? Disgusting!"

I tugged my shirt back down over my boobs. "We're only going to be gone for a couple of nights! How often do you change your bras?" She shot me a disapproving glare.

"Bottoms? Do I even dare ask?"

I wriggled out of my pants, revealing some blue-and-white-striped boy shorts, cotton again.

"Oh my God! A ten-year-old boy called! You stole his underwear. You have to wear my suit."

I shrugged my shoulders. "What? It's late. It's just you two. It doesn't matter, right?"

"Sarah." Kristen pinned my elbows to my sides. "We are going swimming with an available man, and only one of the two of us is available. I know that you have put him in the friend zone, but I am telling you now, as your friend, that you must not go outside in those rags that you call undergarments."

"He is just my friend, and it really doesn't matter."

"Fine! It matters to me, then. I don't want to have to look at that crime against underwear."

I do not own one single string bikini, and it was a new experience to put one on. The side strings on the bottom were working in my favor, since I could adjust them. There was no help for the top, because I'm a D and Kristen is a B. There was no way all of that was going to fit in there. I poked my head out of the bathroom. "I look like a porn star."

"Let me see." Kristen let out a long whistle. "You do look like a porn star! Hot damn! Let's go."

I grabbed a towel off the rack and wrapped it around myself. "I can't go out like this."

"Sure you can. You look amazing."

"I look like Attila the Hun in a swimsuit. Jabba the Hutt going to the beach."

"No!" She poked at my midsection. "You're the teeniest bit squishy here, but men don't mind that. People go to plastic surgeons to have boobs like yours." She paused. "And they're not all fucked up from breast-feeding. Let's go!"

I tucked the end of my towel under my armpit and followed her out. There was a small bar next to the pool, and Jack had already ordered three beers. He was perched on a barstool in some board shorts that had seen better days. Kristen picked up her beer and drank it in one lengthy pull. Jack followed suit. I raised an eyebrow at him. Jack doesn't usually drink very much but was on board for whatever Kristen was doing. "Last one in is a rotten egg," called Kristen and took off at a jog, splash landing in the pool. Jack followed her, with a cannonball that tossed a tsunami in my direction. What was he doing?

"Mr. Donahue," I said. "I think that this is not acceptable principal behavior."

"No one has to know I'm a principal here!" he called, grinning from ear to ear. He appeared to be living out some erstwhile spring break fantasy.

"Get in, Sarah," called Kristen. I clung to my towel.

"Come on," called Jack. I sat down on the edge of the pool, towel included, and put my feet in.

"Get her," said Kristen, and Jack dove under for one ankle while Kristen pulled on the other. I tumbled into the pool with all the grace of a beached whale that rescuers had shoved back into the ocean. My towel floated on the surface as I emerged, spluttering and pushing my hair out of my face. Kristen's hair was slicked back in perfect beachy waves like she had just walked in from the Blue Lagoon.

I wiped the water out of my eyes and just felt tired. They didn't know what I was going to have to face the next day. Neither did I. Maybe she would be thrilled to see us, and all bad memories would be bygones. A lot could happen in twenty years, enough to erase the memory of a high school betrayal. I could only hope that was the case here. Then again, maybe she would slam a door in my face.

I got out of the pool.

"Come on, Sarah. We're just playing! Lighten up!" said the woman who'd destroyed an undergraduate's art project only a few hours earlier.

Jack was gaping at my ensemble, but there was nothing I could do about it since my towel was in the pool. I pulled myself up to my full five eleven and barked, "You want to take a picture? I'd put a towel on, but I don't have one anymore."

"Take mine," said Jack, which would have been gallant if he could have delivered it while looking into my eyes.

"I'm just tired, that's all." I wrapped Jack's towel around me and slunk back up to the room. I fell back onto my bed, tried to read a few pages of the book by the behavioral economist who was coming to visit us next month. It didn't grab me, so this guy may not have quantified absolutely everything. I turned on the TV to watch Jimmy Fallon delivering his monologue. Would Roxanne look the same? Would she look old, and fat? Would she have Botoxed her forehead and filled in the lines around her mouth? Would she still wear skirts that were too short? Would she be there at all?

I dozed off, into a dream where Roxanne was the bandleader on *The Tonight Show*. Her skin was flawless, and her hair shone burnished copper under the stage lights. Jimmy leaned forward and laughed, slapping his desk every time she said something. She looked at the camera, looked at me, and somewhere in the back of those emerald-colored irises, I could see the fear there; the studio audience roared with approval.

I woke up to knocking. I wiped sleep from my eyes and padded over to the door, peeped out of the peephole. There was Kristen, dripping on the floor, no towel, laughing hysterically. "Who's there?" I said.

I watched her dissolve into giggles and opened the door to find out what was so funny. She crashed past me into the bathroom to grab a towel. "What on earth?" I said. "Have you completely lost your mind?"

Kristen doubled over, shaking with laughter. "Not my mind . . . but Jack." She hiccuped and wiped a tear away.

"You lost Jack?"

"No," she howled. "But Jack has lost his swimsuit."

I started to laugh a little, too, without really knowing what I was laughing at. "What are you talking about?" I hoped that Kristen had not talked Jack out of his swimsuit, not that she wasn't capable of it. She was still in her own, so that, at least, was a good sign.

"It's one of those old Jacuzzis, and so, so . . ." She laughed some more, drew in a long snort. "Part of his bathing suit got sucked into one of those jets."

"Wait, he's stuck in the Jacuzzi?"

"No, but he had to take off his swimsuit to get free! And he doesn't have a towel because he gave it to you."

"So, he's sitting down there naked?"

Kristen leaned against the wall for support. This was pretty good. If I weren't so tired, I would try to keep the joke running a while longer, like bring him a towel, but one of those tiny hand towels. We had to go help him. "You need to put on some clothes."

Kristen fished a sundress out of her suitcase and threw it on over her swimsuit. We'd bring him a towel, and then get Jack's room key, which Kristen had forgotten to bring up in her hysteria. I followed Kristen to the pool area, which I could see was not deserted, unfortunately. There was a family with two older children, a girl of about thirteen and a boy maybe high school age. The hotel security guard was there, too. They were all standing around the Jacuzzi. Jack was still inside the hot tub, and his face was bright red, possibly from the heat but maybe not.

"Did the man talk to you?" I heard the mother ask the girl.

The boy was facing the wall, arms crossed. He mumbled, "Let's get out of here."

It was best if Kristen didn't try to speak in her condition, so I walked up to the security guard. "Excuse me," I said. "Our friend is in a bit of a predicament."

"I'll say," said the father. "What kind of sicko gets naked in the pool of a family hotel?"

Jack had nothing to say for himself. He looked like he might faint, in fact. Kristen repeated her story. "His swimsuit got stuck in one of those jets there! It wasn't his fault!"

The security guard didn't look convinced. "That's never happened before."

Kristen picked up the maimed swimsuit, which had been tossed on a pool chair. "See? There's a hole here." The hole, unfortunately, was surprisingly neat-looking, given the trauma the swimsuit had been through, and located in the rear of the swimsuit.

"Dear God," said the mother to the kids. "Thank goodness you didn't get in that Jacuzzi. I'm taking you upstairs." She left the husband to deal with the pervert and his friends, and ushered her children out of harm's way.

"Do you want me to call the city police?" asked the guard. "I think we may need to fill out a report here."

Jack spoke, finally. "My swimsuit was sucked into one of your jets! I did not come down here to take it off! This is not my fault! I am an upstanding citizen!" Kristen started to laugh again, and I pinched her.

"Hey," I said to the guard. "Your pool is a liability. You're lucky it was only his swimsuit. When was the last time that thing was properly maintained, the eighties?"

The security guard squinted at me. "Nothing like that has ever happened before," he repeated.

"I saw on *Dateline* once a story about a faulty jet in a hot tub, and someone sat down on it, and it ripped his intestines clean through his behind. Can you imagine?" I tried to look stern and litigious.

"Me, too! I saw that one!" piped up Kristen. "Turned 'em inside out!"

The security guard cringed. "Get me out of here," shrieked Jack. "Right now!" Kristen tossed him the towel, and everyone turned away as he hauled himself from the water and wrapped the towel around his waist.

"We should sue *you*," I said to the guard. "So, why don't you go ahead and call the police, and we'll fill out a report of hotel negligence while they're here?"

Covered, Jack began to return to himself. He took a couple of deep breaths in and out, and roared, "That was a new bathing suit! You have ruined it, and you have humiliated me! I am going to call my lawyer." Jack doesn't have a lawyer, but I was enjoying watching him lose his shit, which never happens.

At the mention of legal action, the guard backed down. He was, after all, a hotel steward, not much of a law enforcement officer. "Let's just all calm down. What do you say?"

"I will not forget about it!" Jack looked like a toddler throwing a tantrum. "I have been publicly embarrassed, and my property has been damaged." Kristen held up his "property" with a pinky finger. "You have not heard the end of this."

"I can ask the manager if he'll adjust your bill," said the security guard.

"Thank you very much," I said, walking toward the door.

"I do not think that sixty dollars is enough to compensate me for the humiliation I have endured inside your establishment!" shouted Jack. I tugged on his arm. Sometimes, you had to know when to fold 'em.

"Let's just go," I whispered.

Jack put his hands on his hips. "This is not over," he fumed.

We all went back upstairs. Kristen changed out of her swimsuit, and I realized only then that I had been walking around in my pajamas. The hilarity of the incident had transformed into fatigue, but I wanted to know how they had gotten themselves in that predicament in the first place. "What were you doing down there?"

"What do you mean?"

"I mean, naked in the Jacuzzi."

"Sarah, I was not naked in the Jacuzzi, and he didn't mean to be either. What did you think we were doing?"

"I don't know, which is why I asked."

"Maybe you wish you were down there naked, too." Kristen climbed into bed, pulled the covers all the way up. "Your friend there is so nice, such a good man. Why can't they all be like that?"

"What do you mean? That he's graceful while naked in a Jacuzzi?" I snickered. "And I do wish I had been down there. But at least there was someone here to give you a towel."

"You don't know, Sarah, what it's like to come home to a man who cannot talk about anything, who cannot even so much say 'How was your day,' and mean it. You don't know what it is like to live with a pig in shoes who notices you only when he climbs on top of you once a week and then falls asleep. It is just so nice to spend some time with a man who actually knows how to listen." She wiped her eyes again. "I'm halfway tempted to run down the hall and knock on his door. Make sure he's okay after that awful scene."

This sent me bolt upright in bed. "No! Kristen! Stop that right now! You're married to your pig in shoes. This is not a problem the Holiday Inn can solve."

She fell back against her headrest and sighed. "He would probably just think I was drunk and crazy, having a midlife crisis."

"Good." This was true, and she was, but he might still take her up on her offer. She was Kristen, after all. And then, Kristen would go back to her gilded life with her husband and leave Jack pining after her.

"Why don't you run down the hall and knock on his door, then?"

"Cut it out. Go to sleep." I hoped that both of them would return to their senses by the next morning. Kristen had a marriage crisis every few years, but they didn't usually involve my other best friend.

The next morning, Jack and Kristen were quiet at breakfast, both of them nursing headaches, although it might have only been Kristen with the headache and Jack wanting to appear sympathetic. The air had shifted, though, the two of them sitting together while I dug placidly into my bagel. I felt nauseated. We were so close to Roxanne that I could practically smell her spearmint gum, and still, I had no idea what was going to happen.

I went to check us out and pay the bill, and the attendant said, "No charge. Please accept our apology for the inconvenience."

It was easy for me to accept the apology, since I hadn't been inconvenienced at all. Jack was always on the lookout for a good deal, so this would help to balm his wounded ego.

"Ladies, this is it," said Jack. His shirt was freshly pressed. He had to have re-ironed it out of his suitcase for it to look that crisp. Small steps back to dignity. "Are you ready? According to my map, we'll be there in fifteen or twenty minutes."

Kristen and I exchanged doubtful glances.

We loaded the Hyundai back up. I felt a little embarrassed getting into Elvira. Now that we were really here, this idea sounded less funny and more batshit crazy. I took in a deep breath and climbed in. Kristen and I backed out of the parking lot after Jack, not talking.

The closer we drew, the more nervous I got. I wanted to stop to go to the bathroom, but Jack was making good time, on a mission. We crossed into the city of Myrtle Beach, taking an exit with an airport icon on it. Soon, we were driving in the direction of Market Commons, a shopping center with some new-looking condos around it. It had been an air base, remodeled to look like a village. I couldn't stand these kinds of places. They reminded me of a film set, like the time I visited Universal Studios with my parents as a child. The storefronts and houses looked flat, like you could walk around behind them and there would be nothing there.

We turned into the edge of one of these villages. Jack was driving slowly, scanning house numbers. We made a couple of right turns and coasted to a stop. Kristen and I looked at each other in terror. We had just driven ten hours for a ghost, with the biggest prop imaginable. What were we going to find here? Would she be overjoyed to see us? Furious? I wondered if she would even recognize us, but a quick look at the perfection of Kristen's forehead reassured me that at least one of us was well preserved. We climbed out of the car, but Jack stayed seated. "This is your visit," he called out his window. "I'll wait out here." I was surprised he didn't want to trot up those steps behind us, to see what was about to go down. He did have a good seat from where he was parked. Jack is nothing if not discreet—at least when fully clothed and not in a Jacuzzi.

I reached for Kristen's hand. She squeezed like we were girls in a horror film, going to visit a haunted house. Maybe we were. We were moving so slowly, one by one up the stairs, like we were trick-or-treating at the scary old lady's house at the end of the street. "You ring," I said to Kristen. "It was your idea."

She glared at me but slowly lifted up her hand and pushed the button.

We waited for what seemed like an eternity and then heard steps approaching from the back of the house. We exchanged panicked glances. I let go of Kristen's hand so that we wouldn't look like little girls. The door opened, and there she was.

I couldn't believe it, what time had done. She was still beautiful, but so old. Did the two of us look that old, and we just didn't realize it? She wore slim dark jeans, a black T-shirt. Her hair was threaded with gray, frizzier than I remembered it, and the crow's-feet at the edges of her eyes were deep. She had hard lines at the corners of her mouth, and the skin around her neck was loose. I could not speak.

"Can I help you?" she asked. Her eyes narrowed suspiciously.

Kristen sucked in a breath and said, "Mrs. Wilder!"

April 1997
Sewanee, Tennessee

We turned the key a million times. We kicked the car and swore.
We banged the dashboard. But the car is not moving, and smoke is
pouring from the hood.

Our crowd has vanished, including the creepy guy, and the
place is deserted. We go inside to ask the woman at the register.
"Ma'am?" says Kristen. "Our car broke down. Do you know where
the closest garage is?"

"It's twenty minutes that way, but Johnny and Lorraine have
gone down to Daytona Beach, taken the kids. You're not going to
find it open."

A police officer rolls up next to our El Camino and is talking to
Roxanne. Kristen and I run back outside. "Sir," I say. "Do you think
you can help us with our car?"

He opens up the hood and shakes his head. "You're going to
have to tow it. Do you want me to call somebody to pick you up?
Your parents, maybe?"

We look at each other in total panic. It will not help us to have
this phone call come from a police officer.

"You call her," says Roxanne to me. We've got a quarter, and
we use it to call the only parent who is aware that we are here in

a seventeen-year-old car and who might not tell the other parents what we have done.

"Why me? She's not my mother."

"She likes you better than me. And you're the responsible one."

I glare at Roxanne, but I deposit my quarter, take a deep breath, and wait. It rings a few times, and a husky voice comes on and murmurs hello.

"Mrs. Wilder?" I say. "It's, um, Sarah."

"Yes, Sarah?" She doesn't sound glad to hear from me. Impatient.

"So. Hi. Well, um, we ran into some car trouble here. I think we're going to need someone to help us out." I stop breathing for a second.

"Oh." I could hear activity in the background, the rustling of fabric, the pulling open of drawers.

"Um, do you think you could come? We're in, uh, Sewanee."

"Well, I'm a little busy right now. Just getting ready to go out. What about your mother? Couldn't she help?"

I do not want to say that my mother does not know we took the unsafe car and say instead that she is out of town. I hear the tinkle of ice cubes in a glass and a long pause. "Where are you?"

"At a gas station."

She sighed. "Sewanee is two hours away. Do they not have a bus station there?"

"I don't know." I look at Roxanne, who doesn't look the least bit surprised that I don't seem to be getting anywhere.

"Well, that sounds like the best idea. You go on over there, and you girls can call when you're back in town."

"That could be hours! And what do we do about the car?" I hear the hysteria in my voice, but she is as cool as the contents of her drink.

"Well, sugar, sometimes there are consequences for our actions. And that old car was never going to make it far anyway. You didn't really think it was going to get you all the way out to Myrtle Beach, did you?" My mouth falls open, and I hang up the phone.

"Your mother is . . ." I do not know how to finish.

"A coldhearted bitch?" says Roxanne flatly. "I know."

We sit on the curb for a while, postponing the inevitable, and eventually walk down the street to Waffle House in the hopes that food will erase the incident. I order two eggs sunny-side up, and Roxanne orders two waffles. Kristen asks if she can have biscuits, and the waitress says, "This ain't the Biscuit House, sweetheart." We eat glumly, knowing that spring break is over but not wanting to call time of death. Roxanne has a million ideas—hitchhiking, staying for two days in Sewanee and trying to earn enough money (how?) to pay for bus tickets to Myrtle Beach.

"How are we going to make Camino Beach if the Camino part of it stays in Sewanee?" complained Kristen.

But the fate of this car is looking worse by the minute. I start to wonder why we ever believed we could get there in that piece-of-shit car. Worst of all, I know that Kristen's parents really are out of town, and the only ones we can call are mine.

By the time they show up, it's after dark. My mother says, "Well, at least you're not dead," in a way that makes me not quite believe it's true. I start crying.

"Oh, come here," says my mother and gives me a reluctant hug. "It could be worse."

"She's right, Sarah. We'll go another time," says Kristen.

"I don't know when," says my mother. "Sarah is grounded until graduation."

Chapter Seven

I didn't know how I hadn't seen it right away. The eyes had never been the same, the mother's harder, more calculating than the open jewels of her daughter. Everything else was close enough—the color of the hair, the long legs, even the dimpled smile. The vestiges of her former glamorous self were still there.

It would have been awkward if we had come here and found Roxanne, but we had been counting on the joy of the reunion to get us past the initial what-are-you-doing-here that was bound to occur. By the look on Mrs. Wilder's face, we could not have been more unwelcome if we had been Jehovah's Witnesses.

"It's Kristen!" Kristen blurted. "And Sarah."

"From Briley," I added stupidly. "And Roxanne." Kristen shook her head at me and rolled her eyes.

"Oh. Well, hello, girls." Mrs. Wilder took a step back. I would have thought she'd have been happier to see us, or at least pretend that she was. Even though everything had ended badly, even though we had badgered her for an address for Roxanne, even though she made it seem as though she was sending Roxanne away due to our bad influence (a likely story), she still knew us. She had hugged us in her home, high-fived us after football games, told us off-color jokes, and we had fallen under her spell, too. But she didn't seem glad to see us now.

As I got further away from my senior year, I had to revise my memories of Mrs. Wilder. It was hard to explain now, but we had sensed the danger, seen its traces, and chosen to ignore it. I knew, later, that a mother who let us get away with anything, who looked the other way at our cold Zima bottles piling up on the wall of the basement, who had not sniffed the smoke in our hair, and who left the door unlocked for us at four in the morning, was not someone who took care of her child. She didn't take care of us either. We would never know, really, what it had been like every day for Roxanne, with that parade of dates—a revolving door of men, the nights spent alone when her mother didn't come home. We'd had twenty years to think about this, but still, we didn't know what to say when we were faced with Mrs. Wilder.

There is an intimidation that remains from adults who knew you as a child, even though they shrink as you catch up and pass them in size. They hold on to some of their fearsomeness, as if they could still ground you or put you in detention. She had all that. She wasn't much bigger than Kristen, rail thin, and she still knew how to place a hand on her hip in just the right way. I was taller than she was in high school, and I had gained another few inches over her since then. It didn't stop me from feeling small.

I found my voice. "We thought this was Roxanne's address." Kristen and I were lost, bumbling through the awkwardness of this unexpected encounter.

"Well." Mrs. Wilder raked her fingers through her hair. "She did do this one favor for her mama, helped me with my house before taking off. Guess it's still listed as hers."

The first piece of news I'd had in twenty years. Even if we hadn't found our friend, we knew she was at least doing well enough to own real estate, and to buy property for someone else. I just couldn't imagine why she would choose to do such a thing when we knew she couldn't stand her mother.

Mrs. Wilder shrugged her shoulders, which could have meant, *I don't know*, or could have meant, *I won't tell you.* She took in the El Camino parked at her curb. "Well, well, well. You certainly came prepared. Where did you even find one of those?"

"Where is she?" Kristen asked, ignoring the question.

She shrugged again. "I haven't seen her in years."

"How many years?" I said.

She squinted at me. "A few. Now, what is it, exactly, that you girls want?"

Here I felt like shouting, in courtroom style: *The truth! We want the truth!*

Maybe we couldn't handle the truth.

"It's our high school reunion," I offered. "We wanted to find her before then."

"No kidding," she said. "What's that, fifteen years?"

"Twenty," said Kristen flatly.

"I wish I could help, but we lost touch. I don't know where she is." How did you just "lose touch" with your child, like you lost your car keys? How could she not know?

"Do you mind if I use your bathroom?" asked Kristen abruptly. "We've been on the road for a while." We had been on the road for maybe ten minutes.

The hesitation was marked, but it was such a small thing to ask. Mrs. Wilder opened the door a little wider. "First door on the right." Mrs. Wilder gestured to the car as Kristen pushed past her. "Is that one of your husbands out there?"

I snorted. "That's Jack Donahue. You probably don't remember him."

"Jack Donahue! I don't believe it!" Barefoot, she made a beeline across the small patch of yard to the car. Jack climbed out of the car, and she actually hugged him, a hug that lingered. We hadn't gotten hugs. "Which one are you married to?"

"No one," answered Jack.

She slapped him on the arm. "Well, isn't that a shame for them? You have grown! What a handsome man you turned out to be!"

Jack went beet red. He tried to smile back.

"Y'all have driven all this way. The least I could do is give you a glass of iced tea." I noted that she hadn't offered up the iced tea until she saw Jack. Jack and I followed her inside.

I looked around the living room, painted in shades ranging from bubblegum to fuchsia. There were mirrors everywhere—she had always loved to look at herself. A fat gray cat slept on a pink cushion in the corner. A Marilyn Monroe nightmare. We sank into a pillowed white sofa. Kristen came out of the bathroom, mouthing and pointing to something at the door that I couldn't understand. She sat down on a pink chaise lounge, perching awkwardly on the end of it. Mrs. Wilder returned with four glasses of tea on a tray, and Kristen sniffed hers like it might be poisoned.

I remembered our last conversations with Mrs. Wilder. We had stormed her office the day after finding out Roxanne had left. She had been cool with us, making us sit on the hard folding chairs in her office and using her most adult voice. "Girls, you know as well as I do that Roxanne has just been out of control lately. She had all those absences, and I hope you won't tell anyone, but she was just caught cheating. Principal Hunter has had enough."

She stood up then, walked behind her desk. "She'll finish up at a boarding school where she isn't allowed visitors, and I think it's best for you to not see her right now."

The wall of Roxanne's mother had been impenetrable. We thought we'd eventually wear her down, but she left, too, as soon as the school year was over. The Wilder condo went up for sale before we even moved out of our parents' houses, and all trace of them vanished with Mrs. Wilder.

We sipped our iced tea meekly.

"We always wondered," said Kristen. "Where did she go at the end of the year?" What was the harm in telling us now?

Mrs. Wilder swirled the ice cubes in her glass, didn't say anything for a few seconds. "Boarding school," she said mechanically.

"Which one?" asked Kristen.

"Oh, God, it has been so long. It was only for a few months. I can't remember," said Mrs. Wilder.

"Well, what city was it in?"

"Um, Atlanta."

"Was it Clarkson?" asked Kristen.

"Yes, that sounds right. That must be it."

"We called. She wasn't there." There were boarding schools from the Northeast all the way across the ocean to Switzerland. But Clarkson was nearby, and it was known for accepting problem students. Our high school had sent more than one student there, and we knew the name.

"What do you want from me exactly, girls?" said Mrs. Wilder. "That was a long time ago. I don't know why it matters."

I took the opportunity to stand up and go to the bathroom. There was evidently something in there that Kristen wanted me to look at. The bathroom was as frilly as the living room—white lace curtains, mother-of-pearl handles on the faucet. I sat down to pee first, and felt air coming out of one of those squishy toilet seat covers. Ten kinds of bubble bath covered the edges of the tub. When I got up, I went ahead and took a peek inside the medicine cabinet. Prescription meds lined the shelf, from the uninteresting amoxicillin all the way to Viagra (Viagra!) and Vicodin, Percocet and Xanax.

When I returned, Mrs. Wilder was lecturing about "the past being the past" with a dreamy look on her face that I now recognized as

Valium serenity. Kristen had uncrossed her legs and was leaning forward with a scowl on her face that did not bode well for Mrs. Wilder. Jack was holding on to his iced tea with two hands, and looking back and forth between the two of them as if he were following a tennis match.

"You can't really expect me to believe that you forgot where you sent her, and then, you suddenly remembered when I just now said it. And I know she wasn't there." Uh-oh.

"Who can remember these names?" She waved a hand in the air. "I can barely remember the name of that old place. How long were we there, a year?"

"Briley," said Jack. Nobody looked in his direction.

"Fine, so what was she doing the last time you saw her?" Kristen looked exasperated, a policewoman at the end of a tiresome interrogation.

"She has her own life now. Doesn't care about her mama anymore."

"What is she doing?" I asked, in what I hoped was a tone of polite interest rather than rabid curiosity.

Mrs. Wilder stood up, stretched luxuriously. "Y'all. This has worn me out, this talk of the past. I think it's time for you to get back on the road."

"You know! You know, and you won't tell us! Just like the last time! Why won't you tell me? Tell me!" Kristen stood up, too, and put her finger in Mrs. Wilder's face. "Do you swear you don't know where she lives?" she said, like she was going to say *Stick 'em up* or something.

Mrs. Wilder swatted her away, shook her head. "Go on. I don't know and wouldn't tell you if I did. Get in your stupid car and hit the road."

I gasped and exchanged a look of panic with Jack. I didn't need to be told twice. Jack, in his best, most conciliatory voice, asked, "Mrs.

Wilder, please. It would mean so much if you knew anything that could help us."

Now her face was red, from anger, sadness—I didn't know what. "I said no! I don't know anything! Now, please leave me alone!"

"Lady, this is not over," said Kristen. "I'm going to find her."

"Tell her hello," she said, deflating.

"Fuck you. That's what I'm going to tell her I said to you," Kristen yelled. Jack put an arm around her and steered her toward the door. She looked like she might start to cry.

Mrs. Wilder was looking out the window, somewhere else already.

It's opening night of our end-of-year musical, and Kristen and I are sitting in the front row. Even my parents are here somewhere. Roxanne has the lead in *The Music Man*. I do not know how Roxanne is going to pull off being a librarian. She would have made a perfect Roxie Hart in *Chicago*, but no such luck—the main role is Marian this year. I wish I could have auditioned, because I am a pretty good singer, but I just didn't have time, with yearbook, and newspaper, and getting everything ready for college.

Kristen elbows me. "Think she's gonna choke?"

I hope not. We have run lines with her for the past month, and now she remembers most of them most of the time. She has never sung her songs for us, not once, and I don't know how that's going to go. Our practicing may not be enough once she is onstage.

The curtain goes down, and I hold my breath.

When she comes onstage for the first time, knee-length skirt, blouse buttoned all the way to the top, the audience roars, probably out of surprise because of the modest dress. But she looks beautiful, and like a librarian after all.

She flubs a line during the piano lesson scene, and Kristen squeezes my hand. We wince together.

"This is going to be a long couple of hours," says Kristen.

"Shhh. Don't be mean."

Then, Roxanne sings "Goodnight, My Someone," and her voice is quiet and small, but true, and it brings a tear to my eye, and I miss her already, thinking of next year. I look at Kristen, who has mascara running down her cheek.

And then, I'm not watching my friend Roxanne but Marian the librarian, and the rest of the musical is wonderful. We clap and laugh to "Seventy-Six Trombones" and watch her bring it home in "Till There Was You."

When the show is finished, the audience erupts into cheers, and she is second to last to come out for the curtain call. Mark throws her a bouquet of flowers. Kristen and I have two white roses, and we throw them, too. Her face is totally open, transported. I've never seen her look so happy.

I wish she would smile like this every day.

Chapter Eight

"Shit!" yelled Kristen and kicked the curb next to the Camino. She stomped her foot hard, and the heel off that shiny pink shoe broke in one clean motion. "Goddammit! That was Prada, five hundred bucks. Great. Fucking great!"

Jack looked up at the sky.

"I'm sure you have two other pairs in your suitcase," I said. Both probably also five hundred bucks a pop.

"Three," she said.

"Jesus, Kristen, you just went sort of bananas there." I didn't like Mrs. Wilder either, had never forgiven her for leaving us stranded in Sewanee, among other things, but I didn't think she could help us.

"She could help us, and she won't. She was always like that—selfish." Kristen's hands were on her hips, and she was puffing. Jack went back to his trunk, silently, and dug out her suitcase for her. He put it in the back of Elvira, opened it up, and waited for her to make her choice.

"I need a drink," said Kristen, lifting out a pair of flat, strappy sandals. She shucked the remaining shoe and tossed the pair into a nearby bin. I winced. She put on the new shoes and shrank a few inches.

"It's ten in the morning," I reminded her.

Kristen wiped underneath her eyes, where her eyeliner had started to run. "Goddammit. Do you think I should go back in there?"

"No," said Jack and I in unison.

"She knows something she's not telling us. And did you see the pharmacy in her bathroom?"

Jack nodded in agreement. He was faced with little liars on a daily basis and was good at reading intention. "She definitely knows something, but I'm not sure she knows where Roxanne is right now."

"I need to do a full debrief, but with a margarita." Kristen fanned her face.

"Everything is still closed. If you're looking for a bar that caters to normal people drinking at ten o'clock, I don't think you're going to find one. A dive, maybe."

"I'll call Bert," volunteered Jack.

"Who?" said Kristen.

"My college roommate. The one I was hoping to see on this adventure y'all dragged me on." Here went Jack again about the roommate. I was grateful, though, that he had an idea for our next stop. I didn't want to spend one more second in front of Mrs. Wilder's house. I looked back at it, thought I saw a curtain drawn.

"Nobody dragged you," I said. Bert could not be a real person. I had never heard Jack talk about anyone named Bert until we started on this trip. Who was named Bert? Did Jack think I was so helpless that he had to come along? Or was he tempted by the journey with Kristen and maybe even Roxanne? Still, Jack was on the phone already, and someone, a real someone, appeared to have answered.

Jack stuck his finger in his non-phone ear, walked away from us. On the off chance there really was a Bert, I hoped he wasn't hearing about our crazy mission. How would that sound to an outsider? "Wellll, we just bought us a real old car, and it even has a truck bed! We just drove eight hundred miles to find an old friend, and we found her crazy mother instead."

"We're going to drive north, toward Broadway at the Beach." Jack got back into his Hyundai, leaving us to follow.

We piled into the Camino and pulled away from Mrs. Wilder. It was surely the last time we would ever see her. When you were young and everyone was heading their separate ways, you didn't always know that the last time you saw someone was *the last time* you'd see them. We said "good-bye, see you during the holidays," not knowing if we would, and then didn't.

The last time I saw Roxanne was in biology. We were passing notes, making fun of our teacher's habit of picking her nose when she thought no one was looking. In fact, we had wagers on how many times she would pick each day. Roxanne was quieter than usual, but she didn't seem sad. I'd asked myself the question a million times, and I always came up with the same answer. She didn't reveal anything that day. We were all tired in a midterm exam kind of way, and when we left class that day, we were caught in the flow to the lockers. It was just like any other day. The next day, she wasn't at school. Then, or ever again.

We'd had a second chance at seeing her mother, and this good-bye, we could all hope, was final. We'd had a second chance with the wrong person.

"Shit," muttered Kristen again, putting her head in her hands. "I am going to kill that motherfucker of a PI. And he'd better give me my money back! Or at least find the right address."

"I am not going to any address that your private investigator gives us."

"You have any better ideas?"

"No. But I will." I was thinking already. We had never turned over these rocks in the first place, mainly because I was too scared to do it. We had never properly played Nancy Drew.

"We'll think better with a margarita."

"Are you sure you want to be drinking again? I thought you'd had enough yesterday? What a waste of a weekend."

"Why?" said Kristen. "I'm having a great time."

I took my eyes off the road to stare at her. A great time? I knew that life with little kids wasn't always easy, but it had to be better than this. Maybe that was what living with little kids was like, constantly getting yelled at by irrational people.

"Honestly, Sarah, what were you going to do with your weekend, anyway? Work at the store? Hang out with your dog?"

I glared at her and followed Jack off the highway, in the direction of big commerce. We were driving toward a behemoth of ramped-up American retail—a shopping mall crossed with Disney World. There was a sideways-looking museum and a zip line ready for tourist adrenaline rushes looming up in front of a parking lot the size of a small country, which was empty at this time of day. A serene, fake little lake served as the backdrop.

"You may have a point about the weekend." I had to admit it.

Kristen snorted, and I couldn't help it, I began to smile, too. She started snickering, covering her mouth with both hands, as I parked the car next to Jack's. This soon turned into gales of laughter. Kristen had a honking laugh that was so completely unladylike that it never failed to get me going. I got caught up in it, too, and the two of us could not get it back together. I couldn't have said what was so funny, just maybe our nerves finally getting the best of us. Jack started tapping on Kristen's window like a cop with a flashlight. She opened the door, and I rolled out of my side.

"Do not tell me that the two of you started drinking in the car again," said Jack.

"Do you think we have a keg hooked up to the ignition?" Kristen started hooting all over again as we walked toward Broadway at the Beach.

"I do not know what you two think is so funny. I was traumatized by what just happened."

It was "traumatized" that did it. We leaned into each other and laughed some more. "Traumatized," I gasped.

"Where are we going, anyway?" Kristen hiccuped and wiped a stray tear.

Jack inhaled deeply. "I do not know what is wrong with you, but we are going to meet a very good friend of mine at a Mexican restaurant. I would appreciate it if you could behave yourselves."

We looked at each other, suppressing giggles, and then looked away, chastened. Kristen said, "At a Mexican restaurant? Who is this guy we're meeting?"

Off we went again.

Jack turned on his heels and walked briskly ahead of us. I linked arms with Kristen. She was right—crazy Mrs. Wilder or not, we could still have a good time. "Who are we meeting again?" hollered Kristen at Jack's back.

"My college roommate Bert." Jack did not turn around to answer the question. It was already humid outside, but the tourist trap in which we found ourselves was cool and quiet still. It felt like an amusement park, after hours. We walked past toy stores and candy stores, a shop that sold only popcorn, a bar that was still closed. The Mexican restaurant looked closed, save for a lone waitress wiping down some of the outside tables. Standing in front of the restaurant was one of the most gorgeous men I had ever seen—wavy blond hair, slightly unshaven, eyes masked by aviators. His oxford shirt was untucked over khaki shorts, and unlike me, he wasn't sweating at all. He was tall—very. Kristen pinched my arm, hard.

"Ow!"

Jack embraced the handsome stranger in one of those back-clappy man hugs. They beamed and swatted each other about the upper arms like men do when they're happy to see each other but don't want to hug for too long. Kristen pinched me again, and I glared at her.

"I'd like to introduce you to Sarah and Kristen, Bert." Jack held out his arm with some grandeur, as though he expected us to curtsy.

Gobsmacked at Bert's existence, I stuck out my hand for him to shake, and Bert said, "Sarah. I've heard a lot about you," with this devastating megawatt smile.

I could not think of a single thing to say to this, but Kristen had no such difficulty. "We haven't heard much about you! Where has he been keeping you?" She delivered a heavily mascaraed wink, and Jack shook his head as he opened the door to the restaurant.

The hostess wasn't standing at her post, but was still placing drink menus on the table. "We're not serving lunch yet," she called.

"How about margaritas?" said Kristen.

"Y'all can go sit at the bar if you want. I'll see what we can do."

Kristen and I left Bert and Jack to catch up, although Kristen, subtle as a Mack truck, kept nudging me. "Stop it," I said. "I noticed."

"Go to the bathroom and put on some lipstick," she whispered.

"I don't have any."

"Here." She shoved her bag at me.

Jack looked strangely at us. "What are you doing?"

"Sarah was just going to the bathroom," said Kristen, and after she had said it, I didn't have any choice but to go.

Once inside, I inspected the wreckage of my face. I had a couple of things going for me—good skin and hair. As for the rest, I rarely wore makeup, so there wasn't much to be done. I dug through Kristen's bag to see what kind of tools might help me. There was a brush in there, and I plucked a few long blonde strands out of it before raking it through the rat's nest on my head, which improved matters. There were some pots of things that I didn't recognize, and Kristen and I weren't quite the same color anyway. I splashed some water on my face and patted it dry with a paper towel. I scraped the bottom of the tote, looking for a lipstick, and found three garish MAC colors before locating a Clinique tube with a color that seemed closer to nature's range. I had to admit I was somewhat improved with some paint on the barn.

I went back out to the bar, and set the bag on the floor between Kristen and me so that Bert wouldn't notice that I had needed someone else's supplies just to go to the bathroom.

"Looky here," said Kristen. "Much better. Hey, can we get some margaritas?" The hostess had rustled up a bartender. Thank goodness we had found a place that wasn't going to judge us. It was one of those fun restaurants with a bunch of junk on the walls and a TV everywhere you looked. "Break My Stride" was playing, too loudly for early on a Saturday morning. "Four?"

"I think we'll have some coffee, actually," said Jack primly. Kristen and I were sitting on either side of Bert, and Jack might as well have been wearing a cloak of invisibility.

Jack's pious dad routine could get on my nerves, too. He had just been through the same shit we had and was, by his own admission, "traumatized." "No thanks for the coffee. *Los margaritas* for us, please," I told the bartender.

"Las margaritas," said Jack.

"Oh, shut up." I scratched my head with my middle finger.

"I've already had my coffee," said Bert. "Three margaritas."

Kristen and I shot mutual smug looks at Jack, who was fighting the urge to change his drink order but was stuck out of self-righteousness.

Our drinks were gorgeous, a perfect cloudy yellow with chunks of salt dripping down the side, a lime perched cheerfully on the edge. I picked mine up and took a long swig. It was as good as it looked.

"Cheers!" said Kristen, lifting her glass.

"This is a serious drinks outing that you have invited me on. Thank you!" Bert tipped back his glass and drank it in one smooth draw. This might have looked like pathetic fraternity boy behavior, or sexy as hell. With Bert, there was no question—the latter. Kristen and I watched in admiration. I heard what might have been a snort from Jack.

"Woo-hoo!" said Kristen, and finished her glass, too. I followed.

Jack opened up a package of sugar and poured it into his coffee.

"Three more!" called Kristen to our bartender. I already thought of him as our bartender, since it was too early to have to share him.

"What got the two of you drinking at ten o'clock this morning?" asked Bert.

"We might ask you the same question," I said.

"You," said Bert. He was looking at me, but I assumed that it was a collective you, the "y'all" you. He was looking at me, though. Kristen poked me again.

"Who wants to start?" asked Kristen. "I nominate Jack to narrate."

Jack, you could tell, was just dying for the opportunity to be brought back into the loop. Kristen and I swiveled around to listen to him, too, as if we hadn't just witnessed the whole thing ourselves. "Well," said Jack. "It all started with the El Camino."

Kristen interrupted. "It all started when we got our high school reunion invitation."

"No, it all started twenty years ago."

We all jumped into it together, the ending of a friendship, our silly Camino Beach idea, a loopy road trip, and all of us in a Mexican restaurant. We learned things, too. Bert and Jack had been first-year roommates at Emory. They had lost touch for a while after college. Bert had gotten married at a quickie wedding that Jack hadn't attended, and the quickie divorce that ensued happened so fast that Jack never even had a chance to meet the bride in question. I did some mental calculations, and Bert would have gotten married about the same time I did. This was getting interesting.

We told Bert piles of stories about Mrs. Wilder from back in the day after we had described the scene that had brought us here with ever-increasing hyperbole. By the time we were done with it, she was a wild woman, foaming at the mouth and hurling glasses of iced tea at us.

Through all of these a steady parade of nineties hip-hop played in the background—"Funky Cold Medina," "Let Me Clear My Throat," "Mo Money Mo Problems." The bartender knew all of the words and sang along gamely to everything as he readied napkins, forks, and knives for the lunch crowd. The more we drank, the more the words came back to us, too.

"Is it part of your job to know all of these lame old songs?" I asked. I was talking too loudly, but this might have just been because the music was loud.

"Actually, yes. I know all the words to everything. I thought you might like this mix."

"Why did you think that?" yelled Kristen, who was definitely talking too loud, and it wasn't just the music. "I was born in 1983!" Kristen revised her birthday with some regularity.

Someone had given Jack a margarita. Maybe he'd ditched the coffee and ordered it for himself, or maybe Kristen or Bert had ordered it for him. At any rate, he was in the game—finally. And it was only eleven o'clock.

My phone rang, and the name "Hubby," which was how I had entered it years ago, flashed on the screen. I would have changed it, but I'm not very good with the different functions of my phone. Kristen was faster than I was, and my phone was off the bar before I could even decide whether or not I wanted to talk to Matt.

"No! Do not answer that!"

Everyone peered at the phone. "Hubby?" asked Jack. "Is there something you're not telling us?"

The phone marimbaed at us as Kristen hid it behind her back. "You do not want to go there. Hand it over." I held out my hand for the phone. Kristen slowly dropped her arm with a pout, but before I could take the phone away, Jack grabbed it. He had better reflexes than I'd thought.

"Sarah Martin's assistant. How may I help you?" He sounded absolutely professional and was the only one of us who seemed able to control the volume of his voice. Kristen had collapsed in laughter, and a confused Bert joined her.

"She is in an extremely important meeting at the moment," said Jack. "I'd be happy to take a message . . . No, that is not 'Bust a Move.' It must be interference from your phone." There was a pause. "Yes, this is Jack."

Red-faced, I grabbed his wrist and pulled the phone from his hand. "Hello."

"Uh, Sarah? It's Matt. What are you doing?" He did not sound amused.

Kristen was making an awful face at me, and Jack saw her and joined in. Good to see he was starting to loosen up again. "Who?" I said, and they all died laughing. I started to smile, too. This was what happened after two margaritas in the morning. Or was it three?

Matt wanted to find out when his next dog pickup was. It was over a week away. "Oh, well, I'm still in Myrtle Beach. I'll have to let you know when I'm back." Kristen pantomimed a hair flip.

"Myrtle Beach?" Oh, shit. I hadn't told him.

"Yes, Myrtle Beach."

"Where is Rhett Pugler?" Honestly, like I had left him alone in the apartment. "And why are you with Jack?"

"With Mom and Dad. And none of your business."

Silence.

"You could have just left him with me. Have you been drinking? It sounds like you're in a bar."

"Why would I be in a bar?" I yelled. "Look. I'll call you later." Matt would not let me hear the end of this once I returned.

"Well, Sarah, that is an excellent way of managing an amicable divorce," said Jack.

"Hey," said Kristen. "We don't like that guy. He's trying to poison her only child against her."

"Child?" said Bert, with another one of those deadly grins. He had a dimple in the middle of his chin, and I fought the urge to put my finger there.

"He's a pug," I admitted.

"I love pugs," said Bert, and I had to stop myself from throwing my arms around him.

The bartender gave us some chips and salsa. "Y'all going to eat?"

I said yes, and Jack said no at the same time.

"Why don't you give us a few minutes?" said Bert. "It's early. Hey . . . is that what I think it is?"

We listened to the beat for a moment. Jack said, "'Under Pressure.' Queen."

Kristen said, "'Ice Ice Baby,'" which it was. Jack was the only one of us who didn't know all the words, but Bert, Kristen, and I jumped right in. *Stop, collaborate, and listen . . . Will it ever stop? Yo, I don't know . . .*

We were getting loud, no doubt about it.

There was a series of really good audience participation songs that followed: "Sweet Caroline" (*bah-BAH-bah-BAH*), "Margaritaville" (*Salt! Salt! Salt!*), "Piano Man" (*lalalalalalala*). Even Jack jumped in on the last one.

"You have a really good voice," said the bartender to me.

"I know," I said. I was sure that I sounded just like Kelly Clarkson.

"We have karaoke," said the bartender and then shoved a microphone into my hands.

. I cleared my throat and said with as much gravitas as I could muster, "I would like to sing the time-honored classic by Mr. Big, 'To Be with You.'"

I belted it out, to the general approval of all. Bert was watching me with what I was sure was abject adoration, and Jack and Kristen were doing an ironic slow dance. It was too bad that I was singing, because otherwise I could have been dancing with Bert. Kristen was tone deaf, so I would have to hand the mike off to Jack if I wanted a dance. I was imagining how this would work as my song came to a close, when Bert took the microphone away from me. "'Uptown Girl,'" he requested.

Jack stepped in as my dance partner, which was not at all how I had hoped things would go. "You're supposed to be singing, and he's supposed to be dancing," I hissed into his ear.

"That's mean," Jack said. "Besides, he's a terrible dancer." He leaned in closer. "He's not all that great of a singer either." Kristen was back to sitting on her barstool, swaying back and forth, singing along with her eyes closed. Jack was a good dancer. I put my head on his shoulder and felt comfortable and sleepy.

"We should go to the beach," I mumbled. "'I shall wear white flannel trousers, and walk upon the beach.' That's . . ."

"T. S. Eliot," said Jack. "I know. 'Dare to eat a peach.' You weren't the only one to sit in an Intro to Lit class, you know. You're pedantic when drunk."

The place had filled up with families ordering tacos and nacho platters for lunch. The music got turned down, and the bartender, who had seemed so nice just a few minutes earlier, was starting to look annoyed with us. "You all about ready for your check, or are you going to eat some food?"

"What does it matter? I bet we've spent more than that woman over there who is sharing one plate of tacos with her kid," Kristen said, squinting at him.

"Kristen. He was just asking." I wanted to whisper, but it came out really loud, and I slurred it all together—hewuzjussasskin.

"Maybe we should go," said Jack.

"Well, I don't know what for! I'll eat a goddamn taco if that'll make everyone happy," yelled Kristen.

I went over to touch her elbow and took a big sip from my drink. A bubble of margarita stuck in my throat, and it took me a moment to catch my breath. All of a sudden, I could hear ringing, and spots danced in front of my eyes. Everything went out of focus, and I could hear the sound of my own blood rushing through my ears.

In the half second that it happened—it felt more like an hour, like I had fallen asleep and woken up—I was all of a sudden horizontal and in a public place. In the half second, just a half second, everything we had done rushed back through my mind—Mrs. Wilder, Bert, Roxanne. They all muddied up together in my brain, but I felt, for reasons I couldn't explain, a sense of great loss. The craziness of the morning crashed to a halt as I crashed to the floor.

We've only got a few weeks left to go. I haven't done anything but study for exams lately. My parents won't let me do anything else.

Principal Hunter is waiting for me when I get out of pre-calc. He probably wants to review my valedictorian speech or something, make sure I don't go renegade on him. Or maybe he's heard something about my scholarship. I've been accepted for weeks, but I still don't know how we're going to pay for it.

Principal Hunter stands stick straight, gray hair in a military buzz. Even his eyes are gray, and they go all squinty like Clint Eastwood's when he's asking you questions. He looks like an off-duty cop. "How are you doing, Sarah?" he asks me. "Could we have a little chat?"

I nod. What does he want? "Fine." We walk to his office in silence after that. He has an oversized oak desk with a big gray swivel chair, and I have to sit on one of two hard-backed black-painted wooden chairs.

"Sarah, I brought you in here to talk about Roxanne." He leans back in his chair, crosses his arms behind his head.

An alarm goes off in the back of my brain. I still don't know what he wants, but conversations about Roxanne are never good.

"How do you think she's doing?" he asks.

I swallow hard. "Fine," I say again.

"What are her plans after high school?" He leans forward, waiting for my answer.

"I don't know." I really don't. Kristen and I have everything worked out. She's even bought a comforter for her new dorm room. We don't know where Roxanne will go, but she definitely won't stay here.

"See, I have a little problem here, Sarah. And my problem is that you're our best student, but I keep hearing from our teachers that one of our worst students has a tendency to cheat off your work."

I feel all the color leave my face.

"What do you have to say about that?"

I have some trouble getting my jaw to work to formulate words. "I don't know." I am the worst liar I know. I wish Kristen were in here; she could look him straight in the eye and tell him that it wasn't true with conviction. He pulls out Roxanne's statistics test, and mine. "Your paper is an A, and Roxanne's paper is a C. But every now and then, every few lines, one of your answers is the same."

"I'm sure that's a coincidence," I say.

"The problem is," says Hunter, "that you were supposed to show the work on the equations, and only one of you did. The other problem is"—he points at a problem toward the end—"you got one question wrong at the end, and so did she." I want to sit up and see which one it is, and see if I can make an argument for my answer, but now is not the time.

I shrug. Damn you, Roxanne. Why did she have to do that? Here we were at the end of our high school careers, and I have to answer for her.

"But that's not as bad as this one." He pulls out a history paper that I had written weeks earlier, and then a second one—Roxanne's. "The second and third paragraphs are identical to yours." Anger flares up here. I remember we were all sleeping over at Kristen's, and Roxanne had said that she just didn't have any ideas, could she see what I did, she didn't know how to start. I don't know what to say to Principal Hunter.

"Should I keep going?" he asks. "I did my research, and I uncovered some interesting similarities over the course of this past year."

I don't say anything, and I don't know how I'm going to get out of this. I'm furious, furious with her for being such a screwup. Some of us have futures to look forward to! It's not my fault that she doesn't.

"Sarah, if I look at school rules, you are as guilty as Roxanne is, and you could be subject to sanctions, too. These range from community service to expulsion."

"I don't know," I whisper. "I don't know how it happened."

"You don't know how someone looked on your paper for an entire test? You don't know how someone copied your essay directly?" His nice-guy charade is up, and he's all cop now. "For a smart girl, you're not catching on very fast." I imagine that he will call my parents, and that I will be expelled, and that I will have to repeat my senior year. I will not give a speech at graduation. I will live in my parents' basement next year.

"It's too bad, really too bad." He pulls out a letter, and I can recognize the University of the South letterhead from where I'm sitting. My heart seizes. "I just got this letter today congratulating one of our students for being the recipient of their annual merit scholarship. I was looking forward to announcing it." I can't even enjoy the moment, knowing that I can go and we can pay for it, because I am terrified.

"I'm sure this was a simple mistake on your part. But Roxanne. She's been getting in trouble for years, and she is going to have to be punished for this. If this was her idea, well, we could be lenient on you, but I can't know that unless you tell me."

I don't say anything, but I feel a tear start in the back of my eye, threatening to creep around to the front.

"We have a real situation here, and I don't know what the answer is." He looks like he knows exactly what the answer is; he's staring me down like I'm at the end of a gun barrel.

I don't know what the answer is either. What do I do here? I want to say nothing, but not as much as I want to just leave. If we were on *L.A. Law*, I'd call my lawyer, but the closest I'm going to get is my parents, and that's worse.

He pulls out Roxanne's *King Lear* story, which I recognize because I'm the one who wrote it, start to finish. "I'm just not sure Roxanne could write some of these sentences. And your teacher isn't either. She says it sounds an awful lot like you. I may have to write to the university. We are obligated to report infractions that are matters of record."

Oh my God. I'm going to lose it all here. All over a few math problems, a paragraph here, and a paragraph there, a stupid little story. It's too much. It's not fair! And what difference does it make to Roxanne if she gets in trouble. She doesn't have as much to lose. The tear spills over, runs down my face.

Mrs. Higdon recognizing my voice, my signature in an essay—on any other occasion, I would be flattered. I should have known better. I got carried away with the assignment, which was fun. Why couldn't Roxanne just write a fucking short story? What was so hard about that? But we had wanted to go swimming. I saw it all again. Had she asked me to write it, or had I just done it?

"Sarah, I'm going to give you a moment to think about this. I hope your involvement was minimal." He stands up and leaves the room, and I'm here alone, sweating it out. I look at the ceiling, as if there might be cameras there. For all I know, there are.

What is minimal, really? Who decides that? I didn't want to do it. It's not my fault that she couldn't do the work. I see her, a pencil stuck in her hair, lying on the floor. Who does homework on the floor? I do my homework at the library, like you're supposed to. I deserve to go to Sewanee. I deserve it.

Principal Hunter comes back into the room. "I'm going to need your version of the story to make a decision."

Principal Hunter places a legal pad in front of me, holds out a pen. I look at the pen for a long time, and his hand doesn't waver, doesn't move. I take the pen; it feels like a rock between my fingers.

Chapter Nine

Kristen was so close to my face that I could smell the cinnamon of her gum mixed with tequila and lime juice.

"Oh my God," I said. "I cannot believe that just happened."

Jack's hand was under my neck. "Don't move, Sarah. You might have a concussion."

I hauled myself up to a sitting position. "I do not have a concussion." But I did find a small goose egg on the back of my head.

Jack was squatting next to me, so we were eye to eye. "Take it easy. No sudden movements."

Strong arms were already around my waist, lifting me up. Bert. I stared into his concerned blue-green eyes, which were a good couple of inches above mine. "She's okay, Jack. Just a little topsy-turvy incident."

People in the restaurant were staring at us. "Do you want me to call you an ambulance?" asked the manager.

"No!" I said.

"Maybe she would be more comfortable resting somewhere quiet," he suggested.

"We got it, muchacha. We'll get out of here. Go ahead and cash us out." Kristen handed over her credit card. Bert protested, but Kristen waved him away. "I can buy a handsome stranger a couple of margaritas."

Jack flanked me on the opposite side of Bert, and the three of us left, slowly, hobbling a bit, like we were in a three-legged race. "Let's just all go to my house," suggested Bert. "I'm on the beach, and the fresh air will do you good."

We all blinked in the sunlight of the blazing-hot afternoon. Kristen banged out of the restaurant behind us. Her face was all sweaty, and her hair was messed up. Our time in the Mexican restaurant was a serious detriment. "Looks like I'm driving," said Jack, the only one of us still presentable.

"How many margaritas did you have?" I said.

"One. Let's go. We'll come back later for the El Camino."

Bert lived in a cottage next to the beach, and if a bachelor's house could be called cozy, it was—gray wood with a white wood porch all the way around, perched on stilts. The living room was small with a TV so big it was almost a wall. There was a tiny bookshelf with hardbound classics. I leaned over to pull out *Great Expectations* and found that it was actually a cardboard box instead of a real book. Oh well.

There were rocking chairs on the front porch. Rocking chairs! Two of them. I wondered who sat in them with Bert. He read my mind. "This one is mine, and this one is hers." A fat tabby slept in a sunny spot near the railing. "Sit. She won't mind."

And it did feel good to sit, the weight of the long drive, the emotion of the morning, the madcap hilarity of our Mexican adventure crashing down with me. I felt unable to move. "Do you want a drink?" said Kristen.

"No," said Jack.

More quietly, I said, "I just want to sit still for a minute, close my eyes."

It wasn't the first time I had fainted, so I was less alarmed than my friends. I remember fainting at church once as a child. The air-conditioning had gone out, but we went every Sunday, and a little thing like a hundred degrees wasn't going to deter us. I had slithered off my seat like a spilled drink, and I only remember my father lifting me up and waking to the cool air-conditioning of the car. I had also fainted at school; I was coming down with a virus, combined with the stress of the end of the year. It was almost like this was my animal defense mechanism, like a roly-poly curling up into a ball when poked with a stick.

Bert brought me a glass of ice-cold water and sank down into the other chair. The tabby woke up and jumped into his lap. Bert wasn't one of those people who had to talk all the time, and we didn't talk, just sat in a silence that wasn't awkward at all, a silence long enough for me to imagine what it would be like to sit here with Bert on a regular basis. It was not an unpleasant image. Kristen was laughing in the kitchen, too hard. The margaritas were still working.

"Are you going to keep looking for your friend? Or just go home and forget about it?" asked Bert.

What did I want to do? If I didn't want to find her, I had my excuse to give up. But seeing Mrs. Wilder reminded me that if your mom didn't have your back, or at least one of your friends, it couldn't be easy. I wanted to know now. Where was she? It wasn't about the reunion either. If I wasn't going to find my old friend, why bother going to a reunion and running into people I didn't care about? People like Mark.

Mark Johnson.

"Kristen!" I yelled. "Kristen!"

Kristen came running out with her drink in her hand. It was suspiciously murky. "Are you okay? Do we need to go to the hospital?"

"No, no. I'm fine! You know that I faint on a regular basis."

"Yeah, a regular Scarlett O'Hara, you are. What is the matter?"

"Why don't we ask Mark Johnson? Do you think he's still working at the Home Depot?"

"God, I hope not. Let's hope he's at least been promoted from the lawn department."

"Why didn't we ever ask him?"

"Because we didn't like the guy. Also, he was as dumb as a box of hair. I guess I figured he didn't know anything anyway. Surprised that idiot can put his shoes on the right feet every morning."

"He might know something," I persisted.

Kristen was right. Mark had forgotten all about Roxanne once she'd disappeared. He'd stopped talking to us, and he'd stopped talking to everyone else, too. He was going on to play college ball at the University of Tennessee, where he would put himself out of commission by injuring his back as a freshman and flunking out of school the next year. I sort of thought that it served him right, in the spiteful, youthful way that enjoys retribution, and wasn't surprised when I saw him behind the garden counter of the Home Depot a few years later. It never occurred to me that he would have heard anything from Roxanne if we hadn't.

"I guess we could ask at the Home Depot," said Kristen. This was a simple task, no private investigator required. Like playing the Kevin Bacon game, it would take no more than two phone calls to former classmates to figure out where Mark Johnson had landed. Some connections were difficult to shake.

"You don't know anyone who would have kept in touch with your friend?" said Bert. Kristen and I tried not to roll our eyes at him. He didn't know. He didn't know that if anyone would know, that we would know. All he knew was a few tall tales spun over cocktails. He didn't know about the years of shared secrets, midnight powwows, and hours turned into months of girl talk. And yet. We didn't know, not at all. We just shook our heads mutely at him.

"I guess you checked the records at the school, return address, stuff like that."

"They wouldn't give us that, I'm sure," said Kristen.

"It's too bad you don't know any principals," said Bert, and all of us turned to look at Jack.

Jack. Holy shit. It was true that Jack had access that we would never have had before. Jack could pull out all of my shiny old report cards if he wanted, Roxanne's old detention slips. There was an alumni office with a record of everyone who had ever gone to our high school. And I got chills when it just that second occurred to me that Roxanne had not graduated from high school, and if she had ever tried to go somewhere else, had ever requested a transcript, she would have left a paper trail behind in the administrative office of that old school. It would have been confidential, of course it would have been confidential. But we knew the person who could unlock any door he wanted to. The enormity of our stupidity rendered me mute for a moment.

Kristen and I looked at each other.

"I forgot that he did that!" Kristen was getting excited and had forgotten that Jack was sitting right next to her and didn't need to be discussed in the third person. She smacked his arm with an open palm.

"No," said Jack.

"Come on!" I said. "She's not even there anymore! It's not like we're talking about a seventeen-year-old! She's been out of there for years! Who cares, besides us?"

"Jack." I could tell that Kristen wanted to call him by his first and last names, like he was a child, but she couldn't remember what his last name was. She recovered quickly from this. "You were willing to get in your car and drive eight hundred miles in front of an El Camino to help us! Come on!"

"No."

At this moment, I felt exactly like my old high school self, like Jack was being such a fucking loser, such a stickler for the rules. I felt actual disdain for someone who was so married to the system that he wouldn't even go to bat for his oldest friend. I also felt like I might burst into tears. Then, I did.

Bert leaned over to place a reassuring hand on my forearm (reassuring, among other things). I tried, unsuccessfully, not to get goose bumps, but I was too busy being furious with Jack to enjoy the unexpected contact too much. Bert and Jack swooped down on me, and

I would have appreciated the display of gallantry if I hadn't been so annoyed with Jack. I didn't even know what I was blubbering about. I guess I was like an overtired toddler who had gone too long without an afternoon nap. I put the heels of my hands into my eyes and rubbed.

Kristen had some experience dealing with overtired toddlers, and I guess you could call her parenting approach to that behavior no-nonsense. "Stop that, Sarah."

I sniffled, grandly.

Bert said, "Maybe she needs to lie down for a while. She still hasn't recovered from the faint."

Jack patted my arm gently. "Sarah? Let me help you over here to the couch."

"Oh my God! Quit treating her like a baby! Her problem is you." Kristen pointed a finger accusingly at Jack.

If Kristen thought she had the technique down for dealing with misbehaving children, she was outclassed when it came to confrontations with a high school principal, who dealt with low-level drug dealers, petty theft, and cheating all day long. I could see him putting on his principal face (which was not that different from his real face).

"Kristen, I am a Metro employee. It is absolutely not permitted for me to share information in confidential files. I could get fired." He paused and puffed his chest out. "Also, it would be unethical."

"Hey, Jack, you know what? Fuck you. Thanks a whole lot for coming down here with your car and hauling our stuff around like *Driving Miss Daisy* and then when push comes to shove, you won't do the easiest thing in the world." Kristen was spitting mad.

Jack shrugged. "It is beyond my power."

Kristen stood over him and jabbed her finger into his chest. When you were sitting down, she looked tall and a little scary. I peeked through my fingers at all the drama. "It is not *beyond* your powers. It is exactly within your powers, and no one else's. What are you afraid of?"

Jack got up out of his chair and folded his arms across his chest. He towered over little Kristen. "I am not afraid of anything. It's just not something I'm allowed to do, nor am I willing to do it."

"Oh, well, la-di-freaking-da. Aren't you a saint? Don't you care about our friend? Don't you care what happened to her? Don't you want to know? What if she's living in a van down by the river?"

"If she has been living in a van down by the river, she's been doing so for quite some time. Don't kid yourselves that you are going to pull off some big rescue of a forty-year-old woman. You're satisfying your own curiosity. What else you're trying to satisfy, I do not know."

Kristen practically had smoke pouring out of her ears. I thought she was going to throw a Yosemite Sam–style fit and start stomping her feet and pumping her fists. I couldn't blame her, though. If I didn't feel so woozy, I'd jump in there with her. Also, Bert still had his hand on my arm and I didn't want to stand up just yet.

"You know what, Jack. Forget it," I said tiredly. "Thanks for fucking nothing. We'll do it without you. I don't know why we thought you would be any help to begin with."

"For one, your suitcases would be sitting out there in the rain." The skies had suddenly gone gray, and a storm did indeed seem imminent.

"I don't care! They can sit out in the rain! I am leaving!" Kristen grabbed her bag and stomped over to the door. "Come on, Sarah."

I reluctantly let go of Bert's arm. My loyalty was to my friend, and she was right. Jack was being ridiculous. I also didn't want to get in the way of her dramatic exit, even though I was not quite ready to leave Bert. I stood up. "Thanks for all of this. I'm sorry we've behaved badly here. If you are ever in Nashville . . . This was not quite the good-bye I had hoped for, sandwiched in between Jack and Kristen.

"Are you kidding? This is the most interesting Saturday I've had in years." Bert gave me a hug and bent down to kiss my cheek. If I hadn't already swooned, I might have done it here.

Jack said nothing as I slunk out the door behind Kristen. "Can you believe that? All of this way, and he won't even help us! Fuck him! We will get our stuff and throw it in the back. We do not need him." She stormed down the wooden steps, with me trailing behind her.

Except that we did, because we had come in Jack's car and left the Camino at the Mexican restaurant at Broadway on the Beach.

May 1997
Gym, Briley High School

I have gym class next, and I'm hot and sweaty before we even hit the floor. I run some water over my wrists in the bathroom and then just stick my whole head under the faucet. Kristen taps me on the shoulder and I emerge like a Labrador retriever from a pool, shaking the water off.

"Hey, you gotta watch out. Hunter is onto Roxanne, and he'll probably ask you next."

"Ask me next what?" I can barely even hear myself say the words.

"If she's cheating." Kristen pulls her hair in a ponytail high on her head, knots a band around it. "You saw nothing. You heard nothing. You know nothing. Right?"

"What did you say?"

"I said nothing. Jack shit. They can cane me if they want to, biyatch! Not getting through this vault. So, just watch out, okay? We're in the home stretch here."

I swallow hard and nod. We go out to the gym, and Wilder has us running laps today. She's been such a bitch ever since we got back. It's like she doesn't even see us, doesn't remember that we're her kid's friends. She's just done with us. And we're done with her.

I start running, and Kristen's ahead of me fast—she's a much better runner than I am. My shoe is untied and I step on it, flail around, crash to the ground before I've even started. Some of the others giggle as they run past me. I tie my shoe, and Mrs. Wilder yells, "Martin, up, up, up! Let's go!"

I start running again, to the beat of my conversation with Kristen. *You saw nothing. You heard nothing.* She held off Principal Hunter, and here she is, running around like it was nothing. What did I just do? I hear ringing in my ears and I trip again, but I save myself, don't actually fall. I stop running, though, breathe hard with my hands on my hips. "Martin, go!"

I don't move. I feel really sick here, and my ears are still ringing. I sit down, right there on the floor, in front of everybody. I hear Kristen next to me, saying something, but I don't know what. Mrs. Wilder is yelling, "Get up! Get up!" And everything goes black.

Chapter Ten

It was a long, slow walk back to Bert's front door. I suspected that the men were watching the whole time, maybe even laughing at us, but they had the decency to answer the door with straight faces.

"I guess you want me to drive you to your car," said Jack.

"I can do it, if you want," offered Bert, and while I nodded enthusiastically at the suggestion, it was Jack who walked outside with us.

"Sorry I yelled at you," I said, even though I hadn't been doing the yelling and wasn't sorry. It just seemed like the right thing to say to the person who was now driving you back to your car because you were too drunk and ill to drive it in the first place. He just nodded and didn't say anything else on the drive over.

Kristen was still mad, even if she had calmed down—mad enough that she didn't mind throwing her suitcase in the open back of an El Camino. "Could you pop the trunk?" she said. "I need to get my bag."

Jack held up a hand. "Take what you need out of it. I'll bring you your suitcase tomorrow." Neither of us could argue with the magnanimity of this offer.

Before I got in the car, Jack grabbed my arm. "What are you doing?"

"We're going home, I guess."

"Really?"

"Yes, really."

"Look, I came down here to help you if you needed me, and it looks like you need me here. Think about it, Sarah. Do you really want to go digging through Roxanne's file with Kristen? Aren't you afraid of what you might find there?"

I was. I was terrified to find it all in black and white, there with Kristen at my side. But I had come this far, I had looked the beast in the eye (Mrs. Wilder), and I wanted to know now. Was she all right? I felt some of the air go out of my irritation with him. "Yes. Yes, I am, but I want to do it anyway. It's time."

"Are you sure?" Jack scratched his head. "Do you really have to rush off like this? You're going to end up driving at night in that contraption. It's not safe."

"I do not need you to be my dad here, Jack," I snapped.

"Need I remind you what happened to you twenty years ago?"

"No. Besides, you don't know, because you weren't even there."

"Yes, the two of you were a couple of little snots back then and wouldn't invite a guy like me along. And considering your behavior today, I'm not sure you've changed." Jack lifted his chin defiantly at me.

Considering your behavior today. If I had been in high school, I would have imitated him, in that sanctimonious voice of his. "Jack, just . . . just . . . *go home*," I said.

"I'm not going home. You're going home," said Jack reasonably. I couldn't argue with him; I wasn't even making sense.

I sighed and rubbed my eyes. "All right. Let's quit squabbling. I think we got this, so don't worry about us. Go enjoy a night out with your friend. By the way, wow. Thanks for hiding that one away for all the time I've known you."

Jack's faced closed up. "Bert's a fun guy, but he's not relationship material. He has a new girlfriend every time I talk to him. I'm not sure you can even properly call them girlfriends. He's fine for some margaritas at the bar, but he's not someone I would introduce to you."

"Who said I'm looking for a relationship?"

Jack shook his head at me and scowled. "Fine. I'll put in a word for you."

"Okay, tell me what he says," I say.

Jack rolled his eyes at me, waved at Kristen, and headed back up the walk.

"Aw," said Kristen from behind the wheel. "You hurt his feelings."

"What are you talking about?"

"Dummy. He likes you, and you're asking for a setup with his friend."

"He does not." I hoped that wasn't true. I couldn't afford to jeopardize the best relationship I had going for me. I had a neighbor and a buddy and a pet sitter and a confidant all rolled into one, even if he could be a pain in the ass sometimes. What if we hooked up and broke up and all that went away?

"Well, if you want to throw it all away on some other guy, that Bert ain't a bad choice. Whoo! He looks like Ryan Gosling and Robert Redford all rolled into one."

Kristen looked so short sitting behind the wheel that I thought about asking her if she needed a booster seat, then thought better of it. It was late in the day for bad jokes. She pulled out of the parking lot slowly, then abruptly over to the side of the road. "I'm going to need to know where I'm going here."

"Home," I said.

"Which way is that?" We'd had the one extreme, Jack with the GPS and the careful planning, and now Kristen as navigator was like roaming the desert with Moses. Kristen got her phone out, trying to figure it out.

"Hey, we can go through Knoxville. Why did we do it the other way? Oh, because you wanted to, of course. To visit Sewanee."

I didn't say anything. It was about the same, either way. I wondered if she was looking for an excuse to avoid going back through there, a reminder of the incident at the art show.

"I'm really tired," said Kristen.

"At least you didn't hit your head on the floor."

"I should have been so lucky, free rides and lots of attention."

I thought about telling her that she'd had a free ride the whole way here and changed my mind. She wouldn't get it, and I was tired, too. "What do you want to do?"

"Well, we are in Myrtle Beach. Kind of a shame to go home without putting our tootsies in the ocean, don't you think?"

I didn't argue as she pulled back onto the road, toward Ocean Drive. I rolled down a window, stuck my head out. Rhett Pugler would have loved this. I wondered how my dog was doing, how my parents were doing, how the shop was doing. I sent Aidan and Evelyn a text while Kristen drove: **Am I missing anything?**

Aidan, who didn't take a step without his phone, a habit I could do without while he's working, wrote back immediately: **Everything. All is chaos without you.**

I wrote: **So all is good then. See you soon.**

We pulled over near the boardwalk, parked on the strip. We wandered into a few tourist shops, lingered by the Ripley's Believe It or Not!, and salivated outside an ice-cream shop until we gave in and bought cones—doubles. It was a short walk out to the beach. The clouds were breaking.

"Why do you think our parents let us come here for spring break in the first place?"

"To be fair, we never made it."

"Yeah, but they didn't know that was going to happen."

"I don't know. I think one of them did." Kristen shrugged. "Guess they figured we were adults."

"Adults! Ha!"

"Well, we were going to be leaving home in a few weeks anyway. They had to start letting go sometime." Kristen had only gone a few minutes away from home, so there was not all that much leaving to do. She could still drop off her laundry.

The humidity of the day had vanished since our Mexican episode, and the ocean wind ruffled our T-shirts. We were losing daylight, and our return home seemed more and more distant. We'd probably need to stop at some roadside motel again on the way home, or maybe even just begin early the next morning. We walked past a balloon vendor, shook our heads. There was a palm reader camped out behind a card table. Kristen tugged on my arm. "Let's do it!" I let her pull me over to the stand.

The palm reader didn't look like much of a mystic. She had gray hair pulled back in a ponytail, was an extreme shade of tan, and was wearing long khaki shorts. She looked like she could have been out working in the yard next to my mother. I shook my head politely at her. Kristen blurted out, "Sarah wants her palm read," and put a ten-dollar bill on the card table.

"Why don't you go?" I asked. I didn't want to be rude, but I did not want my palm read either.

"Your palm is bigger than mine—more to read."

I sat down hesitantly in the chair and held out my arm as if I were about to get a shot. The palm reader's hands were warm and dry as she took mine. She poked at my hand for a while, tracing its whorls and crevasses. "Love line. You have a fork here. There is more than one great love."

"I'd settle for one," I said. These people always begin with the love shit. Also, don't most people have more than one love? Easy guess.

"You have a fate line. Not everyone does, but there are breaks here, too. You have gone in different directions." I rolled my eyes. We would have been better off with a balloon animal. At least we could take that home with us.

"I want to go!" said Kristen, butting in and holding out her palm.

"Ten dollars per palm." Our fortune-teller sat back in her folding chair, crossed one brown leg over another. Kristen unearthed another ten-dollar bill, put it on the table.

"Straight lines everywhere," said the fortune-teller. "Your future is clear. One love. Long life line, straight."

"What's my fate line say?" demanded Kristen.

"You don't have one."

"What do you mean, I don't have one? How can I have no fate?"

"I think I'd better leave you here, if you have no fate," I said. I was tired of the game, though. I knew that my love line was broken up without even looking at my damn hand, and I didn't think I believed in fate.

"Can you tell us if we find our long-lost friend?" asked Kristen.

"It doesn't work that way," said the palm reader and shrugged.

"There goes twenty bucks." I stood up from the table.

"Wait," said our palm reader. I extended my hand again next to Kristen's, which was indeed crisscrossed with clear, straight lines. My lines were all fissured and fragmented. "You are friends for a long time, I see." Well, any idiot could see that. We nodded together. "See how the directions go the same way; the placement is the same, even if the lines don't look the same."

"Do you think we'll find our friend?"

"I'd have to see her palm, too. But if I had to guess, I'd look at this one's fate line. And I would guess yes."

Kristen was placated by this bit of nonsense, and we walked away, twenty bucks lighter and no wiser.

"Sucker," I said.

"What's wrong with a little magic?"

"I like magic a lot more when it doesn't cost twenty bucks."

"You're such a cynic. You don't believe in anything." Kristen looped her arm through mine, and we walked toward the ocean like an elderly couple.

"I believe in keeping my twenty bucks in my pocket."

We went down to the end of the boardwalk and took off our shoes to walk through the sand. Myrtle Beach sand was not the best sand, dirty and intermingled with bits of sticks. Patrol cars could drive down it, and the sand next to the water was packed and shallow. "We're inches away from making Camino Beach," said Kristen.

"Who's going to bring the sand from the beach to the back of the car? You? Maybe you can put it in your purse."

Kristen gave me a little shove. We made it to the water and put our feet in, let the Atlantic wash over them. It was cool by then, the evening breeze whipping my hair into a frizzy mess. Kristen's blonde mane remained well coiffed, if tousled into waves. I felt the knot that had been building ever since we got into our El Camino loosen a notch. Then, my phone rang.

Matt.

Kristen saw. "Oh, no. Don't answer that."

I was feeling guilty about hanging up on him in the Mexican restaurant. I also didn't want him to be one up on me, to think that I had been out behaving irresponsibly, which of course I had.

"Hello," I said.

"Sarah?" Who did he think it was? He was the one who had placed the call.

"Yes, Matt."

"I was just calling to make sure you were all right."

"Of course I'm all right. Why wouldn't I be all right?"

"You sounded like you were in a saloon earlier." Saloon?

"I was in a Mexican restaurant, Matt. People need to eat lunch, you know."

There was a long pause.

"Well, okay, then. When do I come and pick up Rhett Pugler?"

"Next Sunday?" Hadn't we been over this a thousand times?

"Okay, fine. See you then."

Kristen shook her head at me as I put the phone back in my pocket. "Who does he think he is? You don't have to answer to him anymore."

"I know." It wasn't that long ago, though. Not that long ago that I found myself with a lease in hand and a career change, asking for permission that I had never gotten. I didn't need it now for sure.

"Don't even think about it."

"Think about what?"

"Getting back together with him."

Getting back together with Matt was the last thing on my mind. I had only recently felt my head clear of the cobwebs that had been building since my marriage. I was still acquiring furniture in the new apartment, and I had no intentions of going backward; in fact, each conversation or encounter with Matt reinforced the decision. Furthermore, I had just met an extremely attractive new prospect. Extremely.

"Why would you think that? No way."

"Why are you being nice to him? And why are you taking his calls now? He doesn't even have your ugly little dog. What do you need to talk to him for?"

"My dog is not ugly. What if I called your children ugly?"

"Not the same thing. Answer the question."

I didn't want to do any of those things. I didn't want to hear his voice next to the waves breaking near my feet. But it was a voice from home, someone needing me in some way, someone to be there when no one else was around. There were times when that seemed better than nothing. And there were times when it didn't.

I took my toe, wrote "BERT" on the sand, raised an eyebrow at Kristen, who burst into laughter. "Right?" she said. "That's what you should be thinking about. Think we could ask him to be your date to the reunion?"

"It's a long way to go for someone you spent an hour with, who then passed out and shouted at your friend in your house."

"True dat." Kristen erased my scribble with her foot, sideswiping it. "But no kidding, stop talking to Matt. You've talked to him more than I've talked to my real husband."

"Speaking of your real husband, have you talked to him at all? Doesn't he need your help to know where to go and what to do?" I was surprised that Kristen's phone hadn't been ringing off the hook with questions from Chris.

She was silent for a moment, then said, "He can figure all that out his own damn self."

"Whoa."

"No, well, I talked to everyone before that Jacuzzi/swimsuit hole saga. The kiddos are fine. But Chris can let me go for one goddamn weekend."

"Whoa."

"Whoa yourself. You don't know what it's like to have them all over you like a cheap suit every damn minute of the day. Feels good to be out here with grown-ups, clears my head." All of our drama—the art show, the Jacuzzi, Mrs. Wilder, the Mexican restaurant—flashed through my head. Was this relaxing for her?

"We should probably apologize to Jack, shouldn't we?" Kristen wanted to change the subject.

"I did already."

"No, you didn't. That was a lame apology, and it was clear that you weren't sorry."

She twisted her hair, put it on top of her head in a messy chignon with a clip that appeared magically from her back pocket. "It was nice of him to take my bag, after I was such a bitch. But God, wouldn't it make it easier if he would just break a rule or two?"

It would. Now that the idea had presented itself, we were moments away from discovery—if only Jack would open the door. I didn't know if he really didn't want to break the rules or if he was trying to protect me. Either way, Jack was stubborn, so we would have to find another way. We headed back to the boardwalk, cleaned sand off our feet, and walked the end of the boardwalk barefoot, stomping off the remaining grains. We decided to stay the night in Myrtle Beach and wake up early the next morning for the nine-hour drive. We walked back to Elvira, where a piece of paper was clamped to the windshield wiper. I pulled it off.

"Parking ticket. We forgot to come back and feed the meter."

"Oh well. I'd rather pay twenty bucks than have walked back over here." Kristen shoved the ticket in her bag, where I hoped she would remember to pay it. "Hey, that palm reader might have told us to get back over to our parking meter."

"The palm reader was full of shit. Also, she's the one who took the twenty bucks." But she was right that Kristen's life was filled with straight lines whereas mine held forks and breaks. Kristen had always known where she was going, and I still didn't, not even today. The palm reader said we would find Roxanne, and even though I didn't believe in that sort of thing, I wanted to believe it was true. To trust that my fate line meant that there were still surprises left in store for me, that all of those lines had not broken off and splintered into a future that held nothing interesting at all.

May 1997
Parking Lot, Briley High School

I know that she knows, just by the way she's not talking. It's more than being annoyed that she had to leave work to come and get me after I fainted in gym class. And she doesn't seem to care that I fainted in gym class.

"Rough day," says Mom.

I just nod. I think I'm going to start crying, but then she'll really think I'm crazy. I saw her talking to Hunter while I got into the car, and I don't know what he told her.

"Congratulations. I heard about the scholarship," she says. She doesn't sound as happy as I thought she would. I mean, we basically just won a hundred thousand dollars.

"Thanks."

"He told me about Roxanne," she says. "She may not be in school next week."

I guess I expected that. Will she be suspended until graduation? Will she have to go to summer school? I don't say anything.

"Cheating. Not good."

My mother has seen Roxanne with her homework a million times, books spread out across the kitchen table, me trying to teach her something. And she knows how often I end up doing a problem or two, just to get us through it. She knows.

"Hunter says you won't be punished." I realize that I am holding my breath, and I let it out. I'll get to go to my school, at least. "That short story does sound a lot like you, though. Guess you got lucky they didn't want to take it any further." She sighs. "You know, Sarah, not everyone gets the opportunities that you've had." She puts the car in gear and turns to look at me. "A girl like Roxanne doesn't get to go to university like you do. That's not easy. And she'll have to watch you and Kristen go, while she stays here."

The knot in my chest tightens back up again, and tears come with it, too, rolling down my face, into the corners of my mouth.

"I just don't know if you realize how lucky you are."

"I'm not that lucky!" I yell at her, and she sits back. "I'm not like Kristen with all her money, who gets to go wherever she wants, who will get in wherever she wants, just because her parents can buy it for her! I have to work for whatever I get. So, that's what I did! I did what I had to do!"

Mom shakes her head. "It's not all about money, Sarah," she says gently.

"Well, it feels that way to me!" I turn forward and don't look at her again, and I am not talking about this, not now or ever again.

Chapter Eleven

The next day, I felt like I had been hit by a bus. Or the floor of a Mexican restaurant. Kristen had agreed to a motel outside of Myrtle Beach. There was no Four Seasons or Ritz-Carlton in sight, so she didn't have much choice. We slept side by side, on matching double beds again, the air-conditioning blasting our faces. When we got back on the road the next morning, I drove the first leg of the journey, Kristen the second. With a stop at Subway and two gas station load-ups of junk like Pringles and Twix, we made it back home late the same day. Like all return road trips, the mood was quiet, our eyes heavy-lidded.

Since Jack had driven us to Kristen's house, I didn't have a way to get home, and I consented to a night in her posh guest room. It compared favorably to our roadside motel and to the Holiday Inn. There, I was ensconced in a fluffy, colorful Anthropologie comforter on top of a Tempur-Pedic bed, and I passed out into oblivion, still wearing my clothes.

When I woke up the following morning, it all seemed like a dream, like we had been gone for a week rather than three days. I also felt an odd sense of hopelessness. Our weekend failure didn't really change anything. We hadn't known about Roxanne's whereabouts for years, so we were no better or worse off than when we'd started. I shuffled downstairs in my pajamas, wondering if Kristen was awake yet.

She was not only awake but already in a crisp button-down and khaki pants, in full hair and makeup. My cereal bowl and coffee mug were waiting for me at the table, which gave me a little thrill of pleasure, like coming home from college for a visit with Mom and Dad. "Aren't you bright-eyed and bushy-tailed?" I mumbled, eyes still crusty from sleep.

"Get going. We have a busy day. Do you need to borrow a clean shirt?" I looked down at little Kristen. It was not clear on which of my body parts one of her shirts would fit.

"I think your clothes are too small for me."

"I meant one of Chris's shirts, dumbass." Kristen held up a gigantic blue shirt on a hanger. Chris probably outweighed me by a hundred pounds, but, well, it was the better option of the two. I was wearing a wifebeater over my flannel jammie pants and shrugged into the massive shirt. Kristen rolled up my sleeves to three-quarter length while I tried to maneuver around her to get to my cereal.

"Where is everybody?"

"Sarah! They're at school. And work. Don't you have any concept of what normal people do during the week?"

I had no concept of time at all at that exact moment.

"Can I ask where it is that you think we are going? I really have to go and check on the store, and I don't know if I can do it in this weird shirt. I need to go home and grab a shower and a change of clothes."

"We're going to Briley, where else?"

"Um, why?"

"Duh! To dig through the records. With any luck, we can make it over there before Jack comes in. Who knows? Maybe he decided to spend the week at Bert's."

This was unlikely. Jack knew he had to return Kristen's bag to her, one. Two, he was never late for work. Three, she didn't know about his earlier desires to want to "leave at dawn." He had probably slept at Bert's and then been on the road early the next morning. "I don't think that's a very good idea" was all I said. Jack might be right, too. Was there too much information in this particular file from high school? What would Kristen say if she found out everything?

"Hurry up. I've already backed the car out."

"The El Camino?"

"Who can go incognito in an El Camino? The Rover! It's what school board members would drive."

"School board members?"

"That's what we're pretending to be, and we have a meeting with the school principal."

"No, we don't. And the school principal has already said that we are persona non grata in his records room."

"Sarah! Eat your cereal, and get moving. Just stand next to me and nod, if you can't play along."

Once I put my dark jeans back on, the shirt didn't look as bad. Kristen did look like a school board member, and I guessed I was going as her frumpy sidekick. Our old school was down the street from the store, and on my way home. If Kristen didn't want to drive me back to my apartment, I could always ask Aidan or Evelyn. With any luck, my mother would have dropped Rhett Pugler off at the shop already. Getting in the car with Kristen didn't necessarily obligate me to participate in her scheme.

We didn't talk for the first few minutes of the drive, but the silence was too much for me. "What exactly are you looking for?" She turned to look at me, blue eyes wide. "Watch the road! You're drifting." She snapped the wheel, and we returned to safety.

"A file with her name on it."

"Do you really believe they still have files on all of us?"

"I don't know, but I'm going to find out."

"How much room would that take up, all those files?"

"A binder for every year? All of our taxes for our entire married life fit in two of those. Why couldn't they keep one for the class of 1997?"

My own taxes would fit into a couple of manila folders—a couple of years of married filing separately, then just me. I remembered the old school office well, and beyond the reception, there was a door that occasionally drifted open that led to a room filled with just that—files upon files. There was probably a lot there, not just student records, but employee records, state documents, who knew. Could they have kept those records? Did they have them in that little room?

We had reached Green Hills and would quickly be at the school. Or the store. "Can we stop at my store?"

Kristen banged the steering wheel. "I knew you wouldn't do it! Fine! Go back to your store and forget we ever started this."

I cleared my throat. "If you had just let me finish. I know I have a blazer hanging up in the back room." Who was I kidding? I had to see how this was going down. We were in it together, and we had less than a week until that reunion. Maybe I still had time to make this right.

"Yeehaw!" Kristen hung a hard right into the shopping complex where my store lived and pulled over to the curb.

The doorbell jangled my arrival, but no one in the shop looked up from the books their noses were buried in, which was promising for the day's sales. Evelyn was on the phone but waved at me. She covered the receiver with her hand and said, "Can you believe we only have one Natasha Trethewey book in this whole store?"

I shrugged. "Yes." I don't hold it against my hometown that they don't know the names of any famous poets. Okay, maybe just a little bit. Thank goodness for Evelyn, a retired grandmother with a crackerjack wit, to deal with requests with a smile on her face.

Aidan glared at me when I walked in. There had probably been a lot of cleanup after the weekend's event, and I hadn't helped at all. "Don't say a word," I said, pointing menacingly.

"Hello," said Aidan. "Does that count as a word?"

The relief I felt when I entered my store was palpable. This was what I wanted, when I started this store, somewhere I could relax and feel safe, surrounded by all these great books that I picked out myself. And it was just that.

I remember going to the old Davis-Kidd bookstore as a child and sitting on the floor with a pile of books. Looking back, I don't know if my mom even stayed in the store. For all I knew, she was a block away at Castner Knott's, buying shoes. I always felt happy there among the books. I think I was always searching for that—a quiet place surrounded by something I loved. I didn't find it in my previous jobs, and I didn't have it at home with Matt. When the opportunity came up to invest in my own store, it was irresistible. The investment I turned out to be afraid of was the one I had already with my husband.

An older couple huddled next to the staff recommendations, and the grandpa half was inspecting me like I was a bug pinned to a page. "Are you Sarah?" he blurted.

"I'm Sarah," I confirmed. I occasionally do interviews with the local paper, and I'm the one who introduces authors at events. Aidan blew up a giant photocopy of the last story about us, and there was a huge unattractive picture of me hanging in the front of the store. My hair was up in a big sloppy bun with a pencil stuck in it, and I was about two feet taller than the customer I was talking to. Evelyn charitably said it made me look statuesque, like the goddess Athena. "If Athena had bedhead," Aidan added.

"I've been reading your pick every month. They're always so good!" Grandpa held up the last Allegra Goodman, my choice this month. This never failed to bring a smile to my face, my customers taking our recommendations. It kept the cash register full, too.

I didn't spend as much time at the front of the store as I should. Aidan was good at chatting up the customers. I didn't know how he managed to read anything with the classes he was in; he was pre-law something or other, with a politics and history double major. He looked like he was about fifteen, the perfect foil for Evelyn, and the two of them had become local celebrities in their own right; I recently had to install an Aidan's Shelf and an Evelyn's Shelf under my recommendations. They might outsell me this month.

I made a beeline for the back room, where a navy jacket was hanging on the door. There was a white stain on the elbow, probably powdered doughnut sugar, which I brushed at before throwing the blazer on over Chris's baggy shirt. "I'll be back in a few minutes," I called at my employees on my way out, without looking at them. I couldn't help glancing at the table in front—too much nonfiction for my taste. I grabbed a stack of recent Civil War history books and relocated them to the counter. I knew who was behind that selection. I scanned the walls and chose a nice beach read to replace them. "Can you get rid of those?" I asked Aidan. "When was the last time we sold four Civil War books in one day? The buffs can go look for those in the back."

Aidan sighed. "Yes, boss." He stage-whispered to Evelyn, "I liked her better when she was on vacation."

"I heard that, and I'm coming back soon." The door jingled again as I darted through it and jumped back into Kristen's car. We could have easily walked the block to the school, but walking was not something people in Nashville did. If we were going somewhere, we were driving.

Jack's car was not in the parking lot, a good sign. We were walking in during class; the hallways were quiet, the activity stuffed inside the classrooms. The details of our plan were muddy, at best. The truth was that it wasn't the best idea to follow Kristen, who brought enthusiasm and sass into the venture, but who could not be depended upon to think before she spoke.

I broke the news gently. "Why don't you let me start talking first? Teachers love me."

We had arrived at the main commons area, which was nearly unchanged. There was a massive trophy case, with more trophies than when we were there, and young faces from years beyond ours staring out from behind the glass, memorializing a team, a season, a championship. It was an open, sunny space, windows everywhere, and in the middle was that big clock that normalized our days, telling us when to stop doing one thing and when to start another.

Kristen ignored this request. "Do you think Mrs. Lionel is still at the desk?" Mrs. Lionel was probably sixty when we were in high school, so no, I did not. I hoped not, at least. Mrs. Lionel was a bit of a birdbrain—we had made it past her before, but we needed someone who wouldn't recognize us.

"So, you're going to let me talk?"

"Like the way you talked to Mrs. Wilder? Which was to not say anything at all."

"That was different. I was surprised. And you were hysterical. You were not any better than I was there."

"Okay, if you think you've got this. School board members. Important records. Got it?"

We followed the signs marked "Reception," but we knew the route by heart. Behind a heavy wooden door lay the inner workings of that institution. Unfortunately, we knew all too well that the door to the principal's office was also connected to it. I had a hard time connecting Jack to Principal Hunter. Was he the Hunter for these students? I doubted it. Rule follower or not, he still had a love for education and a love for kids.

"What's your school board name?" asked Kristen.

"Uh . . . Jennifer, uh, Nettles."

"'Uh' is not a first name. Also, Jennifer Nettles is the singer of Sugarland. Oh, boy."

"What's your name?" I asked.

"Lisa. Lisa Novak."

"That sounds familiar, too. Hmm. Wasn't that an astronaut?"

"What?"

143

"I can't remember what happened. But there was a story there. About an astronaut." Why did we need fake names at all? Especially if we couldn't think of any that were actually fake.

"What?"

"Just don't be Lisa Novak. And it's Nowak, I think. The astronaut."

"Fine. I'm Amy Brenneman." Kristen glared at me.

"Isn't that an actress? Why don't you be Reese Witherspoon while you're at it?"

"Fuck you. I'm going in there."

Some things never changed, and one of those things was the front desk of my old high school. There might have even been the same fuzzy pompon wrapped around a ballpoint pen, tethered to the sign-in/out sheet, which you had to inscribe anytime you were late or left early because of a "doctor's appointment." That wasn't the only thing that hadn't changed.

A Tasmanian devil, small and round with a mop of wild gray hair, hurled itself in our direction seconds after we had crossed the threshold. "Sarah Martin! Kristen Calhoun! I'll be! Y'all look just the same! What are you doing here?"

Lisa Novak looked over at me, clearly put out. Jennifer Nettles was also less than thrilled to see Mrs. Lionel, who still looked to be in her sixties, the age I had just placed her in high school. When you were young, anyone over the age of forty was "old," I suppose, and age became difficult to determine. The young did not bother assigning these people a precise age.

Kristen bent down (bent down!) to give Mrs. Lionel a hug. "You look just the same," she oozed. "I bet you're not a day over fifty."

Mrs. Lionel tee-heed at her. "Sixty-seven, would you believe it?"

"And you're still working!" I just wished she wasn't still working at precisely this moment. We were completely screwed. We would just have to say we were in the neighborhood and had decided to say hi. So much for incognito.

"Well, I'm just replacing Becky for the rest of the school year. She's out on maternity leave. Lucky me! I got to run into you two. What have you been up to?" She put a heavily ringed hand on my elbow. "Well, you! I know all about your store. I go there sometimes, but I never see you—always that nice older lady, or the young boy. Isn't that great? You were always such a reader. And writer! Remember when you won the literary award with that poem about . . . was it horses?"

My face flamed. There were so few people who would remember that; even my parents had probably forgotten. Kristen snorted. "It *was* about horses! Why don't you recite it, Sarah?"

"I couldn't possibly remember," I said, wishing the floor would swallow me up.

Kristen put on her pouty face, the one she used when she wanted some guy at a bar to buy her a drink. "That is so sad, such a beautiful poem lost forever. I wonder if there's a copy around here somewhere."

"Well, now, we don't really keep the contest stuff in the library," mused Mrs. Lionel. "I wonder."

"Oh, that's okay, really! It's probably better if it stays lost." I was ready to start inching my way to the records room and forget about my own high school embarrassments.

Kristen stepped on my toe hard, and left her foot there. She was wearing some new pointy shoes, the expensive kind with the red soles. They were only a size six, but it still hurt.

"I mean, you don't keep any files on us, do you? Nothing that old?"

"We sure do! We have a file on every student, but I just don't know if something like that would be in there."

"Oh, I don't know. You used that in your college application essay, didn't you? When you applied for that scholarship?" I had really underestimated Lisa Novak. I felt like I was moving underwater, barely able to recover from the surprise of seeing Mrs. Lionel, and Kristen was a step away from the records room.

"I did." I momentarily had forgotten the name of our guidance counselor, so I brought up our old English teacher and hoped she wasn't still around. "Mrs. Higdon told me to include it with my application, and I bet I would have never received that scholarship if it weren't for that."

"I'll be. Well, who knows? It might still be around here."

"My parents sure would love to read it. They were so proud. Mom doesn't read too much anymore; it's hard on her eyes."

"How old's your mom now, Sarah?"

"Eighty." I rounded up by nine years to a nice, old number. "Yeah, she sure would like to see that."

Kristen nodded encouragingly at me from over Mrs. Lionel's shoulder. "That's okay. She might not even remember it, you know, even though she did love it so much. She has such a hard time remembering things now." We stared somberly at our feet, and I imagined what my mother would say if she could overhear this conversation. She remembered the horsey poem well enough (it was a metaphor for time) and had howled with laughter when she'd read it.

"Well, I guess we could go take a look, but just for a few minutes, 'cause I can't leave this desk unattended. Some of those boxes are on high shelves, too, so I don't know."

"Sarah can reach any tall shelf, right, Sarah?"

I nodded enthusiastically.

"Okay, then, but let's be quick about it!"

Kristen and I exchanged looks of glee and followed Mrs. Lionel into the back room, packed to the brim with binders labeled "Teacher Evaluations," "Detention Log," "English Program 2006–2016." In the back of the room was a spiral staircase that went down. We followed it.

The room was dark, with the dusty smell of dry paper. Mrs. Lionel flipped on a light that didn't help very much, and we walked narrow aisles filled with boxes upon boxes labeled with dates. We were standing near the eighties. "What year are we looking for, girls?" said Mrs. Lionel. "'87?"

"No! '97," said Kristen. From where I was standing, I could see that each year required more than one box. I prayed that *M* had been put with the second part of the alphabet, with *W* for Wilder, and not the first.

I was out of luck.

The box was eye level with me. "1997, *A* through *M*," said Mrs. Lionel. "Let's have a look. Can you lift that big old box, Sarah?"

I lifted it up and placed it gently on the ground. Kristen's eyes were fixed on the box still on the shelf, "N–Z." She looked like she wanted to whack Mrs. Lionel over the head so that she could grab it. I stood back while Mrs. Lionel flipped through the slim files in the box until she found mine. Twenty years later, confidentiality went out the window, I suppose, because she handed it right over.

Of course there was no horse poem in the file. There was no reason for it to have been kept. There was an old photocopied SAT report on top, 1400, which had made me a National Merit scholar, followed by four years of grades. Two letters of recommendation to colleges followed. These had to be requested from your teachers, sealed, and sent directly to the university. I had never seen them, and I couldn't resist the temptation to look now. From Principal Hunter: "Sarah is a gifted writer and a student of great academic promise. She is quite simply the best student at Briley High School in the class of 1997. I hope that her association with students of the scholarly capability that one finds at the University of the South will further help her intellectual development."

I slammed the file shut, red-faced. There was my recommendation letter. It could have said "CHEATER" on it instead, or nothing at all. It should have said "TRAITOR." I stuffed it back into the file, and my voice sounded hollow. "No, it's not here."

"Here. Give it to me. I'll put it back on the shelf," said Kristen.

The box was about as big as Kristen, but she had her hand on the other box, and I hoped that she had a plan. Mrs. Lionel was getting squirmy, and I was running out of ideas. I handed it over but kept my hand on the box. We slid the box onto the shelf together.

Crash.

"Oh, no!" wailed Mrs. Lionel. "Mr. Donahue won't ever let me replace Becky again!"

"1997, N–Z" lay on its side, contents spilled out onto the ground. "Oh my God," I said. Kristen could not stop herself from looking smug. "Did you hear that bell?"

"I gotta go see who that is. Girls, please! Try to pick this up while I go see who's here." Mrs. Lionel scrambled back up the stairs.

"Hot damn! Let's get in there." Kristen rubbed her hands together.

"Was there not a neater way for us to get at this box? Shit, how are we going to get this mess cleaned up?"

Kristen was scooping up documents and just shoving them into folders and back into the box with no regard whatsoever for what went where. "Wait! You are messing all of these up!"

"Jesus, Sarah. Who is ever going to look at this shit? It's taken us twenty years to get down here. This stuff is dead. These are all *N*, *P*, *Q*. Who was named *Q*?"

"Jamie Quincy."

"Oh yeah! Let's look at his SAT score."

"It was probably negative. Keep going." We glanced only quickly at the tops of the pages, putting the documents back in as quickly as we could. Nelson, Trent. Quincy, James. Ryder, Tiffany. Then, we were close. Watson, Wesley, Wilder, Wilson. Wilder!

"Holy shit, I've got it."

I wanted to get to it first, just to see what was in there, but Kristen already had it in her clutches. I held my breath. What would it say about Roxanne's absence? Was there a report? Please, oh, please, let that signed confession from me have been left out.

We blew past three and half years of C and D grades and an extensive detention report. There was an envelope that had once been sealed but had been opened up and shut again with scotch tape, marked "Confidential." Kristen's pink fingernail ripped right through it. The letterhead read "Guidance Counselor." The case history was brief, and some of the key words had been put in bold, which helped us skim through it: "troubled," "acting out." My report was nowhere to be found, and I breathed a sigh of relief.

"Oh shit," Kristen whispered. "Did you know she went to the guidance counselor?" I shook my head. Our guidance counselor was a creepy bald man named Johnny. I think he asked us to call him Johnny because he thought it made him sound younger, but we always thought it just made him sound like a pervert.

We thumbed through her assessment and possible treatment, which was vague. The "subject" had not opened up in the interview, which the interviewer (Johnny, we presumed) deemed insufficient for full recommendations. He did state that regular visits with a trusted counselor were desirable, as "subject feels misunderstood by peers and friends" and "needs an outlet to express her true feelings." The subject needed distance, perhaps separation from "her guardian." There was no report about cheating.

"Oh shit," I repeated.

"Oh shit is right."

We hadn't even heard Jack coming down the steps.

Mrs. Lionel was wringing her hands behind Jack. "I'm so sorry, Mr. Donahue. These girls were just cleaning up. All we wanted was a little old poem that Sarah wrote back in school to give to her poor old momma."

"Poor old momma?" said Jack. He had seen my "poor old momma" a few weeks ago when he'd driven by the house and she was mowing the lawn. I just looked at him—*Please, please.* It was bad enough that he had caught us. We didn't have to also get shown up for the liars we were to Mrs. Lionel.

"A poem? 'Wild Horses Couldn't'?" I did not know how Jack could remember the title of that ridiculous poem. "It's all right, Mrs. Lionel.

I'm sure you meant well. Students are getting out of class, so you go on up. We'll get this mess cleaned up."

"Oh! I knew you would understand! Girls, this one isn't at all like the old one. Just imagine what Roger Hunter would have said if he saw you down here." I did not even want to know.

I put my head in my hands. Kristen snapped the file shut, as if it made any difference at all now. Jack sat down on the floor next to us and sighed. "I tried to stop you."

"You already looked." This was a statement not a question.

"Of course I looked! I checked the file before we left for Myrtle Beach. Come on. Give me some credit, here."

"Why didn't you tell us? Did you really have to give us that bullshit I'm-a-Metro-employee line?" Just when I thought I had Jack figured out.

He sighed. "There was nothing to tell, and there were also no clear indications about where she went. For me, there was nothing in this file but bad memories for the two of you." He looked at me hard. "Also, I thought that you had hired an, ahem, competent private investigator."

All he had tried to do was protect us, protect us while we had broken into confidential records and mocked his position. "I'm sorry. I'm so sorry." I stared at the floor. I should have trusted him.

"How could we have not known?" Kristen smacked one of the shelves with a file. "No one to talk to? Bullshit. She could have talked to us."

"She didn't know that, I guess."

"How could she not have known that? You know, I knew that her mother had something to do with it. She knows something, something she won't say."

"You don't know what it's like for a kid who grows up in a tough home. They don't want to talk to just anyone. Sounds like she couldn't talk to her mother for sure. It's embarrassing. It makes you different, and no teenager wants to be different, especially not someone as cool as Roxanne was. You have to put that stuff deep down inside and not talk about it, and be someone else when you're not at home."

Jack had lived with his single mom when we were in school. I didn't really know what had happened to his father, just that his parents had split up before we had even met him. I didn't even know why he'd appeared out of nowhere in our school in the middle of our four years. By the time Jack and I became close friends, he was an adult with a life of his own; we all were, with our parents being people we visited on the weekends. I had never thought that anyone as easygoing and well adjusted as Jack could have had any major problems at home, but I wondered about it now. I could also not imagine why anyone would ever want to be a high school principal, but that would do it—the desire to watch over all of these young people.

"Dammit. We're no closer now than when we were at the Holiday Inn," said Kristen.

"At least my underpants are intact," said Jack.

"We knew there was something wrong! We knew her mother was bonkers. No wonder she didn't ever call or write." Kristen propped her elbow on the box. "I wouldn't have called us either. We should have helped her, and we didn't."

I stared at the floor. Some of us not only didn't help but also made things worse.

"Hey. She was already an actress, even then. You couldn't have known." Jack rubbed my shoulder. "This may be a ghost you cannot raise. Don't worry about it. Come to the reunion anyway."

"Are you going?" I hadn't even thought to ask.

"Absolutely! I'm forty pounds thinner. And I have no choice, as principal. You should come, too."

"I don't have a date," I grumbled.

"I'll be your date if you can't find anyone." He smiled at me. Kristen was shooting a sad face at me over his shoulder.

"Do you want me to set you up with someone?" asked Kristen. I realized she was talking to Jack, not me.

"Who do you have in mind?"

"I'll have to think about it, but I'm sure I can find someone."

I gave Kristen a dirty look. What if I needed him?

Jack stood up, smoothed the wrinkles from his pants. "So, make sure you clean this mess up, okay?"

Kristen had put the box back together, more or less. "Done," she said.

"Oh, Miss Calhoun. We both know that those files are all mixed up. I'll thank you to put every single document back where it goes. 'Preciate it." Jack straightened himself back up and climbed the stairs again like he did it every day. He did do it every day.

It took Kristen and me another hour to sift back through the files. We didn't do a perfect job, but everyone was restored to semi-alphabetical order. We might or might not have looked at dozens of grades and standardized test scores. "Let's look at Jack's," said Kristen.

"No, Kristen! That's snooping! Cut it out." She had already slid out the first box again and was thumbing through the files.

"Ooh," said Kristen. "Okay. Guess—higher or lower than yours."

I pretended to think it over for a little while, to be polite. "Lower. Put that away. It's not nice."

"Wrong. Fifty whole points."

The shock must have read on my face because Kristen was doubled over, laughing at me. "Why don't we look up yours?" I asked nastily. "If we have no regards for anyone's privacy here?"

"Why not?"

"What did you get?"

"Don't remember."

"Uh-huh." I had always had my doubts about Kristen's college acceptances, which had seemed too good to be true. Her family was well connected, so this had never surprised me, but it did rankle that it was so easy for her to go to the school of her choice. I should have let it go, but I flipped through the files for hers and pulled it out. "Going, going . . . last chance . . . I'm looking."

Kristen shrugged. "Go ahead."

Kristen's grades were on the front page, and while they were not straight As like mine, I had to admit they were pretty good. The top corner of the page said "Class Rank—10." I had never given much thought as to who rounded out the rest of the top ten. My job was to be Straight A Student No. 1. Kristen's was cheerleading co-captain. I kept going. SAT score—1320. It was not as high as mine had been, but it was still very good. It seemed possible that Kristen had gotten into Vanderbilt all on her own.

"Why didn't you ever tell me you did so well?" I said.

"Sarah, you were so obsessed with your own GPA and test scores, you didn't care how anyone else was doing." She was right and I knew it. There was another reason I hadn't been paying close attention to what was going on with Roxanne either. I was so focused on that scholarship and what would become of me when I left high school that I hadn't bothered to notice what was going on with anyone else.

"I'm sorry, gosh."

"Oh well. Water under the bridge, sister." Kristen flashed a pearly grin at me. "Let's get one last look at this Wilder file before we pack it in and go home." She flipped through the counselor's report, the grades, and found nothing interesting. Even though I knew it wasn't there, I held my breath anyway. I noticed a Post-it note stuck to the back cover of the file.

"What is that?"

Kristen plucked it from the back. "7/1/97 4239425120. Huh, wonder what the number is?"

"Read the second one again."

"4239425120."

"Maybe it's a phone number. 423 is the area code for Sewanee. Call it."

Kristen sifted through a giant Louis Vuitton purse for her phone, punched in the number. Her face lit up.

"What? What is it?"

"Marion County High School. Monteagle, Tennessee."

Roxanne and I are completely wasted. I have never been this wasted in my entire life. We are lying on the fifty-yard line of the football field, and Roxanne's head is touching my head, and our feet are straight out in front of us. The grass doesn't feel as soft as I thought it would when I first lay down on it. Like bristles. Itchy.

Nothing has happened yet, and we just went out for the night. I figure everything will be different in the morning, but at least we have tonight. Tonight, we are all best friends, and she does not hate me.

Roxanne brought tequila. I don't drink tequila, only beer sometimes. Not much of that even. I'm a good girl. Not tonight.

Too. Much.

"Why did we do this?" I ask the sky.

"Because it's fun," says the sky, but the sky has Roxanne's voice.

"I smoked so many cigarettes." My throat is aching, and the pack of Camel Lights is lying in between me and Roxanne. I can have another one. I shouldn't. I will. "Where's Kris?"

"With Jeff." Roxanne doesn't sound nearly as messed up as I feel.

I look up, and the stars are perfectly clear, and I have never looked at them like this before. I wish I knew which ones were the dippers, and the bear. All I see is lights, like it's Christmas, and they're all blurring together now. "I love you," I tell Roxanne, and I do. I'll miss her so much. I'll be out of this place soon, and what if she leaves and we don't see each other anymore?

"You love Kristen more." Roxanne's voice is smooth and rich, vanilla in the warm almost-summer breeze.

"No, I don't." I do, though. Just a little bit.

"I love you, too," says Roxanne.

"You're my best friend." I think I might start to cry because our friendship is done for. It's ending. It's never going to be the same. "Both of you."

"You, too. I'll remember you forever."

"Don't go to California and never come back to Tennessee. You can't. You better not. Just don't."

"Oh, we'll see what happens. But I'll always remember you. Always."

This doesn't make me feel better at all. I turn my head and vomit on the round part of the five in fifty.

Chapter Twelve

Monteagle was a two-hour drive away, and we had just been through there during our Sewanee pit stop. Had we been that close, and hadn't even known it? "Let's go! If we leave now, we could still get back home by tonight." Kristen's eyes had a crazy glimmer. She hopped up and slung the box back onto the shelf, teetering on her heels. I did not move from the floor. She kicked me with one of those pointy shoes. "Get up." Where did Kristen get all her energy? I felt so tired from the weekend's activities, and I had some things to take care of at work. I had no idea how the event had gone, if we had sold a lot of books, if Amy had talked with customers. This kind of stuff was important. It got back to agents for speaking tours if readings didn't go well.

"I don't know, Kris. I need a minute here. Maybe we can play detective next weekend?" I wasn't optimistic that this would turn out to be anything but another disaster.

"How are we going to do that? We'll be at the reunion!"

We didn't have enough time to get our friend to attend, if finding her was still even within our grasp. I wasn't going to the reunion. "We need to at least call first. I don't want to repeat the Mrs. Wilder Myrtle Beach fiasco. That's enough miles for me for one weekend." I hauled myself up gracelessly. I didn't know what age it was when you started to have a hard time getting up from a sitting position if you've been there too long. My knees were all stiff, and my back was frozen into place.

Jack jogged down the stairs at about the time I was returning myself to Sarah erectus position. I held on to my lower back. "What happened to you?" He didn't wait for an answer but peeked over to check that the box had been returned to its rightful spot. "I trust that everything is back where it's supposed to go."

"I trust that you missed something when you looked at that file," said Kristen, holding out the Post-it note.

Jack inspected it. "A Chattanooga area code?" Lord. He saw it right away, too.

"This number was in her file, stuck on the back! And it's the high school! It has a date written on it—1997!"

"Kristen wants us to go there. Now." I said this flatly, as if to emphasize how silly it was. I hoped he would tell her that and be more persuasive than I had been.

Jack pulled his phone out of his pocket and took the Post-it note from Kristen.

"What are you doing?" I said impatiently. "We called already. That's how we found out it was the school."

Jack held up a hand to shush me and started dialing. "Yes, Jack Donahue, principal of Briley High School. Could I speak with someone in charge of student records?"

Kristen turned to me, eyes wide, fingers flapping, and mouthed, *I can't believe it.*

There was a pregnant pause, and then Jack reintroduced himself again to some other interlocutor. "I need to close out an old file of ours. We have a student who, I believe, transferred to your school many years ago, and I would consider it a great personal favor if you could give us her last known address."

We waited, breaths held. "Wilder," said Jack. "Roxanne Wilder." Then he motioned at Kristen for a pen, pantomiming writing. Kristen scrambled to dig around in her bag for a pen and a notepad. She pulled out a compact, a protein bar, and finally came up with a receipt and an eyeliner. Jack reached for the eyeliner.

"Yes. You're sure. White? But first name Roxanne? The same one that graduated as Wilder? Yes, of course, it was a long time ago. I doubt it, too, that it would be valid, but it helps me to archive this file. It will do. Thank you so much!"

Kristen hurled herself at Jack's neck and kissed him on the cheek, a loud smack that left a smeary mark. I hit him on the back like he was an old baseball buddy. "I thought that was against the rules," I said. Both of us beamed at him like idiots.

"Who's going to make the call? Or do you just want to go there?"

Kristen cocked a hip and put her hand there. "Oh, Sarah is *tired*. She has *important* business at her bookstore, you know, those old books just won't sell themselves."

"You have to be kidding." Jack stared at me. "I'd come with you in a heartbeat, but I just busted some kid who's been keying cars in the parking lot, and I have to deal with an irate mother and father. Besides, I'm probably not invited."

"Sure you are," I said unconvincingly. We were in his great debt, even if neither one of us felt like having him in tow again.

"What are the odds that she's still there?" Kristen asked.

"Look at it this way. The odds of her turning up at the reunion are zero at this point. This would boost your chances up to about one percent. Still," Jack said.

"How about this? We find nothing, and you get to eat lunch at your favorite little university restaurant again?" Kristen said.

I sighed. Would one more stop be all it took? "Let's call first," I said. I didn't believe it, not really, that we would find anything other than some house where some girl who may or may not have been Roxanne may have lived at some point in her life, closer to twenty years ago than now.

Kristen held out the phone and the number. I took it, dialed—slowly. Jack and Kristen stared at me, breaths held. Ring. Probably would turn up nothing. Ring. This was totally ridiculous. Ring. I could get back to the store. Ring—click, and answering machine. "Hi, you've reached the White house. Leave a message!" in a breathy voice that was incontestably one that I knew. I pushed "End."

"Well?"

I nodded.

"Well?"

"It was her," I said in a small voice. We all looked at each other, and then, it was a frenzy to see who could move the fastest. I went for the keys that were on the ground. Kristen grabbed her purse.

"Call me when you get there," shouted Jack, and we were already halfway up the stairs. I missed one of the steps, banged my knee hard against the ground. Jack was behind me in a second, hauling me up. I massaged the knot but hardly felt it. "Go," whispered Jack, and we were gone, out the double doors, into the parking lot, running like it was the last day of school before summer vacation. I unlocked the car, hurled myself into the driver's seat; Kristen flew into the passenger seat.

This wasn't my car. And these weren't my keys.

"What are you doing?" said Kristen.

"I don't know." I started to laugh.

"Well, you're sitting there, keep going! Drive!" After my precipitation into the driver's seat of the car, it took me a moment to adjust the seat back to my own leg length, fix the mirrors. I pulled out of the school parking lot and tried to calm down.

"We need to think for a second. First, we are driving the wrong car."

"It doesn't matter. Let's go!"

"What do you mean it doesn't matter? That was the whole point." My phone buzzed with a text, but I couldn't look at it from the driver's seat. "Could you see who that is?"

Kristen read, "'Mom—Matt's here for RP. Okay for me to let him go?'"

"Goddammit! He cannot have the dog. It is not his turn yet!"

"Sarah, who cares? That works out better. We've got to go. Pick up your dog whenever we get back."

Kristen didn't understand. This was a custody arrangement, and it was not Matt's week.

"It's on the way," I said, making a right turn on Abbott Martin. "And we have to go to your house to get the El Camino."

"And I have to ride two hours with your fucking dog on my lap?"

"You can get in the back, if you want."

"It's *my* car."

"Then you can drive, and I'll ride with the dog in my lap."

"Is this really how you want to meet up with Roxanne, with a pug in your arms?"

He's all I have, so why not?

My parents' house was not that far away, and we could easily get back on the highway from there. I turned onto Belmont and then followed the back streets until we arrived. Matt's car was still there, so it wasn't too late. I parked the Range Rover in the driveway, and we went through the back door to the kitchen, where Matt was sitting at the table drinking a glass of orange juice with my parents. I felt as if I had interrupted a scene with someone else's family.

Rhett Pugler went berserk when he saw me, jumping off Matt's lap and panting at my feet until I picked him up so that he could slobber on me. "What are you doing here?" I said, without saying hello to my parents.

Matt was wearing this fake expression of concerned innocence. "It just sounded like you were busy down there in Myrtle Beach, where I did not know you were going, and I thought it might be less trouble for your parents if I came to pick him up." Sure, he was just acting out of kindness to the dog, not out of any desire to prove that I had been irresponsible and that he, like always, was doing what he was supposed to do.

My mother filled up Matt's glass with some more juice. "Maybe Matt is right. If y'all are busy this weekend, with your reunion and stuff, maybe Rhett Pugler is better off with his daddy." His daddy? I could have killed her.

"Well, we're back, as you can see, so there's no need."

"Did you get a new car?" asked my dad.

"It's my car," said Kristen.

"Why are you driving Kristen's car?" asked my mother, registering the keys in my hand and squinting at Kristen as if she might not be sober.

"We're just in a hurry, and I just took her keys, and, well, it's not important."

They all looked at each other, complicit. My mother folded her hands, put them on the table. "Why don't you just let Matt keep the dog until next week if you're busy?"

My mouth opened and closed, guppy-like. Why did she always have to be on his side? Didn't she know he was manipulating this situation?

"Who are you bringing to the reunion?" asked Matt. "If you need a date, I might be free." I wrinkled my nose at him.

"She's bringing Roxanne," said Kristen, and we all stared at her.

"Roxanne!" said Dad. "That pretty girl with the red hair. What ever happened to her?" We all ignored him.

"Well, well. So, you found her in Myrtle Beach? What's she doing?" Mom emptied her own orange juice glass in one smooth pull. What to say to that? Nothing would change my mother, or her ideas about my friends and ex-husband.

"It's been real nice seeing y'all," said Kristen, voice sugar sweet. "We're kind of in a hurry here, so we're just going to take the dog and go." Something underneath that sweet tone suggested that she might have a handgun in her purse and that she might be willing to use it.

Matt snapped his fingers at Rhett Pugler, who had descended to snort up some crumbs on the ground. "I thought it was decided. It's really not a problem for me to keep him for a week. Sarah can see him after my turn is finished. So, that's three weeks now."

Kristen is not a big dog fan, but she leaned over, picked up my dog as if he were a baby, tummy up, legs pointing to the ceiling. Kristen's only experience dealing with small mammals was with her children. "We're taking the dog."

The momentum from earlier was starting to return, and just being here was making me itch. My mother shrugged. "Whatever you want."

Matt was turning red, but I could tell that he didn't want to make a scene in front of my parents. "I'm not sure that's best."

"Well, Matt, I don't care what you think is best," said Kristen. "I don't care what you think at all." My mouth fell open. My mother might have been about to snap at her, or she might have been suppressing a grin, I couldn't tell. Her mouth was twitching.

Matt stood up. "You're holding him wrong." He held out his arms, and Rhett Pugler started wriggling.

I felt like King Solomon, ordering the women to cut the baby to decide whom it belonged to. We were losing time. I cleared my throat. "Do not touch my damn dog. I am telling you that right now. Do not come one step closer." Even though I'm a good bit shorter than he is, Matt stepped back. "And you two could back me up every once in a while." I shot an evil look at my parents.

"Hear, hear!" said Kristen, bouncing Rhett Pugler as if she were trying to burp him.

"Honey, we didn't mean anything. He just showed up here." Dad at least looked sympathetic.

"You are making a fuss out of nothing," said my mother.

"Maybe I feel like making a fuss. We're leaving." I took Rhett Pugler from Kristen and opened the door. "I'm making a fuss! So there!" Kristen made a run for it, and I slammed the door behind me. My mother had a wreath of what looked like dead leaves and some sticks hanging on the door, and it fell off on impact. I opened the door and pitched the wreath back inside. "Look, I'm sorry," I called. "Talk to you next week, okay?" I looked at Matt. "Not you."

We climbed back into the car. "Did you really say 'so there'?" said Kristen, starting to giggle.

"Did you just say 'I don't care what you think' to Matt?"

"God, he is such a douche," said Kristen. "I don't know how you stand it."

"Do you mean to say that it wasn't the worst mistake of my whole life breaking up with him?"

"Worst? Are you kidding? Best thing you ever did." I looked over at her in surprise. She had given me a hard time about the divorce, told me to try harder, told me to be sure, to not act too fast.

"Really?"

"You can't breathe around that guy. He would have suffocated you." He already had. I was glad that I only had the dog to share with him, and there were times when even Rhett Pugler did not make it worthwhile.

My mother stuck her head out the door, jogged down the stairs. "Hey, girls!"

They were not getting a better apology. I was fresh out of regrets for the moment. I rolled down my window.

"If you find her," she said. "Just tell her . . ."

Kristen and I leaned forward to hear this. "Yeah, what?" I said.

"I guess just tell her I said hello."

Kristen and I looked at each other. "Is that all?" I said.

She nodded. I was pretty sure this was her way of apologizing without saying she was sorry.

"Hey, Mom," I said. "I'm not getting back together with Matt. Not ever. Just so you know."

"I know that, dear."

"Well, would you quit inviting him over for goddamn orange juice, then?"

My mother leaned in and pushed my hair out of my face for me, smoothed it behind my ears as if I were a little girl. "You have your nice friends, and, well, you have us, too. Matt doesn't have anyone, you know. I guess we feel a little sorry for him, bless his heart."

I looked up at the house, and Matt was leaving, head down, dogless, to go back to his empty house with a half-empty closet.

It was a thirty-minute detour to do the car switch, but we had made it this far. On the off chance we hit pay dirt here, we needed to be able to show off our new toy. When we pulled back into Kristen's driveway, Chris's car was there.

"What is he doing home? It's the middle of the day!" I would have argued that it didn't matter, that we could just pick up the keys to the car and go, but not Kristen, who wanted to barge in and find out what was going on.

Kristen stomped in as if she expected to find a naked model in her living room. Instead, she found Chris in front of the TV, in his boxers and a white T-shirt.

"Hi, Chris," I said. "Thanks for dressing up."

"What are you doing lying around in your underwear in the middle of the day?" Kristen leaned over him, hands on hips.

Chris's big Saint Bernard face wrinkled up. "Did you not ask me to pick up the children?"

"Well, yes."

"I had a dentist appointment at lunch, and then I just came on home. That all right with you?"

"Oh. Sorry. Um, we're going to be gone a little while. We came back for the El Camino."

"Wait, what, hon? Where you going?"

"We're going to pick up Elvira and drive up to Sewanee."

"What? You just got back! What are we going to do for dinner?" Chris had stood up from the couch, his belly hanging unattractively over his boxers.

I could see the hesitation on Kristen's face, the pull of her family, the wear of the weekend, and the weight of her absence there. She was needed in a way that I was not. When she wasn't around, people noticed.

"You know how to call for a pizza, don't you?" I said.

"We did that yesterday!" Chris scowled at us.

Kristen looked back over at me, and if she was out, then this whole crazy mission was lost. "How often do you do what she wants to do?" I demanded of Chris.

"Huh?"

"She just wants to go and do this one little old thing, for one little old weekend, and you don't want to let her out of the house."

"Well, that's not it. It's just time for her to get on home." Chris scratched his stomach.

"One more day—half a day, and then you can have her back," I pleaded. Kristen was grinning, watching me beg for her release. "We have waited for twenty years! Can you not heat up some spaghetti for one freaking night?"

Chris held up his hands. "Fine, fine. Go on." Kristen hugged him suddenly, squeezed tight, as happy as if her dad had given her permission to stay out past midnight. She held up the Camino keys, and we were gone.

Back on the road in no time, we sped down I-24 again. I felt comfortable behind the wheel of Elvira now, and giddy with our escape; we waved at the passengers in other cars who stared at us and our car.

"Do you think we should find some sand?" asked Kristen.

"Aren't you getting a little ahead of yourself? No. The car will have to be enough for now. Let's just check out this address, which could still be a dead end."

"Worst-case scenario, we can go shopping and pick out something to wear to the reunion to console ourselves," said Kristen. I could not imagine anything worse than going to the mall with Kristen. Kristen wore a size two and had a limitless bank account. The reunion had never completely seemed real to me, but it was starting to. What if we found her? What if we could have the reunion we'd always wanted?

The road became narrow and winding, and we took the Monteagle exit, hooking back into downtown Monteagle rather than heading toward Sewanee. The address Jack had given us was off Broadway, and there were row upon row of redbrick houses built in the fifties along narrow, tree-lined streets. It was country out here, an unpretentious, family-centered kind of isolation. If we got the address wrong, we could probably just start banging on random doors and find out just as much information that way.

We found the redbrick we were looking for only by a meticulous search for the number on the mailbox. It was otherwise indistinguishable from every other house on the street. It had a one-car garage and a little front porch with a swing on it, red geraniums in window boxes and stone pots next to the wall. A black Lab came to my door, wagging its tail, not much of a guard dog. Rhett Pugler put his nose to the window.

We had come too far, wasted too much time to linger in the Camino for long. There was a hint of anticipation now, the night-before-Christmas kind. It could happen. But what if I had been wrong? What if it was someone else's voice? It wasn't; I knew it wasn't. I felt sick but ready. I was ready to face Roxanne. I was not sure if I was ready to come clean to Kristen, but I would cross that bridge when I got to it.

The dog followed us to the front door, sniffing at one of Rhett Pugler's paws. "Roxanne always liked dogs," said Kristen.

"Yeah, that's a great clue. No one likes dogs. Labradors are really unpopular, I hear."

Kristen scowled at me and wiped her feet on the welcome mat, preparing to go in already. I sighed, hoping at least if it wasn't her that it was a friendlier informant than we had found the last time. I jerked my chin at her to ring the doorbell. Come on, already.

The button produced a bright chime and a scuttle of activity inside the house—more paws, smaller ones, raced through, toenails clattering. Yippy barking commenced. The Labrador looked at us with sympathy, like, *Oh, please.*

The front door whooshed open, and there she stood, absolutely unchanged.

There wasn't a single wrinkle on her perfect skin, and her auburn hair cascaded almost to her waist. She was wearing jean short-shorts, barefoot. I felt my pulse pounding in my head and the soundtrack start to go dead.

Kristen slung an arm around my waist, as if she could have really held me up. "Honey," she said. "Is your mom at home? We need a glass of water, fast."

May 1997
Bellevue Mall

Mom's driving me to Bellevue to look for prom dresses, and Kristen and Rox are tagging along. We have to pick up Roxanne because she now has no wheels after our spring break fiasco. When we drive up, I can hear a glass shatter and a shriek. I look in the backseat and exchange a look with Kristen.

Roxanne comes banging out the front door, and a dish comes flying out behind her like a Frisbee, erupts in the middle of the walkway. "Get out! Get out and stay out, then! I don't care if you never come back!" Mrs. Wilder is as red as her hair, and a big vein is standing out on her forehead. I have never seen her like this. Usually, she's ice when she's mad.

"You are a whore! Fuck you!" And Roxanne hauls back and spits—straight into her mother's face. Mrs. Wilder looks like a hurricane, contained. But then she looks over and sees us sitting there. It takes a minute for her to turn her face back into the one we know. Roxanne takes advantage of the lull to jump into the backseat with Kristen. Kristen and I are positively bug-eyed.

"I'll have her back at eight!" says my mother chirpily, as if nothing has happened. Mrs. Wilder just nods, slowly, attempts a smile and goes back into the house.

We arrive at the mall, and Mom explains that we are to meet her in two hours sharp. "Girls, if you are not here at exactly four o'clock, I will call the police and report you missing. Do you hear me?"

"Yes, Mrs. Martin," says Kristen.

"Uh-huh," I say.

Roxanne doesn't say anything.

We go to the only store that sells prom dresses, and Mom goes to Castner's. Kristen puts her arm through Roxanne's. "You okay?"

Roxanne just shrugs it off. "Fine." We'll get no more out of her for now.

Roxanne props herself up against a shelf. "Let's go do something."

"We are doing something," I said. I pull out this great black slinky number. I check the tag—size two, and hand it off to Kristen instead.

"Let's go outside," says Roxanne.

"What, to the parking lot?" says Kristen. She's holding up a gold gown with a sweetheart neckline. I couldn't fit my right arm into it.

Roxanne tries again. "Y'all, let's get out of this mall." She tries on a gaudy rhinestone necklace, makes faces at herself in the mirror, braids her hair, but doesn't attach the end with anything. Kristen has decided to buy both dresses, in case she can't make up her mind the day of prom. I'll have to try to sell my mother on something, but I don't know what. There's this amazing silver dress on the manne-quin out front, but the price tag says three hundred dollars.

And lights are flashing, and there's a super loud noise.

I look around, and Roxanne is gone. Kristen is standing at the cash register, looking confused.

The security guard is outside talking to Roxanne, and we go out there, stat.

"Miss, empty your pockets," he's saying. He's not bad-looking for a mall security guard.

"No," says Roxanne, with a slow smile. Kristen and I look at each other in terror. Roxanne has a little problem with taking stuff, although I thought she had gotten better about it.

"I think we both know what you did."

Roxanne leans against the store window and shrugs. "Nope. Can't say that I do. Hey, is there anything fun to do in this mall?"

The security guard is probably right out of college. He's out of his league with Roxanne, but he is carrying a Taser. Kristen and I want to believe that this is a terrible misunderstanding, and that this guy maybe just wants to flirt. We kind of know better, though.

"There's a security camera in the store. I saw you put the necklace into your pocket. Now get it out."

Roxanne slowly reaches in, and a long silver chain snakes out. Oh, no.

"The other pocket, too," he says.

A pair of hoop earrings joins the necklace.

"Young lady, I'm going to have to take you down to our office, and the store manager will decide if he wants to press charges against you." Young lady. He's what—twenty-four?

"What is it you're going to press against me?" says Roxanne with a big grin. It's not working. He looks mad, and he has caught her.

I don't know what to do, and I'm backing out in panic, even though I know I can't go anywhere, and I run right into my mother, who has apparently seen the whole thing. "What's going on?" she demands. She's holding a shopping bag, and it is full to bursting, probably with pants with lots of pockets for gardening tools.

"This young lady has stolen merchandise, and we're going to go file a report," says the guard. His baby face is starting to turn red. "What do you have to say for yourself?"

Roxanne looks at my mother, who might finally blow a gasket here, and I see that Roxanne gets it, finally, that this is not Principal Hunter from school and that she is in big trouble here.

"Is this your daughter?" he asks my mother.

"No," Mom says, a little too quickly.

"We're going to have to call some parents, then," says the guard.

"She won't come," says Roxanne, starting to look worried.

"She'll have to come if we take you to the police station," says the guard.

"She won't come." Roxanne is pale anyway, but she looks like a corpse now.

"I'll pay for whatever she took," says my mother out of nowhere, and I'm shocked. At this point, I was thinking she'd just let Roxanne go to jail. The store manager has joined us. He has a vague hint of a mustache and thick glasses.

"You'll have to ask the manager. If he wants to press charges, I'll have to take her in." The guard crosses his arms and stands up straighter.

"I'll buy the jewelry," Mom says. "And this and this, too." She throws a random shimmery wrap on top. The manager hesitates, if only for a second, and she sees it. "Sarah, that dress." She points at the beautiful silver one. The expensive one. "Is that your prom dress?" I nod violently. I see on the face of the manager that the big-ticket sale has won him over.

"I guess we don't have to go through all that," says the manager. He scratches the shadow of the mustache. "If she apologizes."

The mall cop pauses, stuffs his hands down tight back pockets. He is now firmly in the camp of the adults, no longer attractive at all. "You are a lucky girl. Most stores would have had me haul you in. Your parents will be disappointed when they find out, right?"

"I'm sorry," whispers Roxanne. Kristen and I stare at her because Roxanne never apologizes for anything. My mother takes the pile of jewelry and the dress over to the counter, and the security guard fades back into the mall.

"Oh my God," I gush. "I can't believe he let you go! You are so lucky."

"Geez, what's the matter with you, anyway?" says Kristen.

Roxanne looks at the floor and doesn't say anything. We all hear the total of the sale: "$384.47." My mother is not Kristen's mother, and I do not ever remember buying nearly four hundred dollars' worth of clothes anywhere.

We walk out, and Roxanne says, to my mother's back, "I'll pay you back," and then she hiccups, except it's not a hiccup, and all of a sudden she is crying, big gulping sobs, and she cannot stop. Kristen and I do not know what to do. We should hug her, but she is out of our hands, like this might be contagious. My mother puts down her two bags, the one with the gardening pants and the one with my prom dress, and hugs her. We all wait until Roxanne is done crying.

"I'll pay you back," says Roxanne again.

"Oh, don't worry about it," says my mother. "I'll come back in a couple of weeks and return it all when that twerp is on his lunch break."

I knew that dress was too good to be true.

Chapter Thirteen

I sat down on the porch swing. Why I seemed unable to recognize women of the same family belonging to different generations was beyond me. I had one model of reference and was not mentally prepared to meet anyone else.

"Mom! There are some ladies out on the porch to see you!" Louder: "Mom!" The door banged shut, and the girl thumped through the house, followed by the cacophony of dogs.

She emerged again, green eyes wide with concern, holding a glass of water. "She's coming," the girl explained. "She was in the shower."

"What's your name?" said Kristen.

"How old are you?" I mumbled.

"I'm Sarah," she said. "I'm eighteen. Well, nineteen in September."

"Oh my God," I said softly, feeling my eyes well up. *Sarah.* I reached out to touch her hair as she bent over me, without any regard for how weird that must have looked. Kristen leaned in to inspect her more closely.

She didn't seem to mind. Sarah smiled, cracking gum that smelled of cinnamon, and threw the red locks back over her shoulder. "I know. It's way too long. My mom says I have to get it cut before I burn up this summer."

Kristen and I shook our heads simultaneously. "No, it's beautiful," I said.

We beamed at her as if we had given birth to her ourselves, or like proud grandparents standing behind the glass of a nursery for the first time, watching. The dog had decided that we were to be trusted and nosed my thigh, as if to make sure I was all right.

"Is that y'all's car? That's awesome! I always wanted to get in one of those."

Kristen held out the keys. "Well, don't let us get in your way."

"Seriously?"

"Absolutely."

The door opened again, and out wandered a terry-clothed, turbaned cupcake. It was probably good that we had seen the child first, because we wouldn't have recognized her mother if we hadn't been adequately prepared. Roxanne, while not exactly fat, had gained a good thirty pounds. Her fine, sharp jawline had softened with the extra weight. It was, oddly, not unattractive; she just seemed more approachable. Her skin had held up well, fair without too many spots, and her eyes were still bright, still sparkling, even if all sign of mischief was long gone, replaced by a placid friendliness.

It only took her a second to recognize us. Her hands went to her face, where they flapped around like birds. "Oh! Oh!"

Kristen was closest and was grabbed first. I watched them hold each other long, tight, before heaving myself off my seat for my own hug. My arms sank into her midsection while she held on for dear life. And she didn't smell like she used to but like vanilla and butter instead, of warm things and home. I guess none of us had our old smells, but it was still her, still my friend, and I was holding her again, just like before.

Sarah had retreated from the Camino when she saw the state we had put her mother into. "Mama? Are you okay?" She jogged up the stairs, put her arm around her mother's waist.

"Oh!" Roxanne wiped her eyes and pulled her daughter close to her. "These were my very best friends, Sarah and Kristen." It was just a manner of speaking, and I didn't know why "were" stung.

I couldn't believe it, that we were here, that we were at her house, that she had a daughter! She had named her daughter *Sarah*. I had done nothing to deserve that. Twenty years, and all this time, she had been a couple of hours away. Had she been here when I'd lived here? It seemed impossible. We had just eaten lunch at Shenanigan's the weekend before. If we had driven a few miles and made a few right turns, we would have found her.

Roxanne was so unprepared for this. We'd at least had a few days to reminisce, to imagine what the reunion might be like. This woman had just stepped out of the shower. And she hadn't even seen our El Camino yet. She was still in her slippers, too, matching terry-cloth flip-flops. She hiked up the robe and ran out to the car once she spotted it. "I can't believe it! Which one of you drives an El Camino?" The towel turban tumbled down and fell on the lawn, revealing an impressive head of red curls. She leaned over and looked inside the truck bed, and the robe hiked up unattractively.

"Incidentally," said Kristen, "these no longer cost five hundred dollars."

"It's a long story," I said. "It may take us a while to get through it."

Roxanne pulled her robe back together and came over to us, and we all smiled at each other because we could not think of anything to say.

"I thought you were dead," said teenage Sarah to me.

"Gee, thanks," I said.

"Goodness, Sarah! Where did you get such an idea? I never said that anybody was dead." Roxanne flushed.

"Well, when you talked about your old friends Sarah and Kristen, I just thought they weren't around anymore."

"I wasn't," I said. I wanted to know more, like why, why had she named her child Sarah, but that could wait. We had other business to take care of.

"I think what I meant," said Roxanne, "was that she was a friend from the past." Again, this hurt more than it should have. I guess I would have said the same thing.

"Well, here we are," said Kristen, making some jazz hands.

"Ta-da," I said.

"Oh, come inside. We have so much talking to do." Roxanne pushed Kristen toward the house and grabbed my hand. It could have been senior year, the ease with which she did it. "Your doggie is welcome to come in. I love pugs! Might get one. We got a whole bunch of pets, Dottie the Chihuahua, Hank the Lab, Dolly the poodle, cats—Willie, Lorrie, Pam, and Vince."

We walked into a tiny living room, with a wood-burning stove and a basket with wood still in it, even though it was almost summer. We were led to a plaid sofa for three, or for two people of the larger persuasion. I took up a good portion of it, while Kristen tried to keep herself from falling in between the cracks. There were blankets spread out everywhere, judging by the smell, for the dogs.

"Can I get y'all some sweet tea?" asked Roxanne.

"I don't know about you, but I am in the market for something a little stronger," said Kristen.

"I'm real sorry, but we don't keep any alcohol in the house! If I had known y'all were coming, I could've picked something up, but we just don't have anything lying around."

Kristen wrinkled up her forehead the best she could around the Botox. "Not even an old bottle of JD, with a Coke or something?"

"Nope! Nothing at all. Brian doesn't drink, and, well, I might drink the tiniest glass of sparkling wine on New Year's, but that's about it!" Who was this person, with Roxanne's red hair and green eyes? Sparkling wine on New Year's?

"I'm sorry!" whispered Kristen. "Are you in AA?"

Roxanne pushed Kristen playfully. "You silly! Of course not! It's just not something we do here. We don't really go out much, just stay home and watch our shows. But we play in a bridge league."

Kristen and I exchanged horrified looks as Roxanne went into the kitchen to make us our beverages. Sarah followed behind her and turned to stage-whisper, "They're a little lame." This reincarnation of our friend was as cute as a baby taking its first steps.

Kristen whispered to me, "She has to be in there somewhere if she produced this creature."

"Shhhh!" I shoved her. She was right, though. Where had Roxanne gone, our Roxanne? The one who skipped classes, snuck out at night, did exactly the opposite of what you told her to do. This woman looked like the farthest she ever went was the Piggly Wiggly.

"What happened to her?"

"She got married! She has a child! She has a happy, normal life. That's great, right?"

"I got married and have children, but I'm not sitting around playing bridge with a bunch of dogs."

"I don't think they play bridge *with* the dogs," I said. "I don't think that would be very sportsmanlike."

"Shut up, Sarah."

Roxanne bustled out with our drinks and plonked down in the La-Z-Boy next to us. "I missed you all!" She leaned over to touch our cheeks simultaneously, like a benevolent aunt. She missed us. I looked at her for traces of resentment, found none.

I took a sip of my iced tea and slurped it a bit too loud. They both turned to look at me. That used to be enough to set us all on a laughing spree, but it didn't work this time. I took another sip, a quiet one.

"So, what do you do out here?" asked Kristen.

Roxanne shrugged. "I stay busy keeping the house. It's more work than you think, one kid and a husband. Do you have kids?"

"Three," said Kristen.

"No," I said. "Just the pug."

"Oh, so you know," she smiled expansively, only at Kristen.

"Three is a lot of work, and they're young," said Kristen. "It's not like any of them help to do much." Sarah was bringing us some napkins to put under our tea glasses, which I could see were actually just paper towels. I looked around, to really observe the extent of the housekeeping. The small house was clean but bursting with bric-a-brac. She probably needed to vacuum every day, just for the dog hair. The Chihuahua sniffed my foot, and I gave it a nudge. There was a limit to small, when a thing can still accurately be considered a dog.

"Did you ever try acting?" I said and then hated myself for it. Did she look like she had been acting, like maybe she was just on hiatus from her soap opera?

"That was just a dumb childhood dream, like our El Camino. But you went and got one!" Roxanne tittered. "How about you? Are you a writer now? I keep thinking I'll see your name at our bookshop."

"No," I said.

"Ladies," said Kristen. "Cut the shit."

"Kristen!" said Roxanne.

"I mean, I think we can stop with this bullshit chitchat. Sarah and I want to know what happened! Why you left and never called us! Who cares if we have kids, or if Sarah's a writer!"

I stared at the floor. I could feel my cheeks turning red, the blush spreading to my ears.

"We would have busted you out of wherever you were. But we didn't know where you were! Where were you?" asked Kristen.

Roxanne didn't say anything.

"Roxanne, goddammit! We were best friends." Kristen was getting in Roxanne's face, but pretty soon I was the one who was going to get it.

"I don't know what to say." This just sort of burst out of my mouth and left the two of them staring at me.

"About what?" Roxanne looked at me with this new, bland expression of hers, as if I might have a story to share about my pug.

"You know."

"Not really." Roxanne wrinkled her nose at me, opened her eyes wide, and tilted her head quizzically.

"I never meant to hurt you. I never thought . . ." My eyes welled up, and my nose started running. "I just never thought I wouldn't see you again! I just thought that you'd have detention, and you'd get mad at me, and then we'd make up, and that would be all. I just didn't know that it was *over* all in one stupid moment in Principal Hunter's office when I was eighteen years old."

"Oh, yeah, that." Roxanne laughed, more drily than before. "Bet you sang like a bird. What did he tell you he'd do?"

"He said I'd lose my scholarship." Saying it now sounded ridiculous. Would that have really happened?

"You got that big scholarship you wanted?" Her eyes were wide, as if it had just happened yesterday. "That's great!"

"Great?" She didn't even seem to really remember it, what had happened, but she had to. She had changed schools, left town! If it wasn't my fault, whose was it? "Are you really not mad at me?"

Roxanne shook her head.

"What in God's name are you two talking about?" said Kristen. "Would someone tell me what's going on?"

"I hope you'll forgive me." What I had needed to say for all this time.

Roxanne blew her bangs out of her eyes. "Oh, honey, you've been forgiven for a long time. That was ancient history."

"Forgive her for what?" Kristen looked like she was about to seriously lose it, and I wanted to ignore her for as long as possible.

Roxanne turned to Kristen. "You knew who turned me in for cheating, didn't you?"

"No! No way!" Kristen turned to look at me, and I looked away. "Sarah!"

I ignored Kristen. "Why, then? Why did you leave and never come back? It basically ruined my life then!"

Kristen rolled her eyes.

Roxanne laughed, a low, ironic chuckle. "Ruined your life, Sarah? Your life was about as perfect as anyone's I could imagine."

Kristen nodded enthusiastically. "Golden."

"Golden! That wasn't me! That was Kristen, with the money and the perfect hair! I was working after school to even be able to hang out with her! And you! You did what you wanted and just didn't care. I was always worried about doing the wrong thing!"

Kristen and Roxanne exchanged a look that I remembered, one that said I was going off the deep end. Like parents over a child having a tantrum.

"Why? Why did you leave us, then?" I persisted.

"Yeah, sister, let's hear it already," said Kristen.

"My mother," said Roxanne, "was *seducing* my boyfriend." She said "seducing" in a whisper, with a furtive look over her shoulder.

I clapped both hands to my cheeks, like that *Home Alone* kid.

Kristen leaned in. "Come on."

"I mean, I walked in on those two in the middle of things! I could paint you a picture, but trust me, you don't want to know." Roxanne shuddered and put her face in her hands.

I painted my own picture then: beautiful Mrs. Wilder from the nineties; tall, galumphy Mark in his football jersey and floppy hair. He wouldn't have been able to resist her. It never occurred to me that a seduction could have happened the other way around. It would have come from her. She was more of a monster than we had ever known.

Even Kristen was speechless.

"I can't believe it," I managed. But when I thought about it, I could imagine it.

She was a predator. She could have had anyone, and she had chosen him.

"Ew!" shrieked Kristen, finally. "That is just so awful! What was wrong with him? What was wrong with her?" What could she have wanted with dopey Mark, except that he was the one male in her life who was off-limits? Or who should have been off-limits.

"You didn't get thrown out of school for cheating?" I just had to get that straight.

Roxanne shrugged. "Sure, kind of. Hunter called me in, his usual police act, but pretty soon I was crying, and he forgot all about it. He helped me get into a new school." The Post-it note with that phone number. It was Hunter who had left it there; Hunter who had made that first call.

"Hunter?" Had Hunter done her a favor? And had he known what I didn't all along? And why couldn't he have cut me some slack? "It wasn't my fault," I said, more to myself than anyone else. "It was never about me."

"My goodness, weren't you giving yourself a lot of credit?" Roxanne stood up, tightened her robe. "Who needs more tea?" She smiled brightly at us, as if we had all just finished a game of Scrabble.

Kristen and I held our glasses out. My hand shook a little. Roxanne took them and bustled off into the kitchen. "I don't believe it," Kristen said matter-of-factly. "What a little snitch. And you never said anything about it all this time. I tell you what. With friends like you, who needs enemas?"

"Enemies," I said automatically.

"That's what I said," said Kristen and then lowered her voice. "I've got to hear the details about this Mark thing."

Sarah came in through the back door, so we changed the subject quickly.

"Where did you go, you know, right after you left?" said Kristen, when Roxanne returned with our glasses.

"You're looking at it," said Roxanne.

We exchanged incredulous glances. "Right here?"

"Right here. I stopped at the Waffle House on my way in, and I sat down and ordered hash browns—scattered, smothered, and covered, of course. And before I could start eating, I just started to cry! Real boohooing! Super loud. I didn't even have a change of clothes with me. I'd just left my life, and my best friends, like that. So I started to cry and, y'all, I could not stop. I was, like, wailing, and everybody was looking at me."

The old Roxanne was starting to show through this puffy housewife exterior. You could see that she loved the idea of bawling in a Waffle House with everyone staring at her.

"So this boy in a Sewanee baseball cap comes over and starts patting my back. I keep crying for a while, but he's a good back patter, so I slow down.

I look at him, and he's really good-looking, like a young Kevin Costner, tall, tan, perfect teeth. So I sort of throw myself into his arms and cry for a little while in his neck, and he smells so good. You would not believe it."

Kristen and I looked at each other again, trying to not smile. This sounded like such a Roxanne encounter, all drama and young romance.

"Then what? How did you extricate yourself from this young man at the Waffle House, and where did you end up?"

"I told you! I ended up right here."

"I don't get it," said Kristen flatly.

A door in the back of the house slammed, and a teddy bear of a man ambled into the room. Before acknowledging either of us, he leaned down and kissed Roxanne. A real kiss, more than just a honey-I'm-home peck.

"This is him! I followed him home and never left! This is Brian." Roxanne looked at him with such obvious enchantment that I couldn't help feel a pang of envy. He wasn't Kevin Costner, not exactly, better-than-average-looking, though not by much, but his blue eyes sparkled with intelligence and goodness, and the creases next to his eyes were those of a man who smiled often. "I went to high school in Monroe County."

"Your mother said you went to boarding school."

Roxanne snorted. "I didn't tell her anything! She was the last person in the world I wanted to see. She didn't try to make me come home. Never came up here to find me. Didn't hear from her for years until I found out my credit was busted from the six cards she took out in my name, and the loan to buy that stupid house. I spent ten years building up good credit, and she got rid of it, just like that. At least I have Brian." She smiled up at him. "So happily ever after!"

Happily ever after? This was the most twisted fairy tale I had ever heard.

Brian placed a hand on her shoulder, and it looked as protective as it did comforting. Roxanne grabbed on to his hand. "I was pregnant just a few months after I came here, so that made it easy for him to trap me!"

"Trap you!" Brian exclaimed.

Roxanne swatted him. "His mama took me in, just like a daughter. I went to the new school and finished a few classes so that I could get my diploma. I had to go to summer school, since I'd missed some stuff, but it wasn't like I felt like going to any graduation ceremony."

"So, you were literally right here?" asked Kristen.

"Uh-huh." Roxanne looked pleased with herself. "Honey, you are not going to believe who this is. These are my oldest friends, Sarah and Kristen."

"She means that we've known each other for a long time," said Kristen. "I'm sure you have older friends."

Brian gave us a dimpled smile and held out a strong hand for us to shake.

"Brian, can you and Sarah be darlings and go pick up some steaks at Piggly Wiggly?" Who could ever say no to Roxanne?

"Sure thing, babe. Who's the driver of the El Camino? I had to park in the street." Kristen and I both raised our hands. "Man, classic Chevy. Mind if I take a look inside?"

Kristen pointed at the keys, left on the coffee table by Sarah. "You're welcome to take her to the Piggly Wiggly. Her name is Elvira."

"Why didn't you tell us where you were?" I asked, horrified at Roxanne's proximity for all these years. I still couldn't believe she hadn't told us, hadn't written a letter, made a phone call, had a sudden need to hear my voice in the middle of the night.

"I mean, you just don't know what that feels like. Your boyfriend. Your mother. Okay, I was annoyed at you, at first. But you know, I was pregnant not too long after that, and everything goes away after that. And I had my baby girl!" She clapped her hands together, still in delight over a baby who had long since grown up.

"How did you find out?" Kristen leaned forward like she was watching *Days of Our Lives*. This was actually a lot better than *Days of Our Lives*. "About them."

"Goodness, do we really need to keep talking about this? I want to hear about you! I'm fine now! It's all fine."

She didn't look fine, not in any way that the old Roxanne would have considered fine. You could hardly believe what lurked beneath the surface of the honey-coated shell she had made for herself.

I said, "I mean, what did she say? What did he say? What did you say?"

Roxanne shrugged. "What do you say? I think I ran out. They were in the living room, of all places. Who knows if it was a regular thing or if it was just the one time? I doubt it, knowing her."

"What did Mark do?" Kristen said, eyes wide.

Roxanne laughed, a small, hollow laugh. "He came charging out after me, clothes half on. He said he was sorry, sorry, sorry, he loved me. I told him to, you know, go jump in a lake, or whatever. I stayed out all night, slept on a pool chair until it was time to go to school the next day. I couldn't stand the thought of going home."

"For twenty years?" I said. I understood the need to flee, had felt the same way when I'd gotten divorced. When things went off the rails, you didn't want to talk to anyone, not even the people who should understand. I didn't know if it was embarrassment or grief or just trying to fill the hole that gapes open in the wake of an emotional disaster. But you got through that. I had Jack and Kristen to pull me out of mine, with Rhett Pugler and the store to turn to for comfort. We would have been there for her, of course we would have.

"Did you try to find me?" asked Roxanne.

"Yes!" said Kristen.

"Not hard enough," I admitted. We had to acknowledge, too, that a year later, our lives were so changed that all the urgency had gone out of it. I didn't even see Kristen all that often at that point. A short four years later, we'd had to make the jump again, from university life to the real world, and high school became even more distant. But she had been right here. I could have run into her at the grocery store, at the Waffle House. I knew that the townies didn't really mix with the university students, but I could have seen her at the gas station. We could have passed each other on a run. I could have seen her walking with her dogs. "How did we not cross paths all those years?"

Roxanne looked at me with a small smile. And I knew. "We did, didn't we?" I said softly. "Why didn't you say something? Were you mad at me? How did I not see you?"

"You looked happy. You looked like you fit in there, with all those smart people. I would see you with your backpack, walking across campus. Once, you were at a table at Shenanigan's, and I was at the counter waiting for an order with my baby. It actually made me happy, knowing that you were here being all smart and successful. That was what you were supposed to do! I could have never done that!"

Had I done that? Been smart and successful? Had it felt as good as it had looked? All that time, something had been missing, and it had been right under my nose. If I had lifted my head to look, really look, I might have seen her. But I never saw. I never looked. I just disappeared into a new life, and she sat on the outside and watched me.

We stayed on into the afternoon and for dinner, too, mesmerized by their tableau of ordinariness. We looked at album upon album of family photos, the young Roxanne of our memory holding infant Sarah, and looking very much like a child herself. Roxanne holding Sarah's hand outside of an elementary school. Roxanne, Brian, and Sarah at Dollywood. Roxanne and Brian holding hands. Roxanne, Brian, and Sarah camping. Always smiling, always squished in together for the camera, even through Sarah's adolescence—close, close to each other. What did I have to show for the past twenty years? A wedding photo album of someone I could barely stand. An overweight pug? A binder full of receipts?

We must have drunk a gallon of iced tea, and we found that we didn't really need margaritas to laugh ourselves silly. Sarah sat with us for some of it, long limbs tucked up under her on the couch, eyes closing to listen sometimes. The Chihuahua Dottie had decided that I was someone she liked and had taken up residence underneath my left arm, Rhett Pugler glaring at her from the right. We might have stayed there all night. If we had been invited.

Brian and Roxanne cooked together, and we sat in the kitchen to watch them. They did this often, you could tell, the fine machinery of Brian's chopping the onions and Roxanne's whisking them away, pouring them into a popping skillet, like an assembly line. We had potatoes and green beans with our steaks, nothing fancy, but it was simple and good and there was room for everyone to have a second helping. We would have kept going, but as the dinner wound down, they began to retreat back into themselves and their nighttime rituals. They cleared the dishes from the table, clearing the day away, too, putting a period on our time together. It wasn't that they said we had to leave. We just felt it.

"What are the chances you'll show up next weekend?" asked Kristen. We had told her about the reunion, and she had laughed, her eyes far away. We hadn't thought this through. There were only bad memories there for Roxanne, if you didn't include us. And she had just had that reunion.

"Oh, no. I couldn't."

Of course she couldn't. We knew she couldn't. Mark would be there, I would bet on it, at a table with his old football buddies. Maybe they would show up drunk; they would surely leave drunk. It wasn't that different from prom, really. Hunter wouldn't be there; at least I couldn't imagine that he would, nor would the former teacher she feared most— her mother. At least we could hope they wouldn't be there.

"What are we going to do with this El Camino?" It was useless now, an accessory that we had never needed to find her, good for a moment of laughs and little more. It was never going to be a beach.

"I guess we can just sell it back to Jimmy," said Kristen.

"I think Jimmy needed the money! He won't want to buy it back," I said.

"That Jimmy or some other Jimmy. Who cares?" If Kristen could afford to waste seven grand, I didn't need to be worrying about it.

Roxanne clung to us, one on either side of her, as she walked us out to the Camino. I couldn't help but think she was saying good-bye forever, although that was silly. She lived close by and in a town that I liked to visit. We could see each other on a regular basis. Could. But this Roxanne bore little resemblance to the Roxanne I once knew. I wasn't sure that this woman and I would be friends if we met on the street. In fact, I knew we wouldn't.

"You'll keep in touch?" I asked.

Roxanne nodded enthusiastically. "Of course I will!"

Of course.

I didn't believe her, though, couldn't believe her. I felt the pain of that old story and her wounded teenage self, but the story was old. We hadn't known where to find her, but she had known where to find us. She just hadn't done it. She had her people, her family. Maybe I was still searching for her because I didn't have anyone to anchor myself to. She didn't need us anymore.

We climbed in, and I rolled down the window to tell her good-bye. I had to say something about her daughter; it was too important to leave unsaid. "I'm just so, you know, flattered, that your daughter's name is Sarah. I mean, it means so much to me. If you only knew what I thought, how I worried."

Roxanne didn't say anything for a moment. "Uh, I guess you don't remember my gran, do you?" Roxanne spent most of her early child-hood with her grandmother, I knew, but she had died by the time I met Roxanne. I shook my head. "Gran's name was Sarah."

Kristen snorted in the passenger seat next to me. "Oh," I said.

We waved good-bye, with no idea if we would ever see her again. What was important really, other than the fact that Roxanne was happy? Truly happy. She had found her Prince Charming, and she had lived happily ever after. There wasn't anything wrong with changing, growing up—turning into someone else even.

Maybe I could hardly even recognize true happiness.

June 1997
Briley High School / Roxanne's Condo

It's fourth period, and Roxanne still isn't here. It's too late in the year for her to ditch any more classes. Is it because she's suspended? Is it because she's mad at me? I'm not surprised she's not in school, but we have a presentation to give for art class, and she's my partner.

I go to the gym to see if Kristen has heard from her. She has study hall and is at an extra cheerleading practice.

I wave at Kris from across the gym, and she jogs over to see me. "Where is our juvenile delinquent?" I ask, feeling guilty the moment I say it.

Kristen is out of breath from a back handspring or something and shakes her head. "Still haven't seen her. Do you want me to ask Mrs. Wilder?" I definitely don't want to talk to Mrs. Wilder, so I nod, and Kristen dashes off to her.

I see Mrs. Wilder shake her head at Kristen and quickly turn back to the rest of the girls. Kristen returns to me. "She says she might be out for a while. Dunno why. I asked her if she was sick, and she just walked away."

"Shit. Think she could've called me last night?" Maybe she didn't want to.

"Maybe she's barfing or something? Gotta run. Mwah!" Kristen blows an air-kiss my direction and runs back to her squad.

I trudge off to my locker to collect my painting, a reproduction of a masterpiece. We had chosen a Cézanne landscape, and it's just awful. Roxanne can actually draw better than I can, but it was so hard to get Roxanne to do anything. She sat on the windowsill in my room, smoking a cigarette with her hand dangling outside, while I did most of it. Yet again. I am walking really slowly to class because I so do not want to do this, and I pass Principal Hunter on the way.

Haven't you done enough?

"Miss Martin, have you spoken to your good friend Miss Wilder today?"

Oh my God. He knows good and well where she is, even if I don't. I can see it in his smirky smile. He and Mrs. Wilder can drop dead.

"No," I say, flatly.

God, dude, just let me go to class. I'm not the one missing class. I try a lame yet specific defense. "She's really, really sick. She has a high fever and can't move. You can ask her mother."

"Lying doesn't suit you, Miss Martin." Hunter straightens his tie, lifts his chin, and walks away from me. I hate him.

I'll call her after school. I'll go over there and try to explain. If it weren't for Hunter, none of this would be happening.

I do okay in art class. Everyone else has created terrible paintings, and I'm pretty good at bluffing my way through a presentation. Having Roxanne up there with me wouldn't have been a big help after all. All the boys would just stare at her, including Mr. Moyer. When it's over, I run out of art class to go find Kristen in the hopes that she will be willing to drive over to Roxanne's. I would give anything for my own car.

"What do you want to bet the bitch is faking?" says Kristen.

I wish that were the case.

I spot Mark on the other side of the parking lot. If anyone knows what she's up to, it should be him. "Mark!" I yell. He doesn't look over at me. "Mark!" I yell again. Still no response. I think his head has been hit one too many times during football games. Kristen sticks two fingers in her mouth and lets out an earth-shattering wolf whistle. You wouldn't think someone that small could produce a noise like that.

"Hey, asshole!" yells Kristen. This is not really intended as an insult, and Mark is used to our giving him a hard time. He is so not one of the girls and ruins many weekends, just by existing. At any rate, he turns around. "Where is she?"

He shrugs and gets into the car. If Kristen hates anything, it is being ignored. "That fucker," she mutters. "I'm going over there." She gets out of the car, stomps across the lot, and bangs on his window. Mark rolls it down. "What is your problem?" demands Kristen. "I just asked you a question."

"I don't know," says Mark.

"You don't know she's sick, or you just don't want to tell me?" says Kristen.

"Easy, detective," I say. Kristen can be a real pit bull when she doesn't get what she wants.

"I don't know, is all."

"Some boyfriend." Kristen sniffs. "Well, we're going to go check on her. With any luck, she blew the coop and has been off enjoying the day."

"Okay," said Mark, staring at his steering wheel. Something is clearly wrong.

"Are you okay?" I ask.

He nods and says, "Gotta go. See y'all tomorrow."

"Is it just me, or was that really weird?" I ask Kristen as he drives off.

"Maybe . . . maybe," whispers Kristen, "she dumped him, and is taking a personal day! Wouldn't that be great?"

We're not big fans of Mark, but he's harmless. He serves as Roxanne's personal errand boy, carrying her books to class, buying her lunch, and taking her out on the weekends. She could do better, but she could also do worse.

I jump in Kristen's convertible, which still has that new leather smell, and we drive over to Roxanne's. We ring and wait, leaning over to look in the window. No answer. Kristen bangs, like that's going to help. "I knew it," she says. "Probably at the mall."

"Maybe she's asleep," I offer. "What if she's really sick?"

"Let's go look," says Kristen, and we walk around to the side of the house, where Roxanne's bedroom window looks out on their tiny driveway. This, I thought at first, was excellent organization, because you can go out the window if you want to sneak out at night, but if Roxanne wants to go out in the middle of the night, she just uses the front door. There's a little planter where you could put flowers, but there aren't any here, and Kristen climbs up to peek in the window.

"You're going to scare her to death if she wakes up and sees you," I say, but Roxanne isn't easily frightened. Kristen's chin barely touches the window frame, so she lifts up a skinny arm and bangs on the window itself. "Stop it. Somebody is going to call the police." Kristen turns around and gives me a mean look. In her cheerleader shorts and Briley High T-shirt, she doesn't look like any cat burglar I've ever seen. "Move. Let me do it." I'm almost a whole head taller than Kristen, so I can at least see if Roxanne is asleep.

I look in. The room is clean, cleaner than I've ever seen it, cleaner than it's ever been the whole time Roxanne has occupied it. Roxanne has stuffed teddy bears and kitties everywhere, most of them gifts from Mark. She has so much makeup on her dresser you'd think it was the cosmetics aisle of a department store. She never hangs up her clothes, and there are always piles everywhere. She leaves glasses of water and plates on her bedside table. None of that stuff is there.

"Is she asleep or what?" barks Kristen.

"No," I say.

"So she's not home."

I don't say anything. I just scan that room for something, anything that might signal the presence of my friend. The bed has been stripped clean—no bedspread, no sheets. Half of the closet is open, and there's nothing there. I climb down from the planter very slowly.

"We'll call later. Lucky bitch," says Kristen.

I have to sit down, so I do, right there. I feel a little dizzy.

"What's wrong now?" says Kristen.

"She's gone." *Oh my God, no. Where are you?*

"Yeah, she's probably at the mall. Whatever."

"I don't think she's at the mall. I think she's gone." And she feels gone, so gone, more gone than her jeans and eye shadows packed in a suitcase somewhere, more gone than her feather pillow, and her teddy bear that we bought her when she had the flu for a whole week. She is gone to me, and I don't know if I'll ever get her back.

Chapter Fourteen

The last place in the world I wanted to be was alone in a car with Kristen. It was over. Kristen fired up the engine without looking at me, and without making a snarky comment about making her drive. Kristen cannot shut up for any length of time, and the silence was killing me. We pulled out onto the street and headed back to the highway. Which one of us was going to break first?

"Go ahead and say it," I said.

"Say what?" Kristen's face was perfectly smooth, poised.

"That I ruined everything."

"Sarah, you just don't get it, do you?" Kristen shook her head.

"Get what?"

"It's not all about you."

"So you don't think I ruined everything, and you're not mad at me?" She looked like she was mad at someone.

"I didn't say that."

We drove along for a while longer, without talking. It was dark now, and we had another two hours of this ahead of us. We hugged the right lane while semitrailers blazed past us.

"I'm sorry I didn't tell you."

Kristen made a little noise like air puffing out of a tire, continued to ignore me. "It wasn't just you."

"What wasn't me?"

"It was me, too."

"You turned her in, too?" I couldn't believe it! Why was she giving me a hard time, then?

"No, dumbass. I would never do that, because I wasn't a little Goody-Two-shoes rat."

I decided to let that slide.

"I knew."

"That I turned her in?"

"About Mark."

I couldn't see how Kristen could have known, if I hadn't. "What do you mean, you knew?" It was hard to digest, even now, that a mother could have done that to her own child. I wasn't as surprised as I should have been.

"I saw them once, in her office."

"What do you mean, 'saw them'? What were they doing?"

"I couldn't say, exactly, but it was—compromising. He had his arms wrapped around her waist, and it wasn't like a friendly mom hug either. It was just this glimpse of a moment that was so odd, and so wrong, and I just turned around and ran away. I thought about saying something to Roxanne, but then, what would I say? What did I really see? Was it anything? Except I knew that it was weird. So I didn't say anything."

Now it was my turn to not say anything. Would things have been any different if she had said something? Could we have helped Roxanne? "So I guess you're not the only one keeping secrets." We didn't have much to say to each other at all after that and just rode in silence.

"But you didn't know," I said, after a while. "You couldn't have known. You wouldn't have even thought that she would do that."

"I guess," said Kristen. "You, too. I mean, I was in Hunter's office, and he was an asshole to me, too. But he didn't have anything to hold over me, so I don't know that I wouldn't have cracked if he had done that to me."

It seemed that no one had anything to resent anyone about. Why didn't I feel better, then?

"She's really different," I said, the understatement of the year.

"Can you imagine living with all those dogs?" said Kristen. "Wait, don't answer that. But how about the bridge playing? Spooky, like someone replaced her with a robot housewife."

"What will we do if we go visit her?"

"God, I don't know. Guess we'd better brush up on our board game skills."

It was almost midnight when Kristen dropped me back off in the Gulch. Rhett Pugler had been snoring for the greater part of an hour, and it took some effort to lift him off my lap. We parted without saying anything. I didn't know what to say. I wasn't angry with her, nor she with me. We weren't even the same people we were back then. It was like being angry with a ghost. But that didn't mean we felt like talking.

I was exhausted, the kind of bone tired that comes from too much drama and too much interaction with people. I wanted nothing more than to put my feet on my couch, curl up with a blanket and a beer, and watch old eighties sitcoms until I felt ready to face the world again. This lasted all of twenty minutes before I passed out on the couch, falling into a coma from which I did not wake up until nine o'clock the next morning.

It felt good to be alone with my dog, with the *Today* show on in the background, the screeching of Kathie Lee fading behind the roar of the coffee machine. I decided to run a bath, something I rarely did, to try to soak the remains of the extended weekend away. I got the water hot enough to boil an egg and eased my way in. I could not get over the fact that my friend had been so close for so long and had never gotten in touch, hadn't even said hello when she could have. At any rate, she had a great life now, if not what I would have imagined for her.

It wasn't that I missed high school. It was more that things had never been as good for me as when I was in high school. I had gotten what I wanted, a great university acceptance, but it hadn't measured up. I was queen of my world then; all was possible. I could still win a Nobel Prize for Literature, chair the English department at an ivy-league school. I could still have a real marriage, and a real family. It was safe to say that these things were now out of my reach. My life wasn't bad. I'd just thought there would be more.

We had answered the great question—what had become of Roxanne? Roxanne was just fine, better, in fact, than I was. She might even be better off than Kristen; it didn't seem like Roxanne and Brian squabbled with each other the way Chris and Kristen did. Roxanne had been doing fine without her girlfriends for twenty years. I should have felt happy for her.

I eventually dragged myself from the tub, raisin-fingered and red-faced. I tried to make a small effort with my appearance, since I had been gone a long weekend and had only popped into the store the day before for five minutes, wearing a giant man's clothes, before running out. There was a pile of paperwork waiting for me there, and Evelyn and Aidan couldn't do that for me. Before walking out the door, I called my mother to apologize for absconding with the dog.

"I'm just out running some errands," she said breezily. "If I don't get some stuff in the ground soon, it will be too late."

"Sorry about yesterday," I said flatly. I wasn't sorry, really. Apologizing just seemed like the thing to do.

"What? Oh. Yes, you were all worked up. Goodness, Sarah. The things you come up with. Why don't you come and meet me at the Flower Mart?" I wondered if she could hear my eye roll over the phone.

"What would I buy at the Flower Mart?"

"I don't know. Don't you need some of those box planters to put in that box thing where you live?"

"No, I do not." She had given me more plants than I could keep count of. I had killed them all. Well, Rhett Pugler had eaten one of them, so that one wasn't me. At least she didn't sound mad. "Hey, we found Roxanne."

"That's nice," she said.

"Don't sound too excited about it."

"If you ask me," she said (no one had), "you two were better off without Roxanne. Nothing good was going to come of that girl. You had other things to focus on. It wasn't the end of the world."

"It was the end of my world back then."

"Oh, Sarah. You are so dramatic. You always were."

Despite all my drama, I couldn't help but feel like I hadn't been dramatic enough. Not then, and maybe not now either.

I heaved a sigh into the phone—a dramatic one, I hoped. "I've got to get to work, Mom."

"Will you save me that book about the lilies I wanted? The one with the good photos in it? I'll come pick it up next week."

"Sure thing." I hung up the phone and got ready to get back to real life.

June 1997
Newspaper Office, Briley High School

It's our last issue, and I could not give a shit what we put in it. Roxanne is gone. In a few weeks, I'll be gone, and Kristen will be at Vanderbilt. How's that for a headline? Maybe I'll just make one big black page and call that the end.

Jack is bursting with ideas. He always is. "Why don't we write about the board and the misuse of the school budget?"

"Is the budget being misused?" I have my head down on my desk, and I can't see him.

"Isn't it always?"

"Mrmph," I mumbled. I wish I could go get a Diet Coke from the machine, but we're not allowed to until study hall. I have one more period to go before then. Maybe I can get Jack to go get one for me. I shouldn't. Jack likes me, and I know it.

I can't even spend time with Kristen now; I'm so depressed. Being with Kristen reminds me of being with Roxanne, and we still haven't heard any news. I don't know what school she went to, or even if she went to school. Mrs. Wilder won't talk to me. Maybe it will be like this next year, and I won't make any new friends. Or I'll lose the ones I have.

"Hey, why don't we put your poem in there?" says Jack. "Do you even know what a big deal it is that it was accepted to the *Southern Review*?"

"Oh my God, no. I would die of embarrassment."

"What do you care? You're leaving anyway." Jack is going away to Emory. He didn't get a full scholarship, but he's going to do work-study and take out a loan. That sounds crazy to me, but that's Jack.

"Jack, you decide."

"You're the editor. It's your job to choose what's in the last issue." I feel sometimes like Jack is the only person I can talk to right now. I didn't know him that well until now, now that I'm basically on my own. I don't want to go to any games, or to any parties on the weekend. This is the extent of my social life, hanging out in the newspaper office. Honestly, it's not so bad. Jack's better company than most of my group, and he and I have more in common than Kristen and I do. I only have one more month in this place anyway. One more month, and then what? Who will we become once it's all over?

"I don't care." I prop my chin up on my elbow. Bobby is working on layout on our one Mac computer, and Jen is lying on the ground looking at photos.

Jack bends over until he's eye level with me. "Sarah, you have to move on."

"Move on from what?" But I know what he's talking about. Everyone knows. Everyone asks me every day if I've heard from her, and what happened to her. I can't tell them that I did it, and that one of my best friends won't ever speak to me again.

"Roxanne."

"What if she doesn't come back?" I say, and I feel a tear threatening to march around from the back of my eyeball. I don't want to cry in the middle of a classroom.

"What if she doesn't? Do you want it to ruin your whole life?"

I shake my head, but I cannot speak. I wish I would stop crying, and I'm not going to sniffle and make a big noise, but I keep my head where it is and the tears are pouring. Jack reaches out to hug me, which I don't want him to do. People will see me crying, and people will see me hugging Jack. But I get up anyway and it feels good there, and Jack hugs like he's got nothing else in the world to do. He's all-in. I put my face in that spot between his neck and collarbone and soak the front of his shirt.

Jen and Bobby are staring at us, but Jack pats my back and says, "I'm still here. I'm still here."

Chapter Fifteen

"The prodigal boss!" said Aidan when I finally made it in, clutching my shopping bag. "There are boxes to unpack. You're just in time!"

He turned back to an attractive customer, upon whom he had foisted the entire series of *Game of Thrones*. Their conversation sounded a lot like *Blah blah blah dragon blah blah dire wolf* to me, but am I ever grateful for that series, which does great every week in the store.

"You know what to do, then." I was still the boss here. I headed to the coffeepot and poured right up to the brim of my favorite mug. I sat back and waited for a feeling of satisfaction and completion that didn't come.

Roxanne had a good reason for wanting to leave, a bigger reason than me. Had I spent all of these years feeling guilty for nothing? Hunter wanted Roxanne out, and Roxanne wanted to go. It wasn't clear to me why I had been put on the grill if this was an easy task, something that Roxanne wanted and needed. Only one person knew why.

Hunter. What was he doing now? He would be long retired.

What if I asked him?

He would be an old man now. Would he remember any of us? Would he think I was off my rocker, calling him up out of the blue? But, well, did it matter what Hunter thought anymore? Maybe it just mattered what he remembered.

On impulse, I sent Jack a text: **What is Hunter doing now?**

I had updated Jack late last night about our adventure. He wasn't at all disappointed that Roxanne was so close and so different. He thought we'd get together every few weeks now. I guess we could. We could join a bowling league together or something.

I wandered over to the children's section, easily my favorite place in the store. There were beanbags piled around shelves that went no higher than three stories. All four bags were occupied, I was glad to see. I asked a girl with glasses, maybe nine, what she was reading. She didn't answer, just held up a Harry Potter. I could take a hint, and she was doing exactly what I wanted her to do anyway. A smaller boy got up, followed his mother to the cash register, and I took his place, checked my phone.

Watching Wheel of Fortune and enjoying retirement, wrote Jack. **He's in a home somewhere.**

It was inconceivable that the all-powerful Hunter could be reduced to this. I had thought he'd at least be armchair commanding a fleet of grandchildren, lording over his house. I hesitated for only a moment before doing a search for Roger Hunter in Brentwood. There was only one. I picked up the phone with every intention of hanging up if anyone answered.

"Hello?" screeched an old lady. I didn't say anything.

"Martin Books? I didn't order any books!" Damn that caller ID.

I cleared my throat. "Mrs. Hunter?" I said.

"Yes?" she screeched again.

"Is Mr. Hunter home?" Even though I knew he wasn't.

"Honey, he's been at Meadowland Manor since last year. Who's this calling?"

"Um, this is just one of his old students," I squeaked.

"Honey, he don't hardly know his own name these days. He won't remember you. I'm sorry."

I apologized for bothering her and hung up. Meadowland Manor. If he remembered anyone, I bet he would remember Roxanne.

The children were all staring at me, so I heaved myself up out of the beanbag and took a lap around the other sections. It was sparse—normal for a Monday morning, but everyone seemed deep in their reading, and I had every hope that all would leave with something. No real fires to put out here. I could go on one last fact-finding mission.

I gathered up my bag again and clipped Rhett Pugler's leash on him. Aidan glared at me as I walked past him. Honestly, he got paid whether I was here or not. What did he care? Evelyn was manning the front desk and stared at me, too. It was worse when Evelyn disapproved.

"What?" I asked her.

"Sarah," said Evelyn.

"What is it, Evelyn?"

"Don't take this the wrong way, dear, but you look like you've gone a tiny bit off the deep end."

"Thanks a lot." I pushed some flyaway hairs back behind my ears. "But thank you, really, for keeping things together here. I'm almost done."

"Amy Pritchard is going to be here in ten minutes."

Oh shit. Amy was our most popular author and a hell of a nice lady. From the look of the weekend's numbers, the event had been a huge success, and I owed it all to her. She was about to catch me in emotional disarray, pug in tow. She liked dogs, so that part at least wouldn't bother her. "Why is she coming back?"

"She was dropping off some extra signed copies. I told her we'd put them out front, of course." Before I had too much time to think about this, the door opened wide, and there she stood. Amy was petite with a head of blonde curls, and wore wire-rimmed glasses. She blended right into the background of a neighborhood bookshop, nose firmly in a book like everyone else. It's only when you talked to her that you saw the sparkle in her eyes, and the wit and wisdom I had grown to love.

"Lucky me!" she said. "I found you here." I gave her a quick hug, waved one of Rhett Pugler's paws at her. "You've got your best man with you, too."

She placed a small stack of her latest novel on the counter for Evelyn. When we put a "Signed by Author" tag next to them, they flew off the shelf.

"I wish I could stay and talk to you, but I'm . . ." I paused here because I did not know how to finish the sentence. Going to visit my principal from twenty years ago? Recovering from a quest to find my high school best friend? Shopping for reunion clothes? None of those seemed to be socially acceptable things to say. In these cases, it was best to go with the truth. "I'm on a crazy venture to track down a mystery from the past."

Amy looked at me a little strangely. "Okay, well, good luck with that. I have to get going here." I waved limply as she walked out the door. Oversharing.

"Do you want some advice?" asked Evelyn, the door clanging shut behind Amy.

I generally did not want advice, but Evelyn gave good advice.

"You need to think about right now and quit worrying about things in the past that can't be fixed."

But Evelyn didn't know how long I had swept this particular problem under the rug. I needed closure—preferably before Saturday night. All good books deserved a satisfying ending. I opened the door and said, "I'll do that next week."

Meadowland Manor was only fifteen minutes away, on the way to Kristen's house, but I didn't even think about including her on this errand. I hardly knew what I was doing myself. If I had to deal with an El Camino and a fake identity, it would only complicate matters. What could Hunter possibly tell me? But I had run out of witnesses to my adolescence, and I couldn't tell what was true anymore and what was just teenage hysteria.

Most people hated retirement homes, but I always thought there was something comforting about them, the nice ones like Meadowland Manor, at least. I remember fondly visiting my grandmother in one. The idea of eating breakfast, lunch, and dinner at exactly the same time every day, with someone else to cook for you, the sitting around in comfortable chairs, the going to bed early and waking up early. I would fit right in. Things to look forward to, at the rate my life was going.

I parked in a visitor spot and decided to bring Rhett Pugler in with me on the off chance they allowed pets. We arrived at reception, and all of the employees immediately went nuts over my dog. "Who's the little puggy!"

"Doggie baby, have you come to see us?"

"Wook at dat cute widdle squooshy-wooshy face!"

Rhett Pugler was eating it up, and when the two of them had calmed down, I asked if pets were allowed, which seemed completely redundant, given their reaction. "Our residents love dogs!" one cried. "Who is the lucky one who gets this visit?"

"Roger Hunter?" I said.

The two women exchanged looks. "Really?"

I signed a book of visitor names, received a bracelet. The women behind the desk also put a bracelet on Rhett Pugler, giggling helplessly. I had a sudden apprehension at the thought of approaching my former principal with a pug and asked them if they'd like to hold him for a little while. Would they ever!

Pugless, I walked noiselessly down a hallway decorated with floral wallpaper and wainscoting. Each doorway had a lamp outside, as if they were small apartments and not glorified bedrooms all feeding out into the same area. Most of the doors were open, and TVs were on. I reached the number I'd been given and knocked tentatively. How was it that the past few days had been reduced to knocking on doors and hoping they wouldn't yield unpleasant surprises?

"Come in," barked a voice I knew well. It did not appear weakened in any way, and I edged in, feeling that I had been called into the principal's office, which of course I had.

"My lunch is cold," he said.

He sat in a recliner, wearing a worn gray bathrobe and leather slippers on sockless feet. His hair was still clipped military short. He had lost weight but looked otherwise surprisingly like his former self.

"Oh, I, um, don't work here."

"What are you doing here, then?"

I jumped back. This was a terrible idea. "I'm one of your former students," I said. "Sarah. Sarah Martin."

He looked at the TV. I wasn't sure that he had heard me.

"Do you want me to see if they'll heat your lunch up?" I said. Why on earth I was bothering to help him I didn't know. He ignored me. "Can I sit down?" I looked around for a chair but didn't find one. It was a tiny room, with a bed, giant chair, and big-screen TV all crammed into one space. There was an end table next to Hunter that would have to do.

"I don't know if you remember me."

He didn't answer.

"I graduated in 1997. I know that was a really long time ago and there were so many students. I wanted to ask you about Roxanne Wilder. Do you remember Roxanne?"

"I never get any pie with my lunch."

Dammit, what a stupid idea this was. I got up and picked up the tray. I left the room and wandered around until I found a cart.

"Do you have any pie?" I asked the attendant.

"Sure thing. Go on back to the kitchen down there and say you want a slice. It's apple today, mmm."

They gave me two slices of pie at the kitchen, and I trudged back down the hall. "Here you go. It's apple today."

I put it on the arm of his chair, and he just looked at it. I tried another tactic. "Do you remember working at Briley?"

He stared out the window and said nothing. I decided to go ahead and eat my pie, which did not look bad after all. *The Price Is Right* was on. I wondered if he had chosen it himself or if someone had just come in and put the TV on any random station.

"Do you think I'm stupid?"

"What? No!" An asshole? Yes. My mouth was full of pie. I chewed and swallowed hard. "You do remember me, then?"

"I remember you," he said quietly. "How was the University of the South?" If I squinted hard then and listened only to the cadence of his voice, he was still Principal Hunter. I sat up in my seat.

"Well, fine," I said.

"That's good," he said.

"So, I just wanted to come to see if you remember what happened to Roxanne? Remember how she left school?"

"Roxanne," Hunter repeated.

"We're getting ready to have our reunion, and well, Kristen and I had some questions. We tracked her down. I was just wondering—what happened, really?"

"Roxanne." Hunter turned away from the TV for a moment, finally seemed to see me. "I remember her well. She was a girl with problems. Problems someone like you wouldn't have understood."

"I would have tried. She was my friend!"

"Well, I remember calling her in for some low-level infraction, cheating, I believe, and watching the child break down. She told me about her life with her mother. She told me about everything with her mother. The cheating was a good excuse for a last-minute school transfer. On my books, we just kicked her out. I may have made a phone call to a school to make it easier. When her mother asked, I told her that Roxanne couldn't continue with us and would have to find somewhere else. Mrs. Wilder could figure out the somewhere else on her own, but

I hope she never did. I couldn't get my student far, because my jurisdiction was only in the Tennessee school system. But it was better than nothing. And she jumped at the opportunity."

"Why," I asked slowly, "did I have to turn her in?"

"Did you?"

"Yes! Don't you remember? You said that you had to have a confession! You made me write it down and sign it! I felt like I was under interrogation."

He chuckled, long and slow. "Did I? I enjoyed watching those cop shows. Still do. Well, we punished students quite rigorously for cheating, did right up until the day I retired."

"You said that I would lose my scholarship!"

"Surely not. Your academic career was a feather in the cap of the entire school. We would have done nothing to jeopardize that."

I had never had anything to lose, and I had done it anyway. "Why did I have to do that?" I asked quietly, staring at my pie plate.

Hunter shrugged. "I'm not sure. Only you know that."

The answer wasn't hard, not really. It had always been there, and it frightened me as much as the future of Roxanne. I guess I had always known that Roxanne could take care of herself. She would never be a great scholar, but most people weren't. All she ever had to be was happy. That was enough. I answered my own question, to myself more than to Principal Hunter. "Because I was selfish."

He watched the screen, where someone was coming on down to play the game, waving her arms wildly above her head. I set my plate down next to his and stood up to go.

"Too bad you couldn't fire her mother," I blurted out.

"I did," he said, with a hint of a smile. "Is that all, Miss Martin?"

"Yes. I'm sorry for bothering you."

"Miss Martin?"

"Yes?"

"All high school students make selfish choices. That's what teenagers do."

I laughed. "Is that supposed to make me feel better?"

"If you want. Do you know what else?"

"What?" I asked.

"Many adults learn not to."

I went to go get my dog and get back to real life. The front desk was vacant. I poked my head in a living area with a circle of residents. Rhett Pugler was sitting on the lap of an elderly woman in a wheelchair, surrounded by adoring fans.

"Honey, what a wonderful little doggie this is," said his captor.

"I know," I agreed. I leaned down to pick him up, and he growled at me. The woman continued to stroke him.

"Promise you'll bring him back," she said. "Do you have a parent here? Grandparent? I do hope you will come back to see us. Who did you visit today?"

"Mr. Hunter. He's not my father," I said. "But who knows? Maybe I will come back."

I ignored the growling and picked up Rhett Pugler. "Thanks for taking care of him. He obviously had a great time."

"Come back and see us, dear."

I nodded and made a break for the door.

I am sitting on the end of my row, since I have to stand up and walk over to the podium. I am holding two index cards, and the corners are getting frayed. My parents and grandparents are smiling at me. I am sitting nowhere near Kristen, who would pinch me and tell me to snap out of it.

This is no State of the Union address, just a boring valedictorian speech, and I've only been given a couple of minutes. That's two more than I need.

I hear my name called, and I walk carefully up the stairs. Principal Hunter places a hand on my shoulder as I walk up to the podium. I wish I could slap it off.

"My fellow students . . ." I begin. "Our four-year journey has now come to an end. Our paths will soon diverge." Some of our paths will diverge so far that we'll never see each other again. That's a good thing, for some of us.

"Many of us will go on to prestigious universities." Not that many, actually. "Some of us will join the working forces." McDonald's? Baskin Robbins? "We all carry with us our memories of the time we spent at Briley."

I am so full of shit I cannot stand it. I have been working toward this moment for my entire life, and here it is, and I can hardly bear to hear myself talk. Kristen is watching me. She still loves me for now. My parents look proud, but maybe that's just relief that college tuition is taken care of. Principal Hunter has this oh-so-smug look on his face. He is looking at me like, *I know how you got here*, and they would all look at me like this if they knew, too. My friend is gone, has been gone for two weeks. Her mother hasn't even bothered to show up here today.

I clear my throat. The second index card falls to the ground. I bend over to pick it up, but part of it has gone under the podium, and I have to scrabble for it. It is as if the hard surface of the floor has sucked it to the ground. You can hear a pin drop, or just the sound of my fingers on the floor. I stand up, leave it there.

"But you know, we can't forget where we came from. We can't forget who our friends were. What if we go to all of these places, and we don't know anyone? We're going to be scared and confused. If we were popular, maybe we'll be unpopular. Maybe the nerds will take over at these new places. We're going to have to make new friends, and you know, we might not like them as much as we liked our old friends. Everything is going to be different. Maybe it will be good, but you know, we just don't know."

My parents have stopped smiling. I can see Mom shaking her head at me. Kristen's mouth is hanging open, and Principal Hunter is flat-out glaring at me. Because I am kind of losing it here.

And you know what? I do not care. It is the last day, and I don't have to see any of these people ever again if I don't want to.

"Some of us make choices we regret, bad choices, and we turn into people we don't like very much. And we have to decide, you know, what we're going to do about that when we go to the places we'll go. Are we going to be people we admire, or, like, not? I hope that all of you will think about that." I take a deep breath, and I might even say her name. *Roxanne, Roxanne! Are you here? Do you hear me?*

Principal Hunter grabs the microphone away from me, a little roughly. "Thank you, Sarah. Everyone give Sarah Martin a round of applause." After half a beat, the audience claps weakly.

I walk down the stairs, and I can go and sit in my special little seat, but instead I just keep walking, right out of the gym.

Chapter Sixteen

I hesitated for about a second before heading straight to Kristen's. It was on my way, after all. When I pulled into the driveway, the El Camino looked like the clothes from the night before that you wore on your way home from a one-night stand. Not like I had done much of that lately. I pulled into the driveway and honked the horn before piling out and ringing the doorbell a couple of times. There was a long pause, long enough for me to think about ringing again, and then came Kristen, all Lilly Pulitzered out in crop pants and a pink floral top.

"Well, well," she said drily. "Look what the cat dragged out to Brentwood again. Don't remember the last time I saw you in my part of the woods this many times in a week." All right, so it was possible that I didn't go out to her burb any more often than she came to mine.

"I have to tell you something!" I could hardly contain myself. This news was so juicy. Hunter! After all this time!

She pursed her lips and squinted at me. "You are going to just have to wait for snack time and homework time to be over, and then you can give me your news. I've been MIA for days, and I have a mom time clock I gotta punch here."

"Okay," I said guiltily. "Hey, guys!" Her kids dutifully trotted over to give me hugs, although I didn't know how much they really liked me. Auntie Sarah didn't have any kids, except a dog that was too fat and short to play any games. I had a little trouble getting their names straight. They all have *J* names that corresponded to American presidents, and I couldn't even remember what order the presidents came in, much less Kristen's kids. They were eating a plate of cookies that looked grainy and homemade, too Whole Foods crunchy to qualify as dessert. I sat down at a farm table that probably cost thousands to look like it had been knocked around.

"You can have one, too, you know." Kristen shoved the plate at me. "Quit eyeballing them like they're prey."

I leaned over casually, like I was not starving, and gobbled one down, feeling like Cookie Monster. Not bad after all.

"You eat fast," said James Knox.

"I know," I said, my mouth full.

"Mommy says that I'll get the hiccups if I eat that fast."

"That's just something that mommies say so that their kids don't eat all the cookies."

Kristen plopped down a glass of milk next to me. I stifled a burp. "Can I tell you yet?"

She shook her head. "We have to finish the multiplication table first. We have to have seven and eight nailed for tomorrow."

I hiccuped.

"See," said James Knox.

Jackson and Jefferson had already exited to play in their vast yard, which was fenced in and housed two maple trees so manicured they might have been fake. They had a playhouse that looked as big as some people's real houses, attached to a slide that curved around the back, with a swing suspended on the other side. I stared out at it for a while and wondered what it would be like to play there. I wasn't sure that they would welcome a large playmate like myself who was inclined to steal cookies.

Kristen had her head down, pencil poised, just like when we were in school. Eight times three is twenty-four. Eight times four thirty-two. Forty. Forty-eight. I wondered if they read books at night together. Had

I ever given her books for her kids? Surely at Christmas, birthdays. But there were a lot of birthdays to remember, and I couldn't come up with a single one. The oldest one was March, I thought. I made a mental note to bring over some of my favorite titles, in bulk.

Kristen and James Knox finished their exercises, and he trotted off to play outside with his brothers. Kristen took her sweet time stacking up his little notebooks, aligning the three matching backpacks against the wall. She took out a sponge, wiped down the counter. I had never seen Kristen with a cleaning instrument in her hand before. She finally took a seat in front of me.

"I went to see Hunter."

Her eyes widened. Finally, a sign of interest. "Where? I thought he was dead."

"You think everyone's dead who you haven't seen in a few years. I called his house, and his wife told me where to find him. Meadowland."

"And you just showed up there?"

"Uh-huh," I said, pleased.

"And?"

"And he has no memory of asking me to rat out Roxanne! Can you believe that?"

"Yes," said Kristen.

"What? I mean, don't you think that's strange, this thing from back then, and it's like it didn't even happen!"

Kristen patted around her eyes. She couldn't rub, or she would smear the three shades of beige applied delicately around those cornflower irises. "Not really."

She wasn't going to get rid of me this easily. "It did happen. I can assure you. It changed everything."

"For who? You? Roxanne could have given half a shit. Remember? She had more important things to worry about."

"Well, yes, for me," I said. It was a mistake, coming over here. I don't know why I thought she would be interested. I guess finding Hunter wasn't nearly as interesting as finding Roxanne. It was a fact-finding mission only, with no reward at the end.

"Good, then. Hope that helped you."

"It did," I said, not at all believing it.

"Good."

I kept pushing her, though. It had to be more important than that. "But don't you feel like, this is the beginning of something new? We don't have to worry about the past, and what happened to her. We can, you know, get back to ourselves."

"Jesus, I hope you don't want to turn back into yourself from high school," said Kristen.

I didn't say anything for a minute. Sometimes I did want to do just that. "We just had so much hope then. I mean, we could take the best of ourselves from then. You could, you know, paint again." I hesitated for a moment. "Think about your marriage, what you want out of life."

"What do you mean, think about my marriage?" Kristen snapped.

I had to tread lightly here, but it was important to say. She had seemed so mopey lately, and she had lost so much of who she used to be. She could get that back, too. I could move forward, but there was room for Kristen to rediscover herself, too. "I just don't know how happy you are. And you know, you don't have to stay."

"Oh, looky who's giving marriage advice. Thanks a lot."

"You know what I mean."

"I don't know what you mean." She glared at me across the table, slid the empty cookie plate away from me. She stood up and stomped over to the sink, tossed it in.

"I'm sorry," I said. I had gone too far here, touched a nerve.

"What do you think you know, Sarah Martin?"

Nothing, really. But I did know what it felt like to feel squashed by someone who didn't believe in the same dreams you did. And how hard it was to start over.

"You try being married for almost twenty years, and then you can give me advice. You know nothing about marriage."

"It's just . . ." I didn't know how to say this. "You seem so unhappy sometimes."

"Well, I'm not. Okay? Sure, I'm not happy every second, but each day is a drop in the bucket over a decade or so. We will get past this. We always do."

"Okay, fine! I just wanted you to know. It's a choice."

"A choice! Of course it's a choice! It's a choice that I made already, and let me tell you that I make it again and again, every goddamn day. I'd like to see you do so much. Stand by something."

I stood up. "I'm going to go now."

"That's a good idea."

I turned around and ran straight into Chris. He was a poor reader of a room and gave me a hug. I guess he had forgiven me for taking his wife away for a good part of the week. "Don't go! You gotta stay for a beer," he said.

"Sarah has had enough to drink this week, and she was just leaving," said Kristen.

"All righty! Well, if you say so. Hey, look what I got!" Chris entered the kitchen holding a large box with a picture of a shower on it.

"Oh, you got it! My showerhead. Please say it is brushed chrome. No nickel!" She inspected the package. "Yes! That's it, babe! I love it!" She planted a big kiss on his cheek. He looked pleased, like he had just dragged an animal back from the hunt. "Look, stay for dinner if you want." The prospect of the shower she wanted was working in my favor, too.

"That's okay," I said, face flaming. "See you at the reunion. I decided to go after all."

"Sarah, no one ever thought you *weren't* going."

"Hey, you gonna hook up with that new man from South Carolina?" asked Chris. "Kris told me everything." I doubted she had told him everything.

"I don't think so." Should I call and suggest that he drive ten hours to come and be my date? "I can always go with Jack."

That gray cloud passed over Kristen's face again, and I picked my purse back up. I'd better get out of here. "Don't you dare! Don't you take him as your pity date!"

"That's not it. It's just . . ."

"That you can't think of anyone else?" said Kristen. "Well, if you're not better than that, I can promise you that he is."

I hightailed it out of there when Chris started digging around for a bottle opener, and Kristen, for a box cutter.

I guess I had been out of line. My mother had always said that you don't know what's going on in anyone else's home. Relationships are for the people who are in them. It was true that I could hardly imagine Kristen without Chris, even when he drove her crazy. He had just always been there, and if I were to believe what she said now, he always would be. Maybe she was right that there was something to be said for that.

I could at least call Bert. Calling never hurt anyone.

I had plugged his number into my phone last week, which now seemed a very permanent and hopeful thing to do. What would I say? How did you ask someone to drive ten hours for a date? There was no easy way to do that. I dialed and waited, biting my lip.

"Hello?" Just his voice was dreamy, the rich baritone!

"Hi, Bert? This is Sarah. Martin. From last weekend and, you know, the Mexican restaurant." I winced, hearing this dreadful bio.

"Hi, Sarah! How's it going?" A good sign. He sounded glad to hear from me. "Did you find your girl?"

I launched into an executive summary about the end of our trip and concluded, somewhat lamely, about the discovery of a domesticated

Roxanne in Sewanee. Bert was a good listener and laughed at all the right times. There it was, my opportunity.

"So, you know, I know this is kind of last minute, but I have an event to go to next weekend—a class reunion, actually—and I wondered if you might want to come to Nashville for a visit." I closed my eyes and held my breath. I felt like a teenager again, asking someone to prom.

Radio silence.

"This wouldn't be Jack's event, the thing he has organized for months?"

"Yes! Exactly!" Some background information never hurt. At least he knew what I was talking about.

"Who's Jack going with?"

As far as I knew, Jack didn't have a date, unless Kristen had made good on her setup promises. "Oh, I don't know."

Crickets.

"See, I thought he was going with you." This was a big assumption. Jack and I had made no official plans, although it was true enough that if neither one of us had a date, we would probably take one car over. It was logistically easier.

"Oh, no. Nothing like that. We might have gone together if we didn't have dates, but we don't have plans or anything."

Another long pause. "Hey, look, thanks for the invitation and everything, Sarah. I'd love to see you all whenever I come to town." You all—me, Jack, and Kristen—all of us together. "The timing is not great, though, and I'm pretty sure my buddy has other designs for that evening. Why don't you give him a call?"

I bumbled through the good-bye, red-faced, which I was glad he couldn't see. I felt bizarrely irritated with Jack, who, by existing, had blocked my chance at this date. Of course there was no indication that if Jack hadn't been around, that Bert would have leaped at the opportunity, but now I'd never know.

I would just go by myself.

August 1997
West End Avenue, Vanderbilt University

I'm holding a laundry basket filled with Kristen's shoes and feeling really sorry for her new roommate. I hope that she doesn't have a lot of clothes and that Kristen can get an extra corner of that closet for the overflow. Odds are not good that they'll be the same size. This is it for Kristen, and I'm hitting the road tomorrow for school.

The dorm hallways are filled with activity and new young faces surrounded by bleary old faces. It's weird to see this before I actually have to do it myself. I can't quite muster up any sad feelings yet, although it will come, I'm sure. It doesn't feel real.

I have to get back home, and Kristen has some sorority pledging event to go to anyway.

"Well, I'll see you soon. In like two weeks when I'm back for the weekend," I say.

Kristen laughs, a bit hollow. "Right. We're still here. It's not like this is good-bye."

We go quiet. It isn't, but it totally is.

"Okay, then, bye," I say, and I bend down to hug her.

Her scrawny little arms hold me tight, and we can't let go, neither of us. I had said that I wouldn't cry, but I feel her crying, and now I'm going to start.

"Don't say it," I say.

"Say what?" she mumbles into my T-shirt. This is going to leave a big lipstick mark.

"I don't want to talk about Roxanne."

She pulls back, and so do I. She wipes at the rivers of eyeliner that are cascading down her face. I look bad, but at least I'm not covered in makeup. "I wasn't."

I just nod at her.

"There is no more Roxanne," says Kristen.

"Sure there is. She'll be back. Someday."

"Yeah, whatever. As far as I'm concerned, it's just you and me."

"Don't say that."

"Why didn't she write us? Didn't she know we would worry? I'm so fucking mad at her."

I don't have anything to say here, and I wipe underneath my eyes.

"Promise you'll stay in touch." Kristen hugs me again. "Promise you won't leave and not come back."

"Of course I will. You know I will."

"Just promise." Kristen's voice is muffled.

"I promise."

Chapter Seventeen

Tap, tap. Jack was here. Of course he was. We had no plans, but there was a general understanding that we were attending an event at the same time. I would have had to jump out of the window to avoid him. Jack was wearing a suit that I had never seen before and had ditched the glasses. "Whoa, don't you look nice," I said.

"And you look lovely as always." I had paired a sparkly top with black pants, and even if I did say so myself, I did not look bad.

"Are you supposed to be my date?" I asked. Of course Bert had called him, and of course he knew that I had been rejected. Why else would he be standing there with that patient look on his face?

"If you want," he said. God, I would strangle him if he weren't so nice.

"Do you mind if I wear heels?" I asked with resignation, although about two inches was all I could manage without falling over. Guys sometimes hated it when I wore heels because it almost always made me taller than them. This was not the case here, but almost.

"Suit yourself. Wear them. Then we'll both look like Viking warriors, like we're ready to take over the world."

I put on my shoes, and we were eye level. "Any news from Bert?" I asked casually. Was he going to tell me he felt sorry for me?

"None at all," said Jack, looking away. "You'll have to drown your sorrows. I'll drive you home."

Drown my sorrows. Maybe I would. I had spent four years working for the perfect college acceptance and free ticket to go there. I had let a mystery simmer for twenty years that mattered only to me. Also, I was alone, and even my pug had gone back home with my ex.

"Is Kristen going to drive the El Camino?"

"I doubt it. It has lost its luster, even for Kristen. She took out an ad for it on Craigslist already."

"That seems like a real shame."

"We had our laugh. What else is she going to do with it now?"

"Did you ever fill the back up with sand?"

"No."

"Well, that also seems like a real shame." Jack scratched his head. "You bought a car, drove it around for a week, and didn't even do the thing you wanted to do."

"Hey, I didn't buy it."

"Sure, blame it all on Kristen."

"If you don't shut up, I'm not going."

"Are you ready yet? I've been waiting twenty years."

I steeled myself for the worst before walking out the door.

We had the best parking spot in the joint, "Reserved for Principal," right next to the door. If we needed to make a quick exit, we were ideally situated. I fought a rising bubble of dread, even though I knew exactly what to expect behind those double doors. We walked up to a check-in table staffed by Amy Horton and some other cheerleader whose name I could not remember.

"Sarah Martin!" Amy squealed and ran out from behind the table to hug me. My arms remained resolutely by my sides, but I mustered a smile. "You look amazing! I think you grew."

"I'm shooting for seven feet," I said, and Jack snickered.

Amy held out a hand for Jack to shake. "Is this your husband? I'm Amy." Jack obligingly shook, before pointing out that he had gone to high school with us, too.

Amy scrunched up her face, trying to remember. "Wow, I can't believe I wouldn't remember you."

Jack wrote his name on a sticker with a Sharpie. I took a name tag from Amy but crumpled it up as soon as we were out of sight. I had been in a funk since my Principal Hunter encounter, and in no spirits to deal with high school nonsense. Jack couldn't believe I had gone out there, and in hindsight I couldn't either.

Montana was standing by the door. Without even saying hello, she barreled into me. "Sarah! Did you get your car? Is Roxanne coming?"

"Yes and no."

Jack opened his mouth, as if to elaborate, and then shut it again.

The reunion was held in the gym, not the most sophisticated of locations. The bleachers had been pushed off to the side to make room for round tables with white tablecloths and bud vases with a single rose in each. Jack and I moseyed over to the bar, where he ordered a beer, civilized. I asked for a vodka tonic, easy on the tonic, which I drained in one gulp. Jack said, "I'll drive you home, but I don't think I'll be able to carry you out of here."

"Well, maybe I'll find someone else who will."

"Good luck. Hope the football team has been lifting weights."

I banged my empty glass down and asked for another one. Jack tugged on my arm, to reduce my proximity to the bar. "Let's do another trip out to Myrtle Beach soon," he said, like promising Disney World to a misbehaving child.

I nodded, but didn't really think there was much point in dwelling on a potential romance with Bert, who lived nine hours away and seemed disinclined to make the effort to see me again. Besides, it would take a lot more than a handsome guy to get me to leave my hometown in any permanent way. What had it been like for Roxanne, leaving with only the clothes on her back?

There were familiar faces already. There was Jason Higgins, star baseball player until he tore a ligament senior year. He still looked pretty good, with a young-looking trophy wife on his arm. There was Jeanie Church, math team champion, unchanged in unfashionable glasses and a baggy blouse. There was Nicole Osterman in a sensible pantsuit, who was nice to everyone and had one friend here to show for it, whose name I had forgotten. And there was Mark Johnson.

I was like a Rottweiler pulling at its leash. Jack put a hand on my arm. "Don't."

"Man, do I ever hate that guy." We had made the full lap of the room by this point, and we were back at the bar. I used the opportunity to fill up.

"We haven't even been here for an hour. Slow down," said Jack, still nursing his first beer. "I see some of my old crowd. Will you behave yourself if I go over there for a few minutes?"

I was tired of behaving myself, but I nodded, straw in mouth. Jack's old crowd was immediately identifiable. They all wore matching glasses and fitted plaid shirts. Geek chic had not existed back in the nineties, when it was all one or the other, so in looking nerdy and the same as always, they actually managed to look younger and almost hip. I suspected that their collective income was higher than any other table.

No sooner had he left than our old English teacher Mrs. Higdon waddled over to say hello. "My dear! How are you?" She hugged me tightly, and I tried not to breathe vodka fumes into her ear. "How is your writing going these days?"

"I don't write anymore. I just sell books," I said.

"What a shame! Well, it has to be nice being around all those books at least. I've been to your store, but I never see you there."

Mrs. Lionel joined her. "There you are! My little scavenger! Did you ever find that poem to show your mama?"

I shook my head. Mrs. Higdon waded right in. "Sarah was such a wonderful writer! What a star student, a credit to Briley."

"Well, actually," I said loudly. "I just put my butt in a chair and took freshman composition like everybody else."

The two of them exchanged a look.

"I mean, there is nothing wrong with going to keg parties every weekend. It's fun! Writing poems by yourself is not really very much fun!" I gestured grandly, and an errant ice cube popped out of my drink and fell on the floor.

"I am sure you're right, dear," said Mrs. Higdon. "You have a nice night."

The two of them walked away, whispering to each other about me no doubt, leaving me standing there by myself. Jack was still busy with his former nerd gang, perhaps planning world domination with their collective success. I turned back to the bartender. "Hit me again!" I said, thinking what a stupid thing that was to say.

"Are you sure you're ready for another one?" he asked.

"Oh, I'm always ready," I said. He looked like he was about twenty-five, this bartender, nice smile, longish rocker hair. "You having fun here? I'm having a great time." He was too young to flirt with, probably.

"Looks like it." He put a new drink on the bar for me. I saw Jack watching me from across the room, and I gave him the middle finger. He stood up from his table and started to make his way back over to me.

My face was getting all hot, and something was rising up in my chest. Maybe it was all of the cheap well drinks. The week had taken its toll on me, kicked me straight back into high school, and I might as well have been on spring break, pounding shots like a teenager. I was going to pay for all of this overindulgence; you didn't bounce back the way you did as a kid, not when you were coming up on middle age. But I'd been a good girl for so many years, and this night of all nights, I was sick of being dependable.

226

"Well, well, look what we have here," said Mark Johnson, who had sidled up next to me and had a Coke and something in each hand. He had beefed up quite a bit since high school, more fat than muscle, and his face looked tight and puffy. His sport coat probably hadn't fit well for years.

"Double-fisting it?" I asked. "Classy."

"You, too. So, where's your other half?"

"My other half is doing great! She's married to a great guy! And she's happy! And thank God she got the hell away from you. What are you doing? Still selling garden gnomes at the Home Depot? That must be so hard."

Mark had turned white. "I meant Kristen. Do you know where Roxanne is?"

I was just getting warmed up. "Maybe! But you're not going to find out! Because you don't deserve to find out." I was spitting, but I didn't care. The vodka tonics had finally hit their mark, which, as it turned out, was Mark Johnson.

I felt a hand on my back. "Settle down," Jack whispered. "You're making a scene."

"So what! I'll make a scene if I want to! I should have made a scene a long time ago!"

"This is a private conversation," said Mark to Jack. "Who are you again?"

Jack buttoned his jacket. "I am Sarah's date, and incidentally, the host of this event as the principal of this school." He would have sounded badass if it hadn't been for that fussy principal bit. I was also not willing to argue about the true definition of "date."

"He's my friend, and he can stand here if he wants," I retorted.

"Tell me where she went," said Mark.

"I wouldn't tell you if you were the last person on earth." This wasn't quite true, since he probably did come in ahead of Mrs. Wilder.

"You gotta understand. I loved her. She never . . . I never . . . Where is she?" Mark had lost all his swagger. I might have felt sorry for him if I weren't so drunk.

"You never what? You never nothing! What kind of asshole screws his girlfriend's mother? Disgusting. You're disgusting! That's what I'm sorry for. That I never knew what a disgusting pig you were!"

Jack's mouth was open so wide you could see tonsils.

Mark put a hand on my elbow, tried to move me toward the door. "Just tell me where she went."

"Don't touch me!" The whole room was staring at me now. No one was even pretending not to. I felt like I was outside myself, watching it with them all, this middle-aged woman who had had too many cocktails, losing her shit. I slapped Mark's hand away.

"It wasn't my fault," he whispered. "You don't understand. We were just kids. I was a kid, too."

"You were eighteen." Of course, I knew that Mark's birthday was a month before mine, and I knew—knew absolutely—that I had been a kid then, too: a kid who didn't see what was going on, who hadn't blamed my friend's mother for fucking her life up, a kid who couldn't see anything other than prom and her college applications. I knew all that. It didn't make me feel sorry for him.

"I loved her. Is she okay? Just tell me that she's okay." His piggy little eyes squinted, and his brow furrowed. He looked then like the boy who'd carried her books around the hallways, who'd massaged her feet at the school dances when she took off her shoes, who'd brought her roses on Valentine's Day. But he was also the boy who'd ruined it all.

"You know what, Mark?"

"What?"

I thought about saying that she was perfectly okay, while believing that she was not okay at all. She had gotten over it, raised a beautiful daughter in exactly the opposite way her mother had raised her, triumphed, really. But she wasn't herself. She had had to become someone else, someone nicer and safer, to create a nice and safe world for her new Sarah. Who could blame her? She had done the right thing, the best thing. But she wasn't okay, not really.

So, instead, I took what was left of my drink and threw it into his face. I let the glass fall from my hand, and it shattered on the ground. A collective gasp echoed across the gym.

It was petty and immature, but it felt so good.

"Dammit, Sarah!" Mark wiped the vodka out of his eyes. "What the hell?"

"Sarah, let's go outside," said Jack. All the anger just went out of me. I worried that I might cry, or faint. "Show's over," he called to the looky-loos, who slowly went back to their conversations, which were now about me. I took a deep, long breath. Then another.

"Girl, you have lost your mind!" trilled a familiar voice. I turned, and there she was.

My Roxanne.

She looked nearly the way she always had. Someone had done her hair for her, and she was poured into a red cocktail dress. It might have been a few sizes bigger than she used to wear, but man, do not underestimate the power of curves. I had never been gladder to see anyone in my whole life.

I just about fell into her arms. "You're here." I squeezed hard. "It's you! You're you!"

"Lordy! Who else would I be?"

She was flanked by Kristen, chic in black with an identical blowout to Roxanne's. The vision standing before me could only be the result of a Kristen hair and makeup team, and they had done good work.

I had forgotten all about Mark, who looked like he had just witnessed the Resurrection. I suppose he had. And he was covered in vodka, hair plastered down, soaked through his white button-down shirt. "Roxanne!" He came toward us like we were an oasis in the desert, arms outstretched.

Kristen was out in front of it in one Jimmy Choo step. "No way, mister," she said, jabbing a finger at his chest. "Don't even think about it." She turned to me and stage-whispered, "Did you really just throw a glass at him?"

"Well, I threw the drink part, and I just dropped the glass on the floor."

"You should have just thrown the glass at his head!" Then to Mark, she continued, "No, I mean it. You do not get to come over here. We are here to have a good time, just the three of us, and you are not invited to talk to us." Kristen jabbed again.

Mark ignored her completely and called over her head to Roxanne. Chris was standing behind both of them, to back up Kristen, I guess.

"Hey!" I grabbed Mark's arm. "Leave us alone! Do you want me to throw another drink on you?"

"I don't care," said Mark, looking desperate.

Mark was a whole lot bigger than Kristen, who was starting to look desperate herself. I was thinking we might need to call for reinforcement from Chris, who was bigger than everyone. "I will punch you in the face if you go near her!" shouted Kristen. "I will mess you up!"

Mess you up? I mouthed to Roxanne. Actually, I might have said it out loud. I wasn't thinking straight.

"Go ahead," said Mark and kept moving toward Roxanne. "I have to talk to her. Don't you understand?" He grabbed my shoulders, eyes pleading with me.

"No, you don't," said Jack.

"Man, get out of my way! I have to talk to this woman! You don't understand! I never got to tell her! I never got to tell her!"

Jack put a hand on Mark's elbow. Mark shoved it away and took another step toward Roxanne.

Then, in what was the greatest moment of our friendship, in the entire time I have known Jack, he decked Mark Johnson.

Chapter Eighteen

Roxanne, Kristen, and Chris had already turned tail, and I stood there for a few more moments, mouth agape. Mark scrambled up on all fours and spit on the ground before getting to his feet. Jack was shaking off the punch; his hand now looked limp and only loosely attached to his body. The real show had made its way outside, and as soon as I recovered from the shock, I dashed out to find my friends. I hoped that Roxanne hadn't driven out here just to go back home.

It was quickly apparent that this was not a simple retreat. There was Elvira, and she had bags of sand in her truck bed.

"No, you didn't."

"I couldn't sell her without doing what we bought her for!" Kristen cackled.

"Did you bring two cars?" I asked. "How did you all get out here?" My tongue felt like it was a couple of sizes too big for my mouth. I wasn't sure if I opened it that I would say anything that made sense.

"Nope," said Kristen.

"What did you do? Sit on each other's laps?"

"Nope," said Kristen.

"Look, you cannot put three people comfortably in this car."

Chris stared at the ground.

"Oh, no. You didn't. You rode in the back?" Chris did look a little windblown, come to think of it. We collapsed in gales of laughter. "So back it up here. What just happened? What are you doing here? Am I dreaming?"

"You're not dreaming—just wasted," said Kristen. "What happened to you? I don't remember the last time I saw you this drunk—not even at our last Mexican fiesta. Do you think this is high school graduation?"

"I am not drrunk," I said.

"Let's get our beach set up, and we'll powwow. Chris, cut that bag open!" Chris was already in the back slicing into one of two forty-pound sandbags. Kristen was out of her heels and in the back with him, using her fingers to empty it enough for him to pick up the bag. Chris sprinkled some more sand around, shook the bag to get every last grain out, then opened the next one. Roxanne and I watched in starry-eyed amazement. They had even brought a plastic foldable lounge chair. Kristen had her skirt hiked up and was kicking sand to spread it evenly around the bed. "Hand me that chair." Chris emptied the last of the second bag, and mutely, I handed the chair over. She snapped it open. "Thanks, hon," she said. "Bye, now."

Chris wiped his sweaty forehead and rolled his eyes. "Are we gonna go inside this reunion thing or not?"

"Yeah, yeah, we will. Why don't you go on over to that doughnut shop across the street, and we'll head back inside in a little while. Can you be a sweetheart and get the cooler out of the front seat before you go? You're the best."

Chris hefted the cooler up and over.

"See you, sweetie."

"Y'all got an hour, and then I am wheels up. I have sat in the back of this thing and picked stuff up for y'all all afternoon. It's about time for me to sit down and have a cold one myself. Got it?"

232

"See you, sweetie." Kristen plopped down in the chair. Roxanne kicked off her heels, pushed up the skirt of her dress, and climbed in with her.

"I should go check on Jack." I couldn't get that clean jab out of my head. I hoped Jack wouldn't get in trouble for it. Principals are not really supposed to get into fistfights. That's probably in the contract somewhere.

"Jack's a big boy. He'll be fine. Nice to see you worry about him for a change. Get in here, Sarah. How many times in your life are you going to get to sit in an El Camino beach? Never again. Come on."

I got in.

Kristen popped the cap off a Corona and handed it to me. She pushed the sand around with her toes, stenciled a heart on the truck bed.

"What else do you have in that bag of yours?"

Kristen winked.

"Can, uh, someone fill me in here? How did you get here?"

"I had me a little breakdown, I guess," said Roxanne sheepishly. "I haven't thought about all this for so long."

"It's all our fault," I wailed. "Barging into your perfect new life."

"Sarah, cut the 'all our fault' shit. We're tired of it." Kristen opened her own beer.

Roxanne smoothed her hair back. "It wasn't always perfect. I don't know what I would have done if I hadn't found Brian."

"You're so lucky you found him—and at the Waffle House, too!" said Kristen.

"I didn't find him at the Waffle House. I found him in a homeless shelter. I didn't want to tell you that." Roxanne drained half of her Corona. What happened to "a little sparkling wine on New Year's"? "Those first two months were not easy."

"I juss wish you'd called," I mumbled.

"Me, too," she said. "Me, too. But you know what? Then I might have turned around and gone back, and it was meant to be. I'm where I always needed to be." She put a hand on my knee and leaned forward with excitement. "I got to talking with Sarah. Did you know she got accepted to Sewanee this year? I hope we can afford it. I have to send my baby off to school, even if she's just down the road, and seeing y'all and seeing her going on just made me think it was time. I'm not scared of Mark. He's an idiot, and he was then, too." She took a swig of Corona. I considered pointing out that she had changed her mind about the "no alcohol" rule, but thought better of it. I was just so happy to have her back.

"I saw Hunter yesterday," I blurted.

"What?" said Roxanne.

I hoped I could put a complete sentence together. "I just wanted to know what happened to you. I felt, I don't know, incomplete. I just wanted to know, and so I found Hunter. He's in a nursing home."

"What did he say?"

"He did help you into that school. He wanted to get you away from her. Also, he fired her."

"He fired her. No kidding," Roxanne breathed. "Wow."

Kristen butted in. "When Roxanne called, my hair guy was on his way over. I told her, 'Girl, if you get in the car right now, he can fix us both up!'" Kristen clinked her beer bottle against Roxanne's.

"How do I look?" Roxanne ran a hand through her smoothed-out mane, a coquettish gesture out of practice.

"Amazing," I said.

"Like always," said Kristen.

"I'm a little fat," Roxanne said.

"No," I said.

"Oh, not very much," said Kristen.

I pushed my feet through the sand, enjoying the unexpected roughness of sand in between my toes in a parking lot I knew well. I had never felt sand between my toes in the state of Tennessee. We had a thin layer spread over the Camino truck bed, so I could feel the cold metal of the car beneath my feet, but that was okay.

The gym doors opened, and Mark came lurching out. "Roxanne," he shouted.

"Stella!" I cried, a bad imitation. The alcohol was still working.

Kristen shoved me. "Shut up." She stood up. "Go back inside, Mark. No one wants you here."

Roxanne stood up gingerly and brushed sand off the bottom of her dress. "No, it's all right."

Kristen leaned over and whispered, "Do you think she's going to punch him in the other eye?" We held our breath and waited.

Roxanne walked over to him slowly and took a deep breath. If she put her back foot behind her, she'd have more leverage to throw a good punch. "I forgive you," she said grandly. She might have been on a stage, the regal posture, the uplifted chin.

"Oh my God. Thank you. You have no idea how much I worried. You have no idea how bad I felt. How sorry I was. I loved you. I just fucked up. It was a stupid mistake. Just once. Stupid. Stupid kid."

"I know," said Roxanne simply.

He leaned over to hug her, and she put out her hand. "No."

"I just thought if we could talk about it . . . I just wanted to explain to you . . ."

"That's okay," said Roxanne briskly. "It's been twenty years. No explanation, please."

"I just . . . I'm so sorry. Okay. I'm so sorry. And it was never the same, without you."

"That's fine," said Roxanne and turned back to the El Camino.

"Roxanne, are you coming back inside? Will you dance with me?" Mark looked awful. His nose was off-center, and his white shirt was spattered with blood.

"Mark?" said Roxanne.

"What?" he asked hopefully.

"Fuck off."

December 1997
West End Avenue, Nashville

Kristen and I are drinking two-for-ones at Chili's. She knows the bartender; she knows everyone. She lives just across the street. It's not like I'm far away or anything, but I haven't been back much. One weekend for fall break, once for Thanksgiving.

I'm sitting off to the side, by myself, and she's in a big group of people, the center of attention. I think I'll probably just go home. I fight my way through the crowd to tell her good-bye.

I have to wait around for a few minutes before she sees me. "Kris, I'm tired. I think I'll go on home." We've been out for a little while. We had an early dinner, and it appears we have already run out of things to say to each other. I never thought that would happen.

Kris is talking to this giant dude with shoulders like a refrigerator, a football player, no doubt. But all of a sudden her attention turns back to me, and she pins me with those baby blues. "No! You are going nowhere!"

She claps her hands, and everyone looks at her, even though she's the smallest person in the room. "Everyone, this is my best friend in the world, and she's not allowed to leave. If she moves toward the door, you stop her."

I don't feel quite as tired all of a sudden, and I start to smile. She sticks her arm out, grabs my elbow, and yanks me into the center of the circle. "Hey, Doug, get up off that barstool. Were you raised in a barn? The lady needs to sit." Doug moves, makes a gallant gesture toward the empty seat.

Kristen leans over and grabs my hand. "You're not getting rid of me that easy, girl."

The bartender plops down a round of shooters, and we are suddenly both in the center of everything, and the night is still young.

Chapter Nineteen

I sent Kristen back inside for refills to spare myself the judgment of the young bartender. We were happy on our own, at the beach. Two hours slipped by, and the guests started to trickle out. Some of them noticed our beach and took pictures of it with their phones. We gave away a couple of beers, leading to the drought. But the night was over too soon, drama and all.

I held my old friend close. Chris trudged over from the doughnut shop and climbed back into the driver's seat of the Camino. They could hope some of the sand would fly out on their way home and the cleanup job wouldn't be too bad the next day. "I'll see you again before twenty years, won't I?" I asked Roxanne.

"Yes." I believed her, believed that we would eat sandwiches together at Shenanigan's and walk the tree-lined streets of Sewanee and wave to Sarah. I believed she would go there, and I had a nest egg of my own, so I could make a small contribution to the Sarah at Sewanee fund. But there would be time to figure that out. I believed it now, that we would have time.

"I'm gonna see her next summer," said Kristen. "I signed up for a session with the Sewanee Art Department."

"That's great!" I said. "How did that happen?" Had she listened to some of what I had so clumsily tried to tell her?

"I called that professor guy to see about donating after my big old mess, and we got to talking, and he convinced me to do a class. I'll come over and eat lunch with Rox and company and all their dogs sometimes. So, hey, y'all?" Kristen had already huddled up with Chris to plan our next move. "Chris is still sober and still invested in being our Designated. How 'bout we stop off at the Corner Pub for one more round before we go home?"

I was tired, and the beginning of the hangover I was going to have the next day was starting to seep through my buzz.

"Come with us," said Roxanne, and I could never resist Roxanne, not then and not now. I had to go back for Jack, though.

"I've got to go to the bathroom first. Be right back. Anyone else need a potty?" asked Kristen.

"I'll come with you," I said to Kristen. But I didn't need the bathroom.

Kristen leaned up against me as we walked, closer than usual to my height with her very highest heels on. "We did it. Can you believe it? What a night."

I shook my head. "Think we'll really keep in touch?" I asked. "Could it ever be like it was before?"

"Yeah! God knows you'll use every chance you get to eat at Shenanigan's."

"That's a long way from how we used to be back in high school."

Kristen shrugged. "Who cares? We'll never be like we were in high school. I have everything I need anyway. I got the best family in the world, even if they are a bunch of pain in the asses." She glared at me. "It's true. And the best, best friend in the world." She poked me in the shoulder, hard. "So do you. You just don't know it."

I hugged her, hard. "I do. I do know it."

"Ow! You're hurting me, Gargantua! Now go back in there and get your best guy to come with us."

I was already on my way.

Jack was folding up tablecloths with one hand. Everyone had either left or was standing in groups by the door, making plans for afterward. The principal went down with his ship. He looked tired. It had been quite a night.

"How's your hand?" I asked. He had wrapped a towel filled with ice around it.

"Not great," he said. "I should probably go get an X-ray. Do you think you can drive home? Oh, never mind. No." Jack pulled out a chair and sat down on it. I felt the absurd desire to put my arms around him, let him rest his head on my shoulder. Was it absurd?

"We're going to the Corner Pub for one last round. Come with us."

"Sarah, I really do not think you need one last round." Jack rubbed his eyes. "No, I'm sorry. Your friend's here. Your Camino is here. Go have a good time. I'll see you tomorrow, or whenever."

"I want you to come with us."

"That's okay, really. Consider our date over, which was not really a date in the first place. I can't say that you've been the best date I could have asked for, but it has certainly been memorable." I felt guilty that I had behaved badly; he had tried to help me, and now he was hurt. I couldn't imagine that seeing Roxanne, or Kristen, was worth all of that.

"That was quite a jab. Amazing," I said, and meant it.

"Did you enjoy that? Is that what impresses you?" Jack's tone had gone dry.

It didn't. I couldn't think of anything more annoying than a gratuitous show of male bravado, but with Jack, it was different. He had lost control for a second and done the thing that all of us secretly wanted to do. I loved seeing him come undone.

"Hey, you got to see the famous Roxanne again! And the gorgeous Kristen! All was not for naught," I tried.

"Sarah, I could not care less about Roxanne or Kristen. No offense."

"Well, why the hell have you been tagging along to the ends of the earth here? You just punched out the guy who wronged her all those years ago! Geez, you really need to get out more if you need entertainment that badly."

Jack shook his head. "For someone who's so smart, you're not very smart."

"Excuse me?" I said.

He reached into his jacket pocket and pulled out his glasses, put them back on, turning back into himself. He fixed me with a look that was nothing but kind. "I didn't punch the guy who wronged her. I punched the guy who wouldn't get his hand off your arm. And as for tagging along? I'll go wherever you're going. If you don't know that, well, you're not paying very close attention."

I knew. I had known since high school, but it had been so long, and we had been through so much. But we weren't the same people that we had been in high school. Jack was so much better, and I had done so much worse.

"I just . . . You know, I'm not the same as I was back then," I said. "I don't want to disappoint you." That was it, I knew, suddenly. I couldn't be what I had been when he had first admired me. And he had done everything he had always wanted, and still more. "You know, I'm never going to be that 'star' again. I don't even want to be. I spend all my time at my store and my boring apartment. I have absolutely nothing interesting to offer you."

"I think I can decide for myself if you're interesting enough. Sarah, no one is the same person they were in high school. Who would want to be?"

"Me. And you're so successful now."

"You are, too. You love your store, and everyone else loves your store. It was what you were meant to do. You never could have been happy with that terrible professor husband of yours. And you don't want to write poetry! But it's okay. Don't worry about it. We can still be friends. I'm always your friend. You know that." Jack shook his head.

"It's been a long night. Go out with your friends. I'll get myself home, and we can talk tomorrow. If you want to."

Leaving without Jack was not an option—if it had ever been. "I bet a cold beer would feel good on your hand," I said.

Jack smiled. "You never quit, do you?"

"Yes. I do quit. I quit all the time. You know what? I don't feel like quitting tonight."

"If you're going to take a stand, having a last round seems like an excellent issue upon which to build a platform." Jack reached into his jacket pocket, pulled out a folded piece of paper. "By the way, I meant to give this to you earlier."

I took it, unfolded it. It took me a moment to recognize my teenage signature, but there it was, my confession of Roxanne's misdeeds. "You took it out of the file! You had it, all this time." I wadded the paper into a ball, then pitched it into the closest trash can. I never wanted to see it again. "I don't know how you can stand being friends with a person like that."

Jack smiled. "Well, some of the language was needlessly dramatic, if you ask me. Very *J'accuse*. Principals do have a tendency to get carried away with small-scale problems. I have some experience with that, remember?"

And he saw me for who I was, had always known who I was, and loved me anyway. Who I had been and who I was now, with all my many, many flaws.

"Yes or no?" I held out my hand to his uninjured hand.

Jack waited only a second before grabbing it and standing up. "Was there ever any question?"

"It was touch and go there for about fifteen seconds, frankly."

"Can we go to the emergency room when we're done?"

"Absolutely. There's only one small problem."

"What's that?"

"How do you feel about the wind in your hair and sand between your toes?"

"Pretty good, I would say."

"Well, how do you feel about sand in your hair and wind in your toes?"

"Where is this going?"

"I don't know, but you're going to have to hold on to me in the back of the Camino, since you don't have two good hands. Sound okay?"

Jack beamed, put one good hand and one swollen paw on each side of my face, and leaned in for a kiss. It was a little awkward, overly enthusiastic, too much tooth. I pulled back, took a deep breath. This was Jack, my buddy, my chauffeur, my best friend, my champion. Could he be more? "This is really happening. Promise me you won't let me fuck this up."

"I'll be here even if you do," he said.

I took another deep breath. "You're going to have to follow my lead here. Let's try again, on three. One, two . . ." I closed my eyes, but Jack didn't wait for three. It was a better kiss this time—soft, the answer to the question that had always been between us. He pulled away before I was ready for him to stop.

A single pair of hands burst into applause—Roxanne. "I don't know you," she said to Jack, "but I like you already. Let's go, lovebirds!" I pulled back reluctantly but didn't let go of his hand.

Jack nodded, and we followed her past the balloons, the streamers wilting to the ground.

"What a night! What are you ever going to tell your family?"

"I'll tell them everything. Besides, it's not over yet!" Roxanne's face was flushed. She looked radiant, happier than I had ever seen her when I knew her. She had just realized that she could have her happy family life and still party it up with the two of us.

"You're so lucky," I said. "That daughter of yours."

"You look like you're doing pretty well yourself," said Roxanne as she winked at Jack. She lowered her voice to a whisper. "By the way, my gramma's name was June."

My mouth fell open, then curled into a smile. "Aha! What did I ever do to deserve that?"

"What does deserving have to do with anything? I just wanted to." Young Sarah had ended up very much like her mother, the new Roxanne, after all, and had nothing but good memories to show for it.

We returned to Elvira, our two chauffeurs packed into the cab, and in a couple of clunky moves, Jack and I were in the back with Roxanne, together at the beach. I pounded on the window, and Kristen stuck her head out the passenger side. "Are you ready? Finally?"

I nodded. "I'm ready now."

Epilogue

We'd bought the best seats we could find at the Grand Old Opry. The Opry remained the best country music show in town, and everyone who was anyone in country played there sooner or later. Saturday night was the best night to go. It was hard to know exactly when to buy Opry seats, because sometimes you didn't know who was playing until just before the show, when they announced the really good guests. This was where knowing someone in the music biz came in handy. Chris's business partner had a friend of a friend who lived next door to Brenda Lee, and had called us two days earlier to say just, "She's on."

Kristen and I were up front, and we even had backstage passes. But you never knew about those backstage passes, like how backstage were they really? We needed access. This show was a great one—Marty, Ricky, Vince, those little girls from the *Nashville* show, and right there at the end: her.

The show wrapped up to a roar of applause and a finale that included all the performers. We clapped and sang along with everyone else, as if that had been the only reason we were there. Dolly Parton waved a bejeweled wrist at the crowd and called, "Good night, y'all!"

"She's going to leave." I elbowed Kristen's ribs.

Kristen panicked and hollered, "Dolly! Dolly! Over here!" Dolly waved back grandly, to everyone, really, not just Kristen.

"Oh, shit. That's it," I said.

"No, it isn't." Kristen darted over to the edge of the stage and sort of belly flopped onto the end of it. Oh, no. She was wearing a short minidress, and all of Nashville was about to see her nine-to-five. "Dolly! Dolly!" She was leaning over, waving a piece of paper and a Montblanc pen at country music's greatest lady.

Dolly was on her way out, but she did a slow ninety-degree pivot at this little spectacle and walked back over to Kristen. Marty Stuart came over, too.

Marty said, "Ma'am, you need to get off the stage." Marty was about seventy years old. I didn't know who he thought he was calling "ma'am."

"I need Dolly's autograph because I bought a car and I promised this guy I would get it and we took the car on a road trip and we found our long-lost friend and you don't understand but I just have to have it." Kristen was panting a little, and her face read desperate.

Dolly crouched down gracefully, more gracefully than anyone wearing all that spangle has a right to do. "Sure I will, sugar. You really fell for me there. And I just loooove that sparkly dress you're wearing. What you want me to write?" Up close, she was beautiful, with eyelashes out to there and foundation caked on in a perfect porcelain. My lipstick had left my face in the ride from the house over here, but her wild, glossy fuchsia was still going strong, two songs later.

Kristen could relax. She had Dolly's signature; we had done it. Kristen eased herself back off the stage, hiked down her skirt, and smoothed her hair. "To Jimmy, thanks for Elvira. Love, Dolly."

Acknowledgments

To Katie Hayoz and Paula Read, writing friends who suffered mightily on my behalf.

To Stephany Evans, for taking a chance and believing in my El Camino girls.

To Miriam Juskowicz, for reading over and over and still loving these characters.

To Sara Donahoe, my best beta reader and superfan.

To Isabel Huggan, for mentorship and moral support.

To Susan Tiberghien and her Geneva Writers Group, for the toolbox they gave me.

And to Bret Lott, whose workshops came at just the right time.

It takes a village, and you were mine.

To Mom and Dad, who endured a little girl who always had her nose in a book.

To Thierry, for plot ideas and pep talks, who watched a lot of woolgathering in a blue bathrobe.

To Justine and David, my whole heart.

Love you all.

You put the gas in my old car.

About the Author

Photo © 2016 Athena Carey

Amanda Callendrier is a Nashville native, reluctant world traveler, dedicated scribbler, and caffeine imbiber who teaches writing at Webster University and is a member of the Geneva Writers Group. She attended Tulane and Case Western Universities and holds an MA in English. She currently lives in the French Alps with her family and two pygmy goats. *Camino Beach* is her first novel.